Author's preface: On Writing
of the body.

When I first considered writing this novel, I sought a principal character already fully formed, someone who might step forward from a pre-civilised world, carrying with him a life and culture untouched by the assumptions of our own. I wanted to interrogate values that usually remain invisible, because they are embedded too deeply in the structure of our so-called civilisation.

By chance, or fate, I encountered the story of the Suri people of southern Ethiopia and the massacre of the people of Beyahola. What started as a single novel has developed into two. As yet, there are no plans for more.

Both novels, although consecutive, are very different. Here, the first starts with the genocide. Chár, who narrates both novels, is one of very few who escape. He is taken to France as a refugee, where he lives a sheltered life in the Sologne with adoptive parents. Firstly, learning the language, and then slowly through friendships and loves and lovers, he starts to discover the ways and customs of this strange land and strange white people, whilst at the same time hanging on to what it means to be Suri. The second novel is a political thriller. At times, parts of the spoken text are in French and some, also in a scripted Suri. Both are translated in footnotes. A list of Suri vocabulary is offered at the end of the second novel.

The Suri are semi-nomadic pastoralists. They move with their cattle. They build only what they need. Around their villages, they grow a little food. They possess no written language. Their meanings are not fixed. Words shift, decay, and regenerate with the rhythms of the land and the movement of the body. Their language is not stored, but lived, tied to memory, gesture, voice, and performance. Like nature, it is cyclical: dying, being reborn, transforming.

This is a language that breathes.

The first writing systems were not born for expression in the same sense as oral languages, but for control. They were used to fix debts, taxes, and obligations (Sumerian cuneiform) to make life measurable, ownable, accountable. They were technologies of power, born in temples and palaces, not in forests or firesides; they were exclusive to priests, or scribes, the very few who served the king, the pharaoh or an elite class of nobles. They turned grain into currency, people into units of labour, seasons into journals. They abstracted life from its fluid, local context and froze it into permanent, legible forms.

Writing was a luxury of control, in the hands of a very few scribes/priests in the service of a king, pharoah or imperial élite and as such, its strange incomprehensibility for the masses furnished it great mystique and unknown, limitless power. It flattened oral cultures. It demanded permanence, not for preservation, but for governance. "In the beginning was the Word and the Word was with God and the Word was God." The written word immediately loses context and becomes eternal: "It is written!" The language of St John's gospel is classical Greek and the word, logos, also implies, the law. Hence, the opening of the Gospel should also be understood and read as: "In the beginning was the Law, and the Law was with God, and the Law was God."

Oral cultures, like the Suri, resist this. Their language remains inherently contextual, inseparable from performance, ceremony, and relations. It changes with time. It evolves. It decays. It refuses to be owned. This mutability is not a weakness but a freedom: a fidelity to nature's own ambiguity. Without writing, meaning is always alive and always at risk, but that risk is life.

By contrast, the state, by its nature, demands legibility and control. It invents borders. It standardises time. It categorises humans. It criminalises ambiguity. It declares that meaning must be permanent, roles fixed, history recorded, identity defined.
And so, when language is fixed in writing:

- Myth becomes history.
- Performance becomes dogma.
- Mask become face.
- Storytelling becomes scripture.
- Law becomes eternal.

The state replaces the fluidity of life with the cold permanence of record.

But there is a task left for the dispossessed—for the outcast, the orphan, the slave:

> To recover the mythic,
>
> To refuse fixed history,
>
> To speak again, not simply through the terms of a determined and accountable written permanence of the original established lie, but through the body in performance, touch, memory, and dream.
>
> To acknowledge and celebrate the fluidity of identity, and its masks.
>
> To embrace a language of desire, of poetry, of celebration, that flows, rather than a language of resentment, calculation, and control.
>
> To restore to language its rightful place in the living body.
>
> To name the world again making it 'my own', not to possess it, but to embrace it as living in 'me' and 'me' in it.

Black Leopard I
(being the first book in the Black Leopard series)

Civilisation

Dreams from Nubia

"His skin is night, his features, the stars, and all who see him will renounce the garish light of day, quit its clamorous certainties to take flight into the dark and everlasting arms of his heart, his open heart!"[1]

---

[1] Introduction to the ancient Nubian prediction concerning the end of enslavement and the destruction of the Egyptian Empire along the Nile.

1st Chapter.

I saw a leopard kill a man and walk away free.

I was lying on my belly outside the entrance to my home, propped on my elbows, my feet in the air gently tapping together as the pink fingers of dawn reached across the sky to caress my perfect body. I was looking at a notebook with a pencil in hand. This world of signs I found charming; there was a strange magic to them. They came from those peculiar humans, the aranjinya[2], who visited my village sometimes. They wanted to make pictures in their 'cameras.' Some came with gifts: books, pencils, notebooks, sweets. My friends and I enjoyed playing with them. We all loved showing off our good-looks and how good we were at donga[3]. I know now just how complicated their feelings and judgments are about bodies, naked bodies and perhaps already, at that time, I was beginning to realise it, their shame, embarrassment, guilt, even, - now there's an aranginya sentiment, - so I liked to point out, with an innocent grin, the head of my bhirɛ[4], the best bhirɛ possible, which I had spent a lot of time carving. I made sure the carefully sculpted decorative head looked exactly like the head of my dòrmi[5], and enjoyed watching their faces when they understood what it represented. For us, being naked all the time, and having been naked since forever, we have no such anxieties about our bodies, so I will proceed in this writing, which I have finally mastered, with pleasure, explicitly, being clear and distinct, honest, as if I am talking to my people. I become the wound through which my leopard spirit escapes. And if you, while reading this, have feelings of embarrassment, guilt or any sense of discomfort, perhaps then it would be time to close this book and give it to your children, for whom I have great hope.

"I want you to go to the river, Chár, and take a bath," my mother said as she sat down beside me. "You are being too lazy lying around looking at your little books."

---

[2] White foreigners
[3] Donga: stick fighting competition usually between neighbouring villages.
[4] bhirɛ: a wooden staff, approximately 2 metres in length, mostly used in stick fighting competitions
[5] penis

"It is still too cold! The sun is only just climbing out of the trees into the sky!"

"And . . . I want you to shave. Make the hair on your head look beautiful."

"I can't do that alone."

"Take Bongáy with you. It will make him happy doing this for you. And I want you to shave around your dòrmi and búrré[6]. Better to be clean. Here. Stand up. I want to look."

I stood up, brushed the yellow dust of the forecourt from my legs and belly, and turned to my mother.

She stroked my buttocks, saying, "You are like your father. When I first saw him, I knew he would give me a beautiful son, and he has!" She indicated for me to sit beside her. "I knew straight away I had to choose him, as do all Suri girls looking for a husband. I had to choose very quickly, before the other young women. He was expensive!" she laughed. "My family was from a different village, you know. And since his parents had died and he was cared for by the village neighbours here, all of them wanted a say in how many cattle my parents should offer. They had to give a lot of cows for their permission for him to take me! And lucky he was so well loved because it meant we would be cattle-rich. Will you be the same as him? Strong, handsome, good at making babies? Handsome enough for a beautiful young woman to choose you? What do you think?"

I looked at my mother and laughed at her teasing and wondered who would want a say in how expensive I would be and would I get some say myself. I remembered playing with her loose bottom lip when I was still only a baby, climbing over her belly and breasts as I reached up for her attention. I loved the 'sh'/'zh' sounds in her speech made by the gap in her bottom front teeth, and when she put the clay plate into her bottom lip, she looked quite majestic. She reached inside the door of our house and brought out a bowl of yoghurt, which she insisted I drink down.

"Bongáy! Bongáy!" I called out and burped. Within a minute, my friend Bongáy came running across the compound. I stood up, stretched, and put my arm around Bongáy's neck, pulling him close.

---

[6] Suri for penis and testicles

7

"Let's go to the river."

"Here, Bongáy." My mother offered him a razor blade. "Help him to cut his hair and shave, especially here," she said, pointing to my few sprouts of pubic hair. "What about you? You need to shave there too? Hm. Yes, you do."

"No, he doesn't!" I chanted. "He's not as strong and handsome as me and can he make babies yet?" I glanced at Bongáy with a grin. "His dòrmi and búrré[7] are still too small to make hair even!"

Bongáy made to slap me, and we chased each other out of the village towards the river, leaving my mother to pick up my notebook and pencil and put them inside, above a beam, away from ants and mites.

*   *   *

It must have been the day before we met, Nathalie and Claudine were bouncing from side to side through every rut in the red dust track as their guide and chauffeur attempted to avoid the worst of the thousand natural shocks that humanity has inherited in its struggle against implacable nature.[8]

Claudine looked at Nathalie with an amused smile.

"How much further is this 'Lodge', do you imagine, Natha, darling?"

"Joseph, how far is the Lodge?"

"Maybe another thirty or forty minutes, Ma'am, depending on the road."

---

[7] Penis and testicles

[8] Natalie and I have spent many times, many hours, exchanging stories on our lawn. It was always most amusing and fascinating for me to discover her first impressions of my country, my home. If I relate her tales, her experiences less than accurately, it is only out of my deepest affection. A further note: when I am recording, writing this text, recounting, I give myself the freedom to imagine the thoughts and feelings of these different characters. I understand it is me inventing, but it seems to me apt to allow the words to pursue these imaginings. Hence, a character's mood or sentiments, emerging from the events related, will slip into and colour suppertive descriptions that follow; they would never be my sentiments, but seem suitable at the time of writing to extend understanding of the character who has spoken, to add spice. It is, after all, my world!

Their vehicle tout-terrain[9] creaked and winced in agreement.

"Will we be there before nightfall, do you think, Joseph?"

Joseph thought for a long time. In fact, he was thinking how it would be better not to answer.

Either side of the track were tall yellow grasses with occasional wizened, crippled bushes which appeared menacing in their ancient discontent, as if starved of sufficient water and burnt by too much sun through a lifetime of struggle. In the distance were more trees, forests, even, and pale blue hills so far away that no one could recall their name. For Nathalie, it seemed impenetrable, incomprehensible, impossible to map in her mind, to discover paths, directions, existence even, in that chaos of struggle. Perhaps her nature was unsuited, not inclined to finding its way out there, nor making sense of a complex, voracious and indifferent wilderness.

"Ah, mon Dieu! Look! What's that?" exclaimed Claudine. Joseph was at last relieved of the burden of her initial question.

Out of the long grasses appeared a black shape. Both women wondered for a moment whether it was human or some other animal. Small. With legs and arms. Impossible to make out any features. A child? Maybe the burning sunlight dazzled their perceptions. Even its movements initially seemed feral as it parted the grasses to reach the red dust road. And then it was gone. Their air-conditioned four-wheeled drive all-terrain Range Rover left the elusive figure behind, shrouded in a pall of red dust.

"A Suri boy," said Joseph.

"So black!" whispered Claudine to Nathalie. "And no clothes."

"Africa is hot, ma'am, when you live in the bush." responded Joseph, picking up on the comment.

"So, a Lodge," she murmured sardonically, leaning again towards Nathalie. "I wonder what that means. Mud huts and thatch with no electricity and toilets that don't flush?"

Being in the middle of nowhere, the Lodge indeed had an ethnic flavour

---

[9] Off-road, 4x4, SUV

to its design and décor, with of course, thatched roofed huts for accommodation, an open air but thatched roofed restaurant, so that the birds could arrive to find crumbs, bird eating spiders could hide under the thatch, and chipmunks could scurry to beg from the tourists and even challenge them for the food on their plates.

"Well of course, the food is appalling, darling, but what can we expect in the middle of darkest Africa," Claudine smiled. "At least we can get sloshed this evening and we've even got those cute little kerosene lamps for when the generator is switched off. Surprising they trust drunken foreigners with such things when there's all this dry straw around." she laughed.

"What a lovely evening! A bit fresh, don't you think, the air?" Nathalie observed, changing the topic."

"Well it is January, my dear. They even get frosts sometimes! It's ridiculous, isn't it? And here we are, practically sub-Saharan. Are we sub-Saharan?"

"Claudine, I have no idea! Don't ask me about geography. At least we are not in it. Dieu merci! The Sahara, I mean."

"Oh, look at that little pest. Over there. The chipmunk. They are so naughty. Proper little terrorists! Look at him! Nature is so invasive here, isn't it? Thank goodness we have it under control in France. We've got the suffocation of mosquito nets to look forward to tonight! Ah well, if we want to educate ourselves about the peoples of the world, I guess we have to pay for it somehow! So, what are we doing tomorrow? Going to see those naked people? Hmm! Lovely! I hope they are clean. Do you think they will be clean?"

*   *   *

Nathalie's husband, Charles de Rochebrune, someone I hold equal affection for, like many French, enjoyed hunting. It is said Charles' family had owned forests in the region south of Chambord, known as La Sologne, since the time of Charles IX, a gift from the dying king in recognition of the assistance during the hunts the first of the De Rochebrunes had offered him, and the shelter he had provided to the young king and his mistress away from the spying eyes of his mother, Catherine de' Medici, eventually responsible for his death through

10

arsenic poisoning. She wept as blood seeped out of his skin, staining his embroidered white silk costume a pale pink.

Initially, having married Charles and moving to his family home, Nathalie found the forests impenetrable for the casual stroll. Anyone looking for a pleasant happenstance with Nature would find themselves blocked and frustrated by sudden encounters with fetid marshes, black ponds, intransigent ugly undergrowth, and forests that seemed mournful and sad. Once inside them, with muddied ground, slim trunks too close to each other, without sunlight and hardly coloured, every direction became impossible, any attraction lost, and in fact many had no doubt, over time, disappeared in the madness of unfathomable nature, swallowed, never to be seen again.

She had avoided exploring the wild environment of the forests around her home and instead participated in the affairs of the local community. She had a couple of women from the village come to the house to help out with cleaning and occasional cooking while Nathalie was out, either assisting at Charles's offices or shopping in Paris and visiting family and friends.

Charles de Rochebrune owned and managed land and property in both Orleans and Blois, although the family estate itself consisted mostly of forests between Blois and Romorantin. Charles was able to give a considerable part of his time to organising hunts for wealthy friends and associates. His forests were rich in game, both deer and wild boar. Regularly during the season, Nathalie would organise « des grandes fêtes après chasse pour les amis chasseurs ».[10] For these occasions she engaged the help of some of the wives of local farmers, women from the village. Often there were guests from government and from big business: les grands bourgeois et les nobles de France[11]. Nathalie was quite indifferent to the status of these guests; in fact, there status tended to quickly crumble confronted with the alien environment of the countryside. For her, they were just big kids who liked shooting guns and killing animals. On the occasions I encountered them, I found their company difficult, condescending and vulgar.

Charles knew that his wife was a great treasure. He never really understood why, but she was full of admiration for him. And as I

---

[10] big parties after the hunt for hunting guests
[11] The wealthy bourgeois and nobles of France. 'Grand' means great or big, but in this phrase, les grands bourgeois, it refers to their wealth especially.

watched them, I also could see they were very close, devoted one to the other. The one disappointment for both was that they did not have children. Nathalie's compassionate sentiments tended towards parentless children, just as, in her mind, she was a childless mother.

The last few years, they had been travelling with a long-time friend of Charles, Robert-Louis, a member of the Fontenay family, a major producer of Burgundy wine. He and Charles had studied together at ULM (École Normale Supérieure de Paris). He lived in Paris and during the season regularly visited Charles and Nathalie for hunting weekends. It was the inevitable next step that they should start taking big game hunting holidays together. Initially, he had joined organised hunts with others, but now preferred to organise his own, hiring his own guides.

Robert had his own private plane, so they were free to travel where and when they wished. Over the summer, whenever they met at weekends, the two men planned their next big game trip together. Fortunately, the wives, who were old friends also, were happy to do their cultural tours while the men went off on their hunting expeditions. The men decided on Ethiopia, because of the abundance and variety of big game. They had already visited other parts of Africa, especially the south, but now wanted to try the north east. So many times, Nathalie and Claudine, Robert's wife, had heard the lists of various exotic animals the men were hoping to hunt, and each time immediately forgot every single one, such was their interest. Having stopped in Addis Ababa to pick up guides and equipment, they flew on to Jinka, in the south. The men were now free and the women, who were quite used to travelling together in this way, just the two of them, were equally free.

*   *   *

The morning after Nathalie and Claudine arrived at the Lodge, there was a beautiful, clear sunlight. The early morning was not hot. In fact, the air felt fresh. Their hut was near the edge of the compound of the Lodge and their terrace looked out over a forested valley, peppered with blue flowered meadows. There was an early morning mist which hung in patches. With it being winter, the forests and nearer woodland were not the lush, dense green of tropical jungle, but dry, with patches of brown, the deciduous trees losing leaf, interspersed amongst a darker green, and occasionally the bright red flowers of the flame tree.

12

"You see them all over, those flame trees. How many countries have we visited to find them everywhere?"

Their tout-terrain[12] turned off the red dust road and seemed to be disappearing into the long grasses from which yesterday's black figure had appeared. Were it not for the vehicle, the sense of alienation would have been absolute.

*   *   *

Our Komoro was not a chief or king in that he made final decisions for everyone on all grave matters, and certainly he did not rule. He was just old and generally wiser than the younger men. His role, rather, was to manage debates and discussions amongst the people and to provide a conclusive summary to discussions of any serious nature concerning the welfare of every single person in the village as well as the village as a whole. He was very respected and when strangers or people from other tribes arrived, he was called upon to meet them to listen to their needs, absorb their strange stories about their countries and customs, which he could then relate to everyone else as part of entertainment in the evenings. One thing he found astounding was that none of the foreign men had more than one wife and some none at all! He would look at us teenage boys with a puzzled grin, which told us that despite his age and wisdom, he was completely mystified by this strangely timid conduct? What was wrong with them? He had four wives and had only recently married the youngest.

The Komoro was old enough and wise enough to know that a radically different future was arriving with these aranjinya[13]. Growing up, he was only aware of Suri people, with tools and weapons which had existed since the olden days, and his people had first lived in this land. Then, not so long ago, when his own children were young men and women, traders had arrived exchanging guns for gold. At that time, our people saw no value in gold but many young men were very keen to hold guns, not that they wanted to use them for killing enemies or hunting, but just for the hypnotic power and glamour they seemed to possess.

Then the aranjinya came with strange black people from far away. And all of these people hid their bodies. How could they be beautiful? How

---

[12]   SUV
[13]   white foreigners

could they find a wife or husband? And they didn't even have cows!

As Nathalie and Claudine entered the village, leaving their 4X4 outside the compound, their guide led them to our Komoro's hut. For Nathalie, as she was relating her story, it was with great amusement I noted her reactions to those first encounters. For both her and Claudine the huts looked like pre-industrial hay ricks, round, with cone shaped roofs, but beneath, rather than stacked hay, were low, either mud or stick, walls. They seemed to Nathalie to be pretty flimsy forms of basic shelter with little about them that might be called a home. On the roof of the Komoro's hut were lounging two dusty children, propping their heads with one hand to watch the arrival of the aranjinya. What were they doing up there on the roof? Sunning themselves? One of them rolled off the palm thatch, landing on his feet in front of them and ran into the hut. As she described these moments, I found myself calling to mind those little cheeky seven year olds (I am guessing seven), and remembering their names. The women felt slightly uncomfortable, disturbed by the alien nature of the place and unfamiliar, uncivilised behaviour of these dirty naked children who clearly didn't know how to conduct themselves around . . . roofs . . . or . . . houses even. Soon after, with the same boy, the Komoro emerged wearing a purple cloth around his waist and his favourite old jacket, which he believed gave him an air of authority but in fact was in rags and if anyone had washed it thoroughly, it would have disintegrated. We older boys would sometimes tease him about his affection for this worn out piece of dress, but he didn't care, raising his head and sticking out his chin in mock pride of his apparel.

Nathalie and Claudine had a German tourist photographer with them who had travelled widely throughout the Rift Valley.

By way of polite greeting, Dieter offered the old man welcoming them, a gift. He had visited the village before and met our Komoro and so on this occasion had brought this very smart shirt especially for him. It was clear he was very happy to see Dieter again and congratulated him on finding two beautiful wives. As soon as Dieter understood from the old man's gestures, expressions and smiles, he turned to Nathalie, Claudine and Joseph.

"It's fairly clear he thinks you are my wives."

"I was wondering that!" said Claudine.

"I want him to continue believing that. For a start, I gain status and both you two are protected. Not that there is any problem, but it means you are not available. No one is going to try to seduce you!" He laughed.

"Right! Okay! Good!" agreed Nathalie and Claudine.

"Very good idea, sir!" said Joseph.

Dieter turned back to the Komoro, who was all smiles and who immediately started to fuss over the guest and his wives, offering coffee and what looked like homemade biscuits.

"The Komoro is saying," explained Joseph, "how, when you came before, you had no wives and now you have two. He is so happy for you. To have two wives is very good! Now you are like Suri men!"

"Tell him thank you!"

"He says, you are always welcome in Beyahola. You can stay here any time. The people will always take care of you."

"Ask him about the neighbouring tribes. I know that when I was here before he was bothered by the Nyangatom."

"These tribes are constantly stealing each other's cattle," explained Dieter, quietly, to the two women, while Joseph spoke to the Komoro, "fighting over land. They have their brief alliances and neighbouring enemies. When I was here before he was always complaining about the Nyangatom. That's their real name, but the Suri call them Bume, which means 'fart', or bad smell. Charming, eh? The fart people!" he laughed. "They'll tell you all sorts of stories about how really bad the Bume are. How they would just murder an abandoned child, rather than help it. How they are all liars and thieves, and dirty people. Offensive propaganda every country uses about an enemy. We in Europe and the West are pretty good at that as well, although perhaps not quite so colourful!"

"He says," explained Joseph, " he has problems with the Dizi people. Before, they had great respect for these people. He says that some of the Dizi had special powers to call the rain. They used to offer them gifts in hard times when there was no rain; the two tribes helped each other out.

15

But now, he says, the Dizi have lost that knowledge. They have become Christian, like the people of the north. Now they cover their bodies all the time and think they are better than before. They try to steal the Suri of Beyahola's land and our cattle. He says, they want to be like the city people in Jinka and Addis Ababa, places he has never seen. A few came here with some people from the government in Addis Ababa. They wanted the people of Beyahola to send their children to school and move to different lands. Some of the Suri children went to look at the school, but they had to wear clothes, so they didn't go any more."

A slightly older boy ran into the compound and, panting, explained something to the Komoro.

The Komoro frowned and seemed concerned. He waved his hand and told the two boys who had been lounging on the roof to lead the aranjinya down to the river where they could sit in the shade and refresh themselves.

"What a delightful elderly gentleman, didn't you think, darling? Thank goodness he was semi-dressed! It's difficult enough with all these young men standing around with nothing on, but old codgers – it would be too much, wouldn't it?" commented Claudine. And then, leaning towards Nathalie to whisper in her ear. "Actually, I wondered if he had an erection under that purple cloth of his!"

"Oh, you noticed then!" whispered Nathalie and both started giggling.

"Try not to pay too much attention to their nakedness. It doesn't bother them," said Dieter.

"Yes, we've noticed!" said Claudine trying to suppress her giggles.

"And don't forget, these are proud people. They consider themselves warriors and hunters and not peasant farmers. You must ask before taking photos and make a gift for the privilege, some small change – sometimes I bring beads or jewellery."

"Hmm. What little treasures can we find for them?" Both women opened their handbags and peered closely inside trying to hide their laughter in amongst the tissues and cologne.

"So, Joseph," said Dieter, turning to their guide, "What is this problem with the Dizi people? Traditionally, it has always been the Nyangatom that they can't stand, eh?"

"Exactly, sir. I don't know why they now complain about the Dizi. Perhaps it is because the Dizi have started to send their children to local schools, use government medical centres, to forget the old ways. Sometimes people can be too proud!"

*   *   *

They were walking along a well-used path, slightly downhill, either side, there seemed to be tended gardens, dry corn, banana plants, gourds, types of pumpkin and marrow, patches of what could easily be herbs. They had been joined by a few children, fairly shy and not intruding on their presence, nor seeking attention. All had various coloured paint on their bodies, yellows, rust reds, ochres, white. Of the two young boys told to accompany them by the Komoro, one had run ahead and the other, leading the way, in front of the visitors, had a wreath of dried grasses looped around his yellow painted face and tied at the top above the crown of his shaved head. He was maybe ten or eleven years old, quite tall and thin. He turned to check the foreigners were following and smiled.

"Why do they do that? Put those grasses on their heads?"

"I don't think there is a special reason. They take pride in their looks, these people. I guess it's just decoration. They like to do it for the tourists; to show off their good looks. They love painting themselves, putting flowers in their hair, making crowns of grasses or fruits."

They seemed to turn an eternal bend in the path, which was barely even a path, but a sort of parting in the undergrowth, perhaps in the process of both appearing and disappearing. This is what made it eternal, its transience, its stretching through from an unfathomable past to an unknowable future such that its present existence was barely present. And then almost imperceptibly, the path slowly opened out and disappeared into a bower, at one end of which was a babbling river with tall overhanging trees on either bank and before the river, large rocks and a grassy area shaded on either side. There were children playing in the shallows, others swimming, and several older ones preening and tending to each other.

"C'est le Paradis!¹⁴" exclaimed Nathalie, looking at Claudine with a smile. "On a retrouvé le Paradis!¹⁵"

"Oui, c'est vrais! La beauté et l'innocence!¹⁶"

*   *   *

Three of us older boys—Bongáy, his brother Golɛ, and I—had finished our bath. We had sculpted the hair on our heads and shaved our armpits and the few pubic hairs appearing just above our penises, hardly a major task, since none of us could be said to have suffered an uncontrollable invasion of dense curls, but which always made us laugh with excitement and chase each other around, because at least one of us would find his penis behaving completely out of control and waving at the world. All of that was now over with when the little naked herald arrived to announce some aranginya were arriving. Looking up we saw them emerge from the undergrowth into the fresh open space of the grove, and stepped out of the shallows to greet them.

Claudine and Nathalie almost ran away.

"It's ok. Don't worry!" said Dieter.

We indicated some rocks where the aranjinya could sit, keeping at a distance momentarily to give the two women, especially, time to accommodate to this new and strange place with twelve or fifteen black village children playing games in and around the waters of our mother Kibish.

"Isn't it dangerous for them to be playing in this river?" wondered Claudine, looking towards the younger children still swimming further out away from the shore. "Aren't there crocodiles here?"

"Don't worry," responded Dieter, who was already organizing us for photos, "these children know every centimetre of the land, the river, the trees and any animals around here for several kilometres at least. This is their home; they have grown up here, they occupy it, it is their territory. It is their nature to know it as intimately as they know their own bodies. In English, you say, like the backs of their hands."

---

[14]   It's Paradise!
[15]   we've rediscovered Paradise!
[16]   It's true! Beauty and innocence!

All teenage boys like us, enjoyed showing off their bodies. At least, that is a secret I have been told. None of us knew whether the aranginya boys of similar age also showed off their bodies but all of us Suri children from a very young age were accustomed to painting our bodies with different coloured clays and dyes from plants. Often it was simply to decorate ourselves, but sometimes it was part of disappearing into the jungle, becoming invisible. This was especially important if we were going on a long journey away from the village, facing dangers from the jungle, sudden encounters with big cats, wolves or hyenas, and from desperate strangers. Painting ourselves, we felt safe from those crazy people who might kill children and probably smell bad, and the jungle would allow us to hide from its dangers also. All the colours for painting our bodies could be found here and in the surrounding forest.[17]

*   *   *

Later that evening, back at the Lodge, over several long, icy gin and tonics, the ladies were attempting to assimilate the day's experience, Dieter rambled with slight intoxication as a black snake silently slithered towards the terrace.

---

[17] It has been difficult situating the exact position of the original Beyahola, which was more likely near the Kibish River, not far from the Dibdib forest and bordering south Sudan. Information about the existing village is provided below. Christian missionaries have gained a foothold in the region around Kibish, as noted by the Komoro.

The Beyahola village, inhabited by the Suri people, is located in the Bench Maji Zone of southern Ethiopia. The Suri people live on the west side of the Omo River, which is a significant geographical feature in their territory[3][4].

Key Points:

- **Location:** The Suri people, including those in Beyahola village, are situated in the Upper Omo Valley, specifically on the west side of the Omo River.
- **Geographical Context:** The Omo River is a crucial part of their environment, influencing their semi-nomadic cattle herding lifestyle and agricultural practices.
- **Cultural Significance:** The river also plays a role in their cultural practices, such as body art and decoration, as observed during photography tours and interactions with tourists[1][4].

The Suri people's connection to the Omo River is integral to their way of life, which includes herding cattle, cultivating crops, and engaging in cultural practices that are deeply rooted in their traditional knowledge and practices.

Sources:

- [1] www.jaynemclean.com
- [2] www.jaynemclean.com
- [3] en.wikipedia.org
- [4] www.oryxphoto.com
- [5] rightsandresources.org

"It's disturbing in a way, isn't it," commented Dieter, "the nakedness of these people? They're not embarrassed. In fact, we feel embarrassed. They, on the other hand, are even quite proud."

The naughty chipmunks, as usual scampering between the tables, suddenly stopped and sat on their haunches. They sensed in the air that silent death might be approaching.

"No, Dieter, I did not feel embarrassed," responded Claudine. "I must admit I'd rather not be confronted by painted genitals, but these are no more than primitive hunter gatherers. If they are naked, it is their nature. For me, the issue is: Where is their culture? What is it? There are no paintings, no cave paintings, for example. Australian Aborigines have more than these people. What about religion? Do they have a religion? Of what could you possibly have sufficient in common to even start to strike up a conversation? As for those clay plates in the women's bottom lips! What is the sense in that? Why? It's the most appalling disfigurement, which I am sure is actually disabling, also."

The chipmunks scattered in all directions, climbing up the nearest wooden posts and trees.

"Well, they probably think you're peculiar as well, Claudine, daintily picking your way through the long grasses in those finely strapped summer garden party sandals," Nathalie laughed. "These people seem happy, in harmony with their environment. They seem healthy, well nourished."

"Yes! I know! I'm being too hard! Expecting too much!"

The air had become difficult to breathe and Claudine had to search her bag for her tissues and cologne.

"Maybe they are in harmony with their environment," continued Claudine, "but probably no more than my feeling in harmony with Paris. And anyway, what about infant mortality? How many die from malaria every year? Which reminds me, I haven't taken my medication. What I find disturbing is the relations between us as tourists coming to observe their daily life and these people being observed. Don't you find that disturbing? Taking photos of them is even more intrusive." Claudine had started waving her arms above her head, irritated by local mosquitoes.

"They don't like it either, being observed and photographed," Nathalie reminded her. "The guide had warned us about not simply taking photos without asking permission first and being prepared to make some exchange or a gift."

There was a sudden flash of lightning in the distance, so far away that absolute silence followed.

"This is the constant problem of the photographer," commented Dieter, "The self-consciousness of the observer and the observed."

"For goodness sake, Dieter," Claudine retorted, "you're taking photos of naked teenagers who happen to enjoy painting their bodies and showing off their genitals! So, let's not get philosophical about it. Oh my God! Did you see that?" She shouted.

"See what?"

"There, with that flash of lightning! In the grass!"

"What?"

"I can't see it now." she paused staring between the long dark green blades. "I'm sure I saw a snake!"

There was a long silence as everyone stared hard into the darkness surrounding them. The vista from the Lodge bar looked out over a landscape that was totally black, devoid of any indication of civilisation or even human existence. Even the starlit sky was disappearing behind ominous silhouetted black clouds. Were it not for the wooden chairs they were sitting in and the oil lamp on the table lighting their drinks, they would have understood immediately that they were completely lost, in a hostile alien environment, incomprehensible and indifferent to civilised vulnerability.

In that blackness, the effort of staring produced imaginings. Nathalie wondered if she could see the faces of those children by the river, some of them had strangely and deliberately confused themselves with the vines, shrubs, bushes and undergrowth, a game for them of hiding, appearing and disappearing at will, and for the foreigners of occasionally spotting them at the limits of what might be distinguished from the confusion of vegetation. Some had wrapped themselves in long stems and large leaves of various shrubs and palms, playing a game of sneaking up on these aranjinya to see how close they could get without being noticed.

Glancing around as she had sat on that rock that morning, trying to make sense of this grove, which the young Suri knew very well, she became aware that one of the boys Dieter was trying to organise for his photography was staring at her, staring in a way that was a sort of relaxed, curious contemplation. She felt suddenly self-conscious, becoming the object, the focus of attention. At that very moment, when she met his look, he was standing next to a friend whose right arm was leaning on his shoulder. His friend seemed to be saying something to him and grinning about what was going on with Dieter and the camera. The first, who had been staring at her, was holding a short stick which she guessed he had been chewing, maybe to clean his teeth. She could see small fragments of softened wood clinging to his lips. Most of his head was shaved apart from a narrow circle, and then a round patch of short tufts on top of his head. It was careful and studied.

The decoration on his body  was simple and without the attention and finesse of some of the other children. It was painted with almost one complete movement with two swirls either side of his chest around his nipples and central to the design was . . . . and then she realised . . . the cheeky eroticism of a sort of abstract art, genitals, the painted penis pointing down towards his own.

I was looking at the one woman sitting on a rock at a distance from the others. The man was busy with his camera taking pictures, and the other woman was occupied by some mosquitoes. The first, the focus of my attention, had long dark red hair, which I had never seen before, tied in a knot with sticks, revealing her shoulders, the colour of pink apples as they ripen, and then lower down it faded into white before disappearing under her blouse. I could see, nevertheless, that she had beautiful big breasts, even though they were hidden. She was a big woman, taller than me. Again, her legs were covered but strong, and her bare feet had been decorated with red paint on her toenails. I wanted to meet her.

The moment I saw she was looking at me—I actually caught her glance—I knew I had to approach. The older boys had told me that

22

when a woman looks at you, you have to dive into her eyes like into the river. She has given you this chance moment, which you must take. It is law. Otherwise, you will always be weak and never become a man.

I stepped away from Bongáy and Golɛ, and walked out of the shallows, directly towards her without turning my eyes away. Nathalie smiled. I was carrying a wrapped green leaf packet, which I offered with a wide smile, showing my perfect teeth as I leaned forward.

"Hallo!" I held out my hand with the leaf packet.

"Bonjour! Thank you!"

Nathalie took the leaf-wrapped packet I was offering. It was a large leaf of a variety unknown to her, folded triangularly with the three sides held together by a small thin stick.

"These damned mosquitoes love me!" complained Claudine, then added, "Oh, what's that?" noticing the offering.

"I have no idea."

"Well, aren't you going to open it?"

During this hesitation, I leaned forward, my head so close to hers she could feel my warmth as I carefully removed the stick so that the leaf unfolded in her hands.

"Hmm, how beautiful! What are they?" wondered Claudine.

There were two soft and wrinkled, very ripe . . .

"Oh, well, these two are figs, but the smaller ones are a bit like red cherries. I don't know what they might be."

"I think," said Dieter, turning away from Bongáy and Golɛ but still clicking away at Nathalie and Claudine with me, "I think they could be the fruit of coffee bushes. Do they grow coffee in this area? Who knows? Maybe wild."

"You're not going to eat them, are you?" wondered Claudine.

I stepped back and stood upright. Putting my hands behind my head, I stretched my back and chest, turning my head to face the sky. My only form of dress was the band around my head, dark beads wrapped several times around my neck, and a loose string of pale yellow and blue beads around my hips resting on my buttocks. I brought my hands down from behind my head and rested them on my hips, the fore and middle fingers of my right hand playing with the yellow and blue beads which moved up and down just above my supra-pubic bone. I couldn't help smiling to myself when I realised what my beads were doing.

Being so close to my nakedness was disconcerting for these innocent aranginya since, sitting on a couple of rocks, their eyes were at the same naked level.

"Of course I'm going to eat them! They're a gift. Would you like some? Take a fig."
"No, no, no! Thank you!" Claudine said with horror and disgust. "No, you mustn't either. Look at his hands! Where have they been?"

The fore and middle fingers of my right hand had moved down, oblivious of my being naked, to scratch between my legs. There was no deliberation on my part, I can swear.

"Oh, for goodness sake, Claudine! He has just taken a bath!" she responded irritably, biting into one of the figs. "Hmm, delicious! Are you sure you don't want one?"

"Could I try one of the red ones?" asked Dieter. "Oh, wow! So sweet!"

"What is your name?" I asked, looking directly at Nathalie. I had chosen another rock to sit on so that I was at eye level with her, putting my elbows on my knees and leaning forward.

"Nathalie. This is my friend Claudine. This is Dieter."

"Nathalie. Claudine. Dieter. My name is Chár."

Claudine was still bothered by mosquitoes but nodded and tried to smile.

"Bongáy!" I called out. Bongáy ran to join me. Speaking in Suri, I instructed him to find some leaves to stop the mosquitoes biting and looking towards Nathalie said:

"Friend." Then I asked, "What is your country?"

"I am from France. What is your country?"

"France," I repeated nodding as if I knew of that place. "I am Suri."

"What about Ethiopia?"

"Ethiopia." I repeated and then gestured with the palms of my hands turned towards the sky and quizzical eyebrows as if to express incomprehension.

"If he's heard of France, he must have heard of Ethiopia surely!" commented Dieter.

Bongáy had returned and was crushing the leaves to a paste between two stones. He offered some to Claudine and I indicated for her to rub it on her bare legs, arms, and face. Claudine looked slightly horrified.

"It must be for the insects," said Dieter.

"How kind!" said Nathalie.

"I'm not using that!"

"Why not?"

"It might give me a rash! I don't know." She looked exasperated. "I might try it on my legs but I'm not painting my face green!"

"Why not? What's wrong with that here in the jungle? They paint themselves for all sorts of reasons including insects."

"Yes, but they look handsome and I would look just stupid."

Claudine took some of the paste and applied it to her legs, which immediately felt cooler. Bongáy approached and let it be known he wanted to put a little on the bites on her face. Claudine gave in. The green was a lot brighter on her white skin than it had ever been on mine but I resisted laughing and smiled in approval.

"Don't worry, Claudine! You look beautiful with your green as well as red spots," laughed Nathalie.

*   *   *

Reflecting on that delightful moment that evening back at the Lodge, the three aranjinya[18] were on their second or third gin and tonic.

"Quite honestly," said Claudine finishing her gin and tonic and indicating to the waiter to serve more, "I wish I had more of that green paste now. I hate using those chemical insect spays you can buy back home. I always feel they are burning my skin. Perhaps I'm allergic. The paste was actually quite refreshing and even eased the bites.

"What was his name, the boy who decorated my face with green spots? I could've almost become a member of the tribe!"

The three tourists were happy with these memories and finally even Claudine, after her few gin and tonics reflected on how their day had been trying, but great fun.

"I think he was called Bongáy."

"And who was the other one who spoke a few words of English?"

" Chár."

"He really liked you, didn't he?"

"Here, look at the photos," said Dieter, opening his iPad, "I took a few while they were talking with you."

Dieter seemed to have great skill at capturing quite relaxed and unselfconscious portraits of all the people they had met that day and at the same time, the surroundings of the river and vegetation framed the figures in such a way that the place had become a paradise, Eden. The lives for these young people were truly before the Fall of Man, before knowledge of sin, before the Exile, before the condemnation by God to spend their lives in toil and struggle, before the enslavement to need, greed and fear.

---

[18]   white foreigners

Claudine owned and managed Galerie la Farge in Paris. She had studied art on leaving university and had even done restoration work. Robert-Louis had bought the gallery for her, which was on the Rive Gauche not far from Musée D'Orsay[19]. As a consequence of her professional experience, it was very difficult for her to be complimentary towards any unknown artist or artwork and although she was able to appreciate great photography, for her it was a lesser art, more of a skill than an art. For her, photographers were not artists.

"Well, it is very beautiful," she admitted, "and entertaining also. It is so much like, and no doubt deliberately so, Dieter, so much like the hundreds of Renaissance paintings of The Judgement of Paris."

Dieter smiled.

"The colours and detail are fabulous and structurally the same as all those representations. Here in the foreground you have the three young Gods. Of course, in the Renaissance paintings they were Goddesses. And to one side you have Nathalie, sitting in judgement taking the place of Paris. And you even have a young nymph in the background taking a bath in the river. All of this scene is encircled by beautiful overhanging trees. It is remarkable, Dieter, and I have to admire your skill and vision. I was there also, but I did not see what you saw and photographed. I apologise if I have been rude about your photography before."

Thank you, Claudine!" Dieter was encouraged. "So, Nathalie, Claudine has given you the role of Paris, which one did you judge the most beautiful?"

"I am not passing any judgement," Nathalie smiled. "For one thing, I don't have a golden apple as prize and for another, the whole setup of the Judgement of Paris was a trap to sow discord into the world and cause ten years of war and I am not about to do that. Besides, all three were very handsome."

The black snake, which Claudine seemed to have forgotten, slipped silently behind their chairs, across the terrace and towards the back of the kitchens on its nightly patrol for vermin. The chipmunks were well out of reach in the branches of the nearest cashew. The heavy humidity felt threateningly loaded with static charge.

---

[19]   on the Left Bank (of the Seine) not far from the D'Orsay Museum.

Nathalie remembered the moment of the photo. All three boys were standing in front of her, their arms around each other's shoulders, smiling and whispering secrets to each other about the aranji lady as Nathalie surveyed them. Rousseau had been right, she thought, there were clear stages of development from birth to adulthood and each stage reached its own perfection before giving way to the next. For example, children of eleven or twelve years of age had reached a perfection of childhood development in which they were certain of their physical abilities to run, climb trees, embark on adventures and were completely confident in the uses and strengths of their bodies. Then of course, the arrival of pubescence and the awkwardness and uncertainty that that entailed until all those difficulties had been mastered and a physical and psychological perfection met before the responsibilities and anxieties of adulthood had arrived. These teenage boys, almost-men, had reached that perfection.

There was another silent flash of lightning across the sky, as if confirming her realisation.

"And now this one," said Dieter, swiping a finger across the screen, "with the fruit, a picnic scene."

"Oh, my goodness Dieter," exclaimed Claudine. Now we've got 'Déjeuner sur l'herbe', Manet, except the naked figure is reclining instead of the artist. Which one is it, Nathalie? What were their names?"

Nathalie looked at the photo of the group (she has a copy at the house), with me in the foreground, lying on one side, propping my head with one hand, and one knee raised, as relaxed and at ease as could be.

"Chár. The one who gave us the fruit."

"Hm. Handsome boy. You seemed to take a bit of a shine to him and he certainly did to you."

"Nonsense!" said Nathalie. She felt herself blush, although the night was too dark for the others to notice.

*   *   *

That night, Nathalie didn't sleep well. The raucous laughter and a bunch of gangly teenagers jumping around desperate to check out photos of themselves had been exhausting. The oppressive humidity and ghostly, silent flashes of lightning disturbed her sleep, filling dreams with subterranean fears. She remembered there was to be a stick fight the next day, when different tribes met to resolve differences, disputes over cattle, and for the men to show off in front of the young women. Bongáy and I had tried to explain to Nathalie about the stick fight; we even showed her how good we were at fighting. Then, strangely, in Nathalie's semi-conscious rememberings, Bongáy put his hands to his head to make horns and charged at me while I growled like a cat and clawed up the nearest tree. I am not sure how much of this was the exaggeration of Nathalie's anxious dream state, but in her fitful sleep, she sensed a terrible anxiety for us boys. It seemed to her that she had been trying to call out in her sleep, but it was as if her voice had been stopped as if she were momentarily made mute, frozen, her entire body locked in immobility.

"What is your name! What is your name!" we repeated as we growled and bellowed at her in her dream. Suddenly, I leapt from the tree onto Bongáy's back to bite his neck.

"Which big African cat climbs trees to wait for prey to pass?" Nathalie asked at first light, seeing that Dieter had been unable to sleep also.

"Leopard," Dieter said.

And that is my name. Chár is leopard. I am Chár. I am Leopard. I remembered telling her my name, meeting her at the Mother Kibish, but now she had discovered my spirit, its meaning.

*   *   *

In Beyahola, the same night, I also could not sleep. I lay on the mud floor of our family hut next to my father, who was so deeply unconscious that he felt as solid and heavy as one of the large rocks by the river. I couldn't sleep because my penis was standing up. It seemed to stand up all the time nowadays, and although I was quite proud of it, there were moments when it stood at the wrong times, such as now while my immovable father was pressed up against me, quietly snoring.

My mind wandered to the aranjinya. I wondered if I would see them

29

again the next morning. Would they want to see the big Donga? My eyes had been captured by the lady with dark red hair. I had never seen someone like her before, and her surprising beauty had taken hold of me. Her face was lovely—kind and loving—but I sensed a slight wound to her spirit and couldn't help but wonder what it might be.

I smiled at the memory of dancing for her. For me, stick fighting was like dancing, which was why amongst the older boys, I was the best. I danced as I wielded my stick, skipping to avoid being hit and kicking up dirt in dramatic expressions of pride. My legs would straighten, my buttocks tighten, and my back arch as I spun the stick above my head. I knew that when I finally entered the big Donga for the first time, many girls would be watching me.

The stars were fading slowly as the black of night shifted to a dark blue, heralding the dawn, and excitement coursed through me like wildfire! I planned to paint myself into my name! For me, my name should become my body. The custom of my people dictated that a father names his child after the first thing—a plant or creature—that he sees after birth. My father had been in the forest with his cattle when a young boy came running from the village to tell him about my arrival into the world.

Just then, as he learned he was a father, a leopard slipped from a branch above him, flashing its teeth while hissing and growling. He had sensed danger to his herd but hadn't seen the big cat hidden among the foliage. The boy's shout startled both my father and the leopard; in a panic, it leaped toward them both. To save the boy, my father thrust his fighting stick through its heart. At that moment of pure joy, the birth of his son, chance had intervened and fatefully so for the leopard.

"Go and speak to the Komoro and ask him for the cutting stone," he said quietly to the boy.

"My son will be called Chár," he declared with a heavy, but proud heart, "and I will carry the spirit of this animal back to him. He will sleep on this skin so that the spirit can know where to rest." There was an overwhelming sadness in his heart as he contemplated that lifeless carcass. It felt right that he should name me after such a magnificent creature; its strength and fearful majesty would pass to me and never be forgotten. My heart's strength should also be my responsibility, the care of another spirit's nobility.

As I lay there, that fading night, those thoughts swirled in my mind like leaves caught in a tempest. Tomorrow would hold new challenges and perhaps even new memories with that enchanting lady with dark red hair. But first, I needed to find sleep amidst this whirlwind of a young mind and spirit's dreams and desires.

*   *   *

At the Lodge, first thing in the morning, Joseph, the guide, changed his mind. He didn't want to take the tourists to the Donga anymore. He looked pale and worried. Dieter tried to pry out of him exactly what was wrong, but Joseph was always too vague. Some of those young men might have guns, but as far as Dieter was concerned, those guns were merely for status. He had been to a Donga before and knew the fights were formal and organized under traditional stick fighting rules. The point of the Donga was to resolve disputes without descending into all-out warfare.

Dieter had already tipped Joseph generously and now offered him a considerable bribe. He couldn't understand why Joseph, who had been so enthusiastic about the Donga just days earlier, was now emphasizing how the government had made Donga fights illegal and insisted they shouldn't go.

Dieter was close to losing his temper; it was getting late in the morning, and they needed to leave. He declared he would be going without Joseph anyway and would find transport through the lodge. Joseph relented, pocketed the money being offered, and they all piled into the truck with a condition: if he felt it was becoming too dangerous, he would decide when they should leave.

*   *   *

I was excited to see my aranjinya friends again, along with Bongáy. Our young men, eager for a fight, immediately captured Dieter, reminding him, as we had said, that he had two wives and was now Suri. Laughter and teasing erupted as they dragged him away. He managed to give his cameras to me, and I handed them to Nathalie. The young men needed to prepare for the fight and wanted Dieter to join in—not in the fight itself but in the preparation. Before any battle, we would drink river water infused with juice from a plant that acted as an emetic, inducing

31

vomiting to make us more alert during the fight. Dieter, uncertain of our intentions, guessed we wanted him to partake in the emetic and drink some cow's blood for strength and endurance. He had witnessed this ritual before. Though he wasn't looking forward to vomiting, he resigned himself to it just to make us happy and be part of our camaraderie rather than turning away and turning us down. He had had experience of vomiting as a purgative in India while staying in a Hindu temple, forcing oneself to vomit to eliminate toxins or bacteria from the stomach. He also knew how important it was to drink plenty of water beforehand to avoid bruising the stomach while regurgitating whatever might be there.

Dieter was dying. According to his doctors, he had maybe two years left. Between treatments, he had decided to travel as widely as possible. He told us he had visited Ethiopia several times before his diagnosis. The point of his return, especially among us Suri, was that familiarity—being recognized and recognizing others—gave him profound insights into our humanity, even the nature of humanity itself. Many of us remembered him from previous visits, and he remembered us too. This simple endearment had become profoundly moving for him.

We wanted him to remove his clothes, claiming that both vomiting and drinking blood could ruin them. He agreed to take off his shirt, shoes, socks, and shorts with the intention of bathing afterward, but out of modesty, he kept his boxers on. We teased him but didn't mind too much; we wanted him to feel comfortable among us.

Everyone wanted to jostle, push, and drag Dieter around. All of us wanted our hands on him, around him, our arms, soft but firm with tight muscles, moving in coordination with one another, our legs pressing against his, our hot genitals brushing against his thighs. Did he think we were entirely unaware of this sensuous touching? Since his diagnosis, he explained to me later, every experience had become more intense for him. He wouldn't allow the singular event of purging his stomach or being dragged to the river to overshadow the intensity of every moment as it arrived and passed. I wondered many times afterward if we had also felt that intensity too, if we had experienced as intensely our skin on his. He reached out to grasp and stroke the backs and shoulders of those next to him and turned to laugh at one who grinned back, as I quickly turned to kiss Dieter on the cheek to whoops and cries erupting from the crowd.

The vomiting was easy for Dieter. He had experience and drank plenty of water before taking the emetic. As soon as he felt queasy, he let go, forcing himself beyond it. Everyone cheered and clapped at the volume of vomit he produced. He emptied his nose and rinsed his mouth while we collected some blood.

Two of us took hold of a cow by its horns to control it while Golɛ, armed with a small bow—more like Cupid's bow for piercing a heart—fired from close range into a large vein in the cow's neck. The skill was astounding; the arrow pierced only the external side of the vein without going deeper into its neck. Another pulled out the arrow while holding a bowl underneath to collect the blood as it spurted out. Soon the flow diminished; Bongay was putting pressure on the vein elsewhere to stop it, while Golɛ rubbed the small wound for a few seconds until the bleeding stopped.

Immediately, we offered the bowl to Dieter and urged him to drink it all without stopping. Nothing could be more unpleasant than vomiting again, so he tried, and as he swallowed, our cheering grew louder. He managed half of the bowl.

We began dancing—a dance consisting mostly of jumping up and down on the spot—and singing in praise of ourselves: our strength, courage, and superiority in battle. Of course, we dragged Dieter into the dance, but soon he dropped out; the weight of the thick blood in his stomach made it too difficult for him.

Nathalie and Claudine stood back with the women and children. As the clatter of excitement increased, I made sure Bongáy and I were standing on either side of them, painted and bloodied, bearing our own bhirɛ— the Donga war-lance. We stamped our feet in the dust while repeating our improvised battle song.

Afterward, I made my way to the river for a bath and later saw Dieter sitting on a rock with his head in his hands. I approached him and noticed tears in his eyes. I put my arm around his shoulders, feeling and sharing the pain in his heart—though at the time, I was ignorant of its cause—and led him back to Nathalie and Claudine. Suddenly everyone surged forward through the surrounding undergrowth into a clearing.

*　　　*　　　*

On reflection, it was wildly dangerous that I should even let them attend the stick fight. For the foreigners, it seemed completely chaotic and out of control, although for us, accustomed to these events, when does anarchy become chaos? The young men, either completely naked or mostly so, decorated to show off their bodies and eager to display their strength and bravery, quickly turned things into a tempestuous, noisy display of male sexuality, strength, and prowess. The young women were equally well adorned, ready to be seen and to attract the attention of the many handsome young men. Immediately, several eager young men found opposing combatants and started fighting with ferocity, sticks whipping through the air and cracking legs, arms, shoulders, and heads. Some were suffering severe wounds, blood streaming down their faces. Then, when a moment of anger caused one to ignore the acknowledged rule not to beat his opponent once down and submissive, I heard a few shots fired from one of the AK-47s. The crowd spontaneously scattered and then seemed to regroup.

"Nathalie, we shouldn't even be here," Claudine shouted. "There are too many of these young men with guns."

Bongáy ran forward to see what was happening. I took the arms of the two women and led them away at a hurried pace across the field back towards where their truck was parked. Joseph dragged Dieter away from the crowd to follow us.

"Sorry! Sorry!" was the only aranji[20] word I could think to say, repeating it over and over as we hurried through the bushes and trees. Terrifyingly, the gunfire did not stop as it had in the past at other Dongas when only a few foolish young men had gotten too excited. I feared something wicked was happening.

Dieter and Joseph soon joined us at the truck; both were pale with fear. The crackling of guns had increased, and we could even hear the squawking commands of a loud hailer and the distant cold revving of engines. What on Earth was happening?

Stricken by panic, our little group of foreigners suddenly realized they were in an alien and dangerous world. They felt lost with only Joseph and I, Chár, this black naked teenager to cling to for help. They felt . . . white.

As they started to clamber into the truck, I realised they were safe and I could return to my village and the Donga.

---

[20] White foreigner

34

"He's not going back!" said Nathalie. "Whatever is going on, he is not going back; it's too dangerous!"

She was holding onto my arm and trying to indicate to me through desperate gestures.

"Stay! Stay!"

"You can't keep him!"

"If he goes back now, who knows what will happen to him!"

Joseph addressed me in a Suri dialect. Almost every village in our land had its own dialect, style, expressions even.

.

"He wants to find his family. He is worried for them. He says he will come later."

"Where? The Lodge? How will he get there? He's only a child."

There was a terrible pain in Nathalie's heart as she became aware of all the impotences created by her foreignness to this place, this jungle, the red dirt beneath her feet, the hard blue sky which looked on with silent indifference, and the crackling of gunfire.

"Come back, come back," I said, responding to Nathalie's concern. I slipped out of her grasp and ran into the trees.

*   *   *

Now was the time to be invisible, soundless, lying in wait in long grasses, to become a shadow amongst dark shadows, disappear. When I reached the field of the Donga and later my village and home, everything I should have recognised had been destroyed.

Mihret, the captain of this legion of the insane, clearly believed himself vastly better, more intelligent, and far above and beyond the miserable, worthless Dizi foot-soldiers. His Khaki uniform made him stand out from the chaotic ugliness of the jungle and his stripes, braid and faux-medals distinguished him from his fellow khaki draped murderous hired-for-the-day militia. He stood up at the front of his personal jeep, holding on to the windshield with one hand, and his AK47 before him in the other. With his cohort of jeeps and trucks full of his Dizi military, it was not difficult to round up and terrify my people. The Dizi hated us and were enthusiastically killing anyone who resisted being trussed and tied together, The strange horror of watching a living body suddenly collapse like misshapen baggage, into the dirt greatly amused him. The mass of captives moved back and forth in waves until it eventually calmed, too terrified to resist. They had become pathetic in their collective hysteria, which made it easy for the Dizi to enjoy the mass slaughter. They separated a few and forced them to pick up the dead bodies and pile them into a couple of the trucks. Women started wailing and would only stop when shot, children too. His cruel indifference to their terrified screams made Mihret laugh with contempt.

He had sent a small cohort of wild madmen to the village itself to round up the few women, the old and infirm left behind, and burn the huts. Mihret despised the Dizi as much as he despised the Suri. The Dizi were so easy to persuade to murder the Suri, it was laughable, promising them cattle, guns and the status of uniforms. For him, they were all silly, ignorant, sub-humans, with their stupid clownish gestures and movements. He knew very well that, not too far into the future, they too would lose their land and their primitive little lives. Finally, a way of life, a people who had been there since eternity, was being swept away.

"The Komoro and the Chagdo[21] have spoken with me," whispered my wounded my mother, her voice feeble.

The village was burning. There was nothing left of my house and the homes of neighbours and friends. It was deserted. I had seen the beaten, broken body of the Komoro and had run around the ruins of these old men's lives knowing my mother had stayed behind to take care of them.

"Listen to me," she struggled to speak. "You must not go back to the Donga, you can do nothing there. The Chagdo and the Komoro have told me you must go to the aranjinya, the white people. They will help you. You can see, everything is finished here. I also am finished."

I reached down to gently caress my mother's breast as I used to do when I was a baby. She smiled and breathed a sigh of relief. The wound through her ribs had almost stopped bleeding. I could see the life slipping out of her. Tears ran down my cheeks and dripped onto my hands as I

---

[21] Soothsayer

36

tried to hold her.

"Go with the white people. They will help you. Our people here are finished. You have to make a new family, a new tribe. We all love you, remember. We are all in your heart . . ."
She started panting, as if she could not catch her breath. Her head suddenly fell to one side onto my empty hand.

I lifted my face to the sky and howled: "I cannot see! I cannot see!" And many miles away in the Dibdib jungle, a black leopard and his golden, black spotted mate heard my heart break.

*   *   *

I watched the contempt on the captain's face as his Dizi driver who was also his guide, responsible, if you can ask that of people innocent of military skills, precision and efficiency, for leading them into the jungle and more importantly out of it again, as this driver repeated the name of the forest where they were headed.

"Dibdib!' repeated Mihret with contempt at the bisyllabic name. My people were now tied neck to neck and arms trussed, many battered and bleeding. A child was crying, so Mihret shot it. It fell like a collapsed balloon. Their infant vulnerability made it too easy to murder at will. They were, in any case, all going to disappear.

Bongáy? My father? Where were they? All my neighbours? My family? It was not difficult to follow the trail of devastation and brutality being smashed through the jungle, blood and broken branches, sometimes damaged bodies, made unrecognisable in death, partially hidden in the undergrowth by large wild banana leaves and palm fronds. With every death, I knew I was also dying. And when nothing and no one was left, I would also be dead.

Bongay's brother, Golɛ, tried to escape, but was caught. Mihret ordered his mindless troops to hang him by his right arm from the branch of a tree and himself had pushed a bhirɛ into his right side and through his heart. Everyone started howling and moaning in terror.

It was the screams, the howling and cries of the children that was driving their captain mad. The way these cries resounded against the darkening sky, bending the branches and leaves down towards these crying babies, was starting to disturb the Dizi, that and the gloom of the fetid jungle to strip Mihret of his authority. This was far enough. The chain of the bound and beaten and the vulgar, screaming of their captors halted.

From behind the foliage and hanging roots of a banyan I could see the dawn of panic when to every cursed madman, every clownish joke policeman, it was almost night even though according to their captain's watch there should have been at least another three hours of light. He ordered them to start digging a trench, while he took four of his men and rounded up the children. They had come to the Akobo river, so his driver and guide told him. For efficiency and speed, Mihret and his men cracked the skulls of the children while the horror and pain in my heart turned to predatory calculation. Even the Dizi realised they were already in hell as they dumped them there, in the Akobo. In the horrific silence that followed, a few of his men came to him, frightened:

"Captain, sir, Captain! There's something following us, sir. Something from the jungle. My brother! I can't find him! He was just at my side only a moment ago!"

"Yes, sir! I saw something moving in the bushes. It was too dark to see well."

"What's wrong with you?" he shouted. "Don't we have guns? What can a wild animal do to us? All you ignorant jungle people are just weak cowards! Shut up! Stop feeding your silly nighttime fears!"

He also was unnerved. The light was failing. Where was his so-called guide?

"Where is my driver?" he demanded. The others looked around, wide-eyed, at each other, fearfully hoping someone would know. But no one, no one had seen him since the cracking of skulls.

"Maybe this fucking jungle has eaten him!" he shouted in anger rather than conviction.

"Yes, sir!" several chorused. "The jungle! Maybe the jungle has eaten him!" They were beginning to suspect so and were looking around nervously, believing their captain.

38

In the jungle shadows and failing light, their numbers seemed to be diminishing. Were it not for their uniforms, they would hardly have been visible.

Mihret quickly turned away from his frightened policemen to return to where the trench was being dug. It was still far too shallow, they were encountering stubborn roots and dense clays. They all badly needed to leave this place soon or it would be too late, and they would have to camp overnight.

This was the last thing the Dizi wanted. By now they would usually be in the little enclosure of the compound of each tiny hamlet, with its few huts, sitting around a large fire away from lions, hyenas and any wild creature that might decide to take their lives. But here, only terror reigned. Everyone knew they were being watched. Watched by the trees, rats, lizards and frogs, and every bigger creature eager to tear their flesh and crack their bones. One of the men screamed, staring at the huge puddle of blood which had suddenly appeared between his legs. A silent leech had slithered inside his trousers and filled itself with blood before falling, bloated, back to the jungle floor, to digest his feed and await the next to pass by. The small wound facilitated by the leech's anticoagulant was pissing red blood into his khaki shorts. Distant thunder threatened and a few heavy drops of rain fell. Mihret gave the orders of execution, regardless of the fact that the trench had barely been started. When there was no longer movement, the guns stopped. They stood, transfixed by the blood and carnage, astonished that the once living bodies, in lifelessness, had become unrecognisable.

I waited until the shooting had stopped and they had abandoned their guns for forks and shovels. When it came to it, they just couldn't hide all the bodies in the trench. Insufficient soil had been removed to bury them all. Hastily, they were covered with branches and brush wood. By now, it was dark, and they would have to make camp. Mihret rounded up his troops. Counting them, the size of his command had clearly diminished. No one knew why. Where had the disappeared gone to? Driven mad by the jungle? Had they run away into the glowering penumbra? The remainder had to quickly make fires to protect themselves during the night from wild animals which would certainly kill them. Everyone was frightened of snakes. Their creepy silence and indifference to human existence made them monstrous. The blackness of night echoed with invisible cries and screams, turning sanity into nightmares.

It amused and pleased me knowing the few Dizi people who came out of the Dibdib jungle that night would have only tales of horror and insanity, and would spend the rest of their waking days with nightmares, screaming in terror at daylight hallucinations.

The great fear started with the discovery of two bodies of their soldier policemen, lying neatly side by side with their throats ripped.

"A leopard, sir. Black as the night! I saw it in the trees!"

"No animal did this!" declared Mihret. His contingent of so-called police seemed to be getting smaller and he suspected some had already run away for fear of whatever was hunting or haunting them, or both. Howls of madmen blinded by panic, as they stumbled, fell and wounded themselves against vicious thorns and branches, never lasted long before their necks were broken by lions, hyenas or their own terror. It was easy to be superstitious in this place. Even the creaking trees, waving and clattering with the arriving storm seemed to moan and cry out. Who could know whether the howls of pain were the Suri, still dying, or the desperate cries of those who had run off in amongst the trees and found themselves completely lost? Or were they the haunting cries of the already dead and murdered, slowly eaten by dark monsters somewhere out there?

The final blow to this colony of the insane came when, so tales would tell, the black shape following them, an animal, a shadow, no one could be certain and there were conflicting hallucinated reports, stories and imaginings, but something slowly killing them. Had there actions disturbed chthonic demons, emerging from the ground itself, to chase them into death or madness? Suddenly now, it fell from the sky, as if it had been waiting, onto the back of their captain. Mihret dropped to the ground and the creature seemed to jump back into the undergrowth and disappear. The few remaining watched as their captain, screaming in pain, tried to stand up. In the light of their last fire, they could see vertical cuts clawed into the cheeks, eyes and forehead of his contorted face. Both eyeballs had been split open and their gelatinous liquid and tiny striped retinas were slopping down his Khaki shirt, mixing with the blood already staining his badges and silly medals. It would be a mistake to say he saw nothing, since now, in his brain there were the red and yellow flames of tortured hell. He staggered, arms reaching out, and bounced off a tree trunk. Struggling to his feet again, unaware of the last few of his men encircling him and watching in horror, he wandered, picking his feet in strangely high steps, away into the bush, falling again and again until eventually crawling, they saw him enter a small space among the trees where the ground was slightly raised and covered with what seemed like dead leaves. An ant's nest. There was no possibility of any of his men coming to his rescue any longer. They simply stood back and watched with their few brushwood torches, throwing the pattern of their flames up into the branches and leaves of the trees, as Mihret, their captain, whom they had come to hate even more than the Suri, arms and legs flailing, writhed in the agony of the attack of the hundreds of thousands of angry ants. His screams continued for a long, long time into the night as the remaining Dizi people disappeared in the different directions of hysterical panic. Eventually his screams became moans until by dawn they had stopped.

*   *   *

I could feel the rasping scratching of a cat's tongue licking my face. I opened my eyes and saw the yellow and black face of the female leopard right next to mine. She looked into my eyes, without anger, hunger, or greed, and then closed her eyes again with a gentle expression, as if she were cleaning one of her offspring. I felt no fear, being already dead, and let her continue to lick me for a while as my aching body woke up. The faint light of early dawn illuminated the patches of sky visible through the trees. Slowly, I sat up and noticed her black mate watching from a short distance. The female started rubbing her big head affectionately against my shoulders and face. I couldn't help but smile to myself at the strangeness of what was happening as the black male approached to join in, rubbing their scent onto my naked body. The rain had not come, only its threat, so the air was still hot and humid. I stood up stiffly and started walking. The two big cats walked with me at my side, so large that their shoulders were almost level with my hips. They followed me— or led me; however it may have happened—until we reached the edge of the forest, where they stopped and watched as I disappeared into the long yellow grasses.

Back at the ashes of Beyahola, I covered with giant leaves from the forest as many of the bodies as I could find—my mother, the Komoro, the Chagdo, some babies, and other older women. After this task, which tore my heart, I needed to take a bath in sheep's blood, as was the custom. I had been too close to the dead and dying, and this was the only way to purify my body. Back at the devastated gardens of my village, I found a

41

lonely bleating creature. Taking it with me down towards the river, I pulled some liana out of the trees, tied its back legs, and hoisted it over a low-hanging branch. Finding a sharp piece of obsidian, I reached up and cut its throat. Warm blood poured down over my head and shoulders as the sheep struggled. Eventually its twitching body slowed, drained of life. I made sure every part of me body was covered by that thick, sticky liquid.

I remembered to thank the dead sheep, acknowledging its sacrifice. As I stepped into the river to wash away the blood of purification, I noticed Dieter, who had just arrived. No one spoke. Dieter just watched in silence as I washed away the blood covering my body and with it any presence of death clinging to my skin.

I stepped out of the river, and Dieter stepped towards me. He put his arm around my shoulder, and I leaned my head against his chest.

* * *

For Nathalie, Claudine, and Dieter, the night after the massacre had been threatening. Everyone had suffered through the humidity; the electricity—and hence the air-conditioning—had failed. Distant thunder and occasional heavy drops of rain broke the silence. It was only around seven in the morning when Nathalie heard Dieter becoming more and more impatient with Joseph.

"Ms Nathalie, tell Master Dieter I cannot let him go back to Beyahola village. It is too dangerous. We would both die."

"What happened there, Joseph?" she asked.

"I cannot say. The servants here are full of stories. Who knows the truth? All I know is that the local police have said to stay away."

"Look, Nathalie," said Dieter, turning to speak to her privately, "you know the boy who brings us coffee at breakfast? When I saw him first thing, he was as white as a sheet and didn't want to speak. Usually he is so chatty, right? So I pressed him to tell me what was wrong, and breaking down in tears, he said that Beyahola village had disappeared and even many of the police who were there had disappeared as well.

"The government says the Suri people must not have these Donga

42

fights," he said, "because trouble always happens. The police came there to stop them."

"Something bad has happened, Nathalie, and I want to find out," he insisted. "He said the police were taking away some bad people when they were made crazy by ghosts. All of this is just nonsense, but I want to see for myself. I've known the Suri for a few years now and I know they have problems with the central government . . . . Who knows what has happened? I've got to go."

Nathalie immediately thought about the people she had met, especially me and my friend Bongáy.

"Well, just take the truck yourself," she said. "Don't stand here arguing with Joseph. The truck is ours; we've hired it and Joseph is just a local guide. You don't need to argue. Besides, I'm sure everything is fine now that their fight has been broken up. I'll come with you. We can both put our minds at rest. All this business about ghosts is just wild imaginings of people who have nothing to do but serve coffee all day. We'll go and make sure all is as it should be."

Her matter-of-factness silenced the disputing men but hardly calmed her own personal anxieties; she hadn't slept. In her heart she feared the worst—the unknown always brings fear. She worried for us children, and my repeated words "come back" haunted her.

"Joseph, you stay here and take care of Ms Claudine when she wakes up. We'll not be long."

"Ms Nathalie, please, you must not go. You don't know what is happening! This is not your country. You do not understand."

The dirt track leading to Beyahola was deserted. The ground was a darker red with the few heavy drops of rain. Recognizing the countryside, they were supposed to arrive in the village, but there was nothing there. It had disappeared. The smell of burning hung in the morning air from the ashes of thatch and bits of wood that used to make up walls and fences. A chicken was scratching in the yard where it usually hung out. Dieter suggested Nathalie stay in the truck while he wandered around taking photos of the desolate destruction.

"I'm going to walk down to the river," he said, returning to the truck.

"You wait here."

Nathalie sat with tears in her eyes, astonished and horrified. What had happened to all those lovely people she had met? Where were they? Was that it? The simple humanity of connecting heart to heart reduced to blood and ashes!

She couldn't stand waiting any longer and descending from the vehicle made her way towards the river. As she turned the bend to look down towards the river bower, she saw the silhouette of a sheep's carcass hanging in a tree, Dieter standing at some distance, and my black shape stepping out of the water.

She knew immediately who I was and started running, her heart pounding with anxious trepidation.

"Chár!" she called out. Dieter was holding me next to him. I turned my head to look at her, tears running down my cheeks, and held out my hand. Nathalie put her arms around both of us.

"Let's get away from here—all of us."

In the truck on the way back to the Lodge, I sat slumped between them, silent. I felt so small now, just a child. What was going to happen for me? I couldn't even start to worry about that. These aranjinya were deciding for me.

Claudine and Joseph were waiting for us with worried looks. Nathalie helped me out of the front of the truck. During our journey back, my body had stiffened with all the knocks, cuts, and blows it had suffered during that previous night of horrors. She helped me to a lounger and laid me down while the servants looked on wide-eyed.

"Dieter, go with Joseph to the nearest town and buy him some clothes— everything: shirts, trousers, jeans, T-shirts, pants, socks, trainers— everything! A toothbrush too! And a suitcase! He is not staying here! He is coming with me." Nathalie handed Dieter a wad of cash.

"Claudine! Where is our medical kit?" No one dared speak nor offer an opinion.

Chapter 2.

Rémi

Ah, the wonderful, yellow-haired Rémi!

I didn't know it, but I was about to return from dying. Of course, I had never seen a house before, especially one so big, made of stone, as if it would be there forever. So different to the little fragile shelter, always needing repair, which had been home before, although, in truth, home had been the entire village, the river, the forests and the blue sky. In France, I was empty. I had died with my people and my empty shell of a body wandered around this solid, aged house, feeling nothing, l let Nathalie direct me. I didn't think, and couldn't even.

This occasion, there was no time for feeling empty. Nathalie had tried to let me know visitors were coming soon, although I was simply puzzled by her gestures.

And then they arrived. Claudine and Robert I had known from my own country, but now there was a new person, I was guessing their son.

It was Rémi. He straightaway loved the way I had completely upset life here in Charles' and Nathalie's home, I could feel it. He had been accustomed to coming here with his parents, Robert and Claudine, and being completely bored for the whole weekend while the men went hunting and the women sat at the kitchen table peeling vegetables and talking about stuff that was so tedious he couldn't even remember the topic within seconds of the conversation starting. He would usually sneak off to a sofa in the salon to play Call of Duty or Grand Theft Auto. And then his mother, Claudine, would come to moan at him for being exactly what he was, a teenager.

"Why don't you go hunting with your father? Why don't you go on a bike ride around the countryside? Why don't you go swimming at the pool in town? Why don't you blah, blah, blah? Come and peel some potatoes with us."

There was no escape.

But now, everything was completely different. His mother was quite reserved, conflicted in her feelings about my presence, believing Nathalie had created problems for herself she could do without. On the other hand, Robert adored me. In spite of this open affection, Rémi still felt annoyed with his father. Every occasion that they arrived, his father would exclaim:

"Où est mon petit nègre?" or "Comment va mon petit nègre?"

I would run and jump at him to give him a hug while Rémi would every time complain:

"You can't say that, Papa! T'es raciste, ou quoi?[22]"

"Je ne suis pas raciste du tout! Il est noir. Il vient d'une tribu en Afrique. Alors, il est un nègre!"[23]

"Call him by his name, for goodness sake!"

Both Rémi's parents were racists, so he thought, even though they believed they weren't, but what could he do?

The first time Rémi and I met, we knew we were going to be friends. He was sixteen, soon to be seventeen, and guessed I was the same. Even though I had an Ethiopian identity card and a passport both with birth dates on them, no one knew my real date of birth. It was thanks to Rémi's father that I had a long stay visa and, through his and Charles' help, would eventually have a Carte de Séjour and finally French nationality. The whole affair sounded absurd and corrupt as far as Rémi or any other observer might think, with Robert thoroughly enjoying pulling strings and wielding his influence over these petty bureaucracies. According to Rémi's parents, the French Consulate in Addis Ababa had been most helpful once they found out what had happened to my village. Dieter had been present with ample photographic evidence. Robert made a few phone calls to Paris to politicians in government whom he knew, reminding them of the respected reputation of La France, unlike their English neighbours, of welcoming all refugees of any nationality. Consequently, the French Consulate in Addis Ababa was expecting us and had been directed from Paris to help. The advice they gave was to

---

[22] You're racist, or what?
[23] I'm not at all racist! He is black. He comes from a tribe in Africa. So, he's a negro!"

somehow obtain both an identity card and passport. They even provided the name of the director of the Addis Ababa Government Acts and Civil Status Document Registration Office, who, for a fee, would help them. Since it would be impossible to tell these Ethiopian authorities the truth that I came from a village that perhaps they had destroyed, or at least turned a blind eye to whatever was going on with foreign investment, they employed their guide Joseph to act as my father, paid him plenty, and handed over considerable sums in bribes to petty clerks.

"I knew my father could be useful sometimes." Rémi commented.

We had only arrived in France a week prior, when Nathalie had phoned Claudine out of desperation. Could they come to the house for a long weekend to help and advise how to manage this new person in their midst? I was lovely and loving, Nathalie had claimed; it was just that we couldn't converse, even at the simplest level. How could she communicate just the basic customs of Western living, basic manners, how to use a knife and fork, even? I was as limited as a baby, almost, although practically a young man. They were lost!

In spite of my eventually knowing we were going to meet and having seen photos, it was nevertheless a big surprise for both of us. Rémi saw my young, handsome African face, so black—surprisingly black—with high cheekbones, beautiful full lips, and a wide smile staring at him. And I, amazed, saw a beautiful young aranji with curling yellow hair like the morning winter sun. I had seen many aranjinya but never one like this, with skin like cream and ever so slightly pink cheeks. I had lost my best friend, Bongay, and badly needed new alliances with someone my own age; I knew Rémi was the one. My spirit leopard was telling me and so were the two leopards who had saved me in the Dibdib forest.

"I am so glad you are here, Rémi," said Nathalie. "I need you to help me."

"I like Chár's hairstyle," he said, looking at me with an admiring smile and indicating my hair by pulling at his own.

"He knew you were coming; we had told him, and he wanted to make an effort. It is the same style as when we first met him. He had shown us how he felt about his appearance—that he was disappointed and he felt ugly; his hair was growing too long. All of this was with gestures, a mirror, pulling faces to express his disgust. Honestly, it's so difficult!"

"Did he do it himself?"

"Well, that's why you should be here, Rémi, to do things like that. Charles had to help him. Already shaving his head was difficult enough, but Suri men are very proud of their appearance and they don't like body hair."

I could see it was dawning on Rémi what the problem was from the grin that started to appear on his face. I had wanted to shave my armpits and hair elsewhere. Since it's not exactly straightforward, I had asked Charles to help me.

"Help him do what?"

Nathalie couldn't help expressing a certain impatient frustration: "Do I have to say it out loud? His pubic hair! Shave between his legs!"

Rémi was in fits of laughter.

"Did you do it, Charles?" asked Robert.

"Bien sûr que non![24] Merde![25]"

"So, Nathalie, you want me to shave his arse then?" asked Rémi with mock seriousness.

"Stop it, Rémi!" his mother demanded. "Don't be so vulgar!"

"It's fine. I'd be more than willing to help," he said, winding up Claudine.

"Rémi, stop now! It's one thing for people in Africa to do this, but here is different," said Claudine.

"Ne parle pas comme ça! T'es incroyable, Maman! T'as pas honte?"[26]

"Nathalie, my dear, how did you expect to teach a teenage boy about personal hygiene when he doesn't even speak your language? What have

---

[24] "Of course not!"
[25] Shit!
[26] "Don't talk like that! You're unbelievable, Mother! Aren't you ashamed?"

you done?" demanded Claudine, exasperated. "I told you it was a mistake. He would have been better off in his own country and you forgetting him. I mean, what about such things as . . .." Claudine stumbled, realising the trap she had led herself into, ". . . .er . . private cleanliness?"

Rémi was almost falling off his chair with laughter. "You mean wiping his arse? Don't worry, mother; don't worry, I'll show him all that!"

"Please. Please. Obviously, a lot of that is fairly easy—showing him towels, toothbrushes, et cetera. How a toilet functions—but toilet paper..." said Nathalie, trying to bring some sanity back to the conversation. "He would probably be horrified at having to use it; he's never seen it before and no doubt used water when he was living in his village."

"I was not going to show him how to use toilet paper," said Charles. Then trying to show how just a little rational practicality can solve most difficulties: "We've had hoses installed next to each toilet so that he can wash and then use tissue to dry."

"Great!" said Rémi. "So now you can give yourself an enema any time you want!"

"Stop being so disgusting, Rémi!" said Claudine.

All this time, I was listening and watching the exchange. There were a few words I could understand, but certainly not a sense. I loved how Rémi could laugh so much at the serious grown-ups.

"Goona nanu, Rémi!" As if almost talking to myself, I suddenly brought the group of noisy French people to silence. All eyes around the kitchen table turned in astonishment and incomprehension towards me.

In the lengthy silence, I repeated with the same quiet purr:

"Rémi nanu, goona nanu."

I was looking directly into Rémi's eyes, a smile in my eyes at his surprised incomprehension.

"What's that? What does that mean?" Rémi looked straight back at me with his hands turned upwards and a quizzical expression on his face.

I crossed my middle fingers over my forefingers then hooked my forefingers together. Rémi stood up and, indicating for Charles to move out of the way, sat down next to me, put his arm around my shoulders and pulled me towards him.

"Yes, you are my brother," he said quietly.

"Thank you, Rémi," said Nathalie, her eyes slightly tearful. "Chár must feel so lonely."

"T'es un type bien, Rémi," said Robert with a proud smile.

"He feels safe here with us. But he has no friends."

"Tell them how you know he feels safe," interrupted Charles with an amused grin.

Rémi tightened his embrace, for me to lean into his warm body.

"He feels safe with us, we know, because . . ."

But of course, they couldn't know how much I had suffered, what I had suffered, nor even what I had seen and been through.

"Let me explain," said Charles, inviting everyone's attention.

"On our return, Marie Jeanne was here already. You know Marie Jeanne. She helps out around the house three or four mornings a week. You've met her already. She already knew he was coming with us, so she had prepared a room for him, upstairs, at the end of the house, next to our room. We explained that he was a refugee and that he was going to stay here with us. Of course, we explained what had happened so that all the neighbours, the people of the village and the surrounding area would know, thanks to her, what he had been through. She gossips! She knows everyone's business in the village!

"Finally, at night, we were completely worn out and went to bed immediately. In the middle of the night, I felt like it was too hot, and besides, I couldn't move. I was there, under the sheets, with Nathalie on one side, and discovered Chár on the other, who must have crept into

50

our bed in the middle of the night! And as well," continued Charles, "he was completely naked!"

"I told you not to do it, Nathalie, bringing him here! I just knew you were making trouble for yourself and everyone else." Claudine could no longer contain herself. Rémi would have fallen off the bench with laughter, were he not holding on to me!

"So, what did you do?" asked Robert.

"I turned over and went back to sleep!"

"It's normal!" Robert reached out to rest a hand on my forearm. "He has never slept alone all his life. In poor countries it is always the family together."

"And anyway," said Nathalie, "we don't know if he suffers night terrors, what his fears might be, his being lonely. So, Rémi, Marie Jeanne has made up the lit-cage[27], the folding metal bed, in his bedroom for you. What do you think? Is that OK? Keep him company while you are here. I am sure you can help him feel more at home."

"Yeh. Of course."

Claudine didn't seem to be very happy about the idea but said nothing.

"It'll be good," insisted Rémi.

Finally, the evening broke up and everyone disappeared in different directions to their bedrooms. Rémi kept me behind with him in the kitchen. It was a communication of gestures with one or two accompanying words.

"Wait."

He found a . . .

"Jug."

---

[27] Lit-cage. These metal-framed single beds were designed specifically for apartment living; they could be folded in the middle, and, on casters, could be pushed against a wall, for space.

"Jug." I repeated, "kâdӡàrói."

and filled it with . . .

"Water."

"Water. Má."

"Take these. One glass. Two glasses."

"Glass. Bùrcúkù."

"One . . two . . glasses."

"Two glasses."

Rémi opened the cupboard next to the fridge where provisions were stored and picked up a bottle of red wine.

"Wine. Red wine. Mmm! Good!"

"Red wine. Mmm! Good! Chàlli!" I repeated, grinning. The game of language had begun.
Rémi smiled, found a corkscrew, an ashtray, and took me by the arm to lead me in the direction of my bedroom.

The air was fresh but not cold. Rémi opened the windows and, partially, the shutters of the room. He wanted to smoke. First, he undressed himself down to his boxers, and I followed his example. I sighed with relief, finally free of my clothes. Fortunately, there was a little bedside lamp near my bed, shaped like a candle, which gave an almost orange glow. We sat on the windowsill, which was wide enough to accommodate the two of us, the wine bottle, the glasses, and Rémi's tobacco. Rémi opened the bottle and served two glasses of wine. With my new French parents, I was allowed one glass at every meal, and for special occasions, maybe two. I had tasted wine only once or twice since arriving here in France.

There was a silence. We both looked at and assessed each other's bodies. Neither seemed bigger than the other. We were both at that cusp when adolescence was giving way to manhood. Of course, we were still not men and retained that characteristic of youth, an instinct for experimentation. Our bodies were swimming in change, like young wolves—stealing, playing at fighting, but wanting to hunt. Like any wild creature, neither of us would give alliance, friendship, or devotion easily, but we were both aware of a shared will to do so. All those drives of which Rémi was less aware were far more obvious to my conscious mind; I had lived all my life in a world full of wild nature, of which I was a part. I wanted to ask Rémi about cattle, the most important thing for Suri men. Whenever we met and greeted each other, the convention was to ask about each other's cattle—how many we had, their health, how many calves we had, and milking cows. I lifted my fists to either side of my head, my forefingers raised, made a mooing sound, and then pointed to Rémi.

"Non! Non! I don't have any cows!" Rémi laughed and then pointed to me, "And you?" realizing immediately this was a big mistake.

I felt a shadow fall across my face as my head fell forward, and I knew I was slipping away into the pain and horror of the past, and the guilt of still being alive.

Rémi reached forward to touch my sculpted hair and let his hand slide down to stroke my cheek and then took hold of my shoulder, pulling me in towards him. Holding me close, he could feel how every muscle in my body had become tense and rigid. I was no longer breathing. Then I felt the first shake. He pulled me in tighter and with the second shake, I could feel tears wetting his shoulder.

"Tu peux! Tu peux pleurer!"[28] he insisted gently, his own eyes welling up. He heard stifled moans of agony as my body shook again, both of us clinging to each other while Rémi gently rubbed one hand up and down my rigid back. Soon, I pushed myself back upright.

"Hey!" said Rémi, gently tapping my cheek. "Drink! Drink some wine, Chár." He quickly filled two glasses. "On trinque! À nous deux, les jeunes.[29] To us, the young and happy of the house!" he insisted, looking with determination into my sad eyes.

He encouraged me to repeat with a gesture of his hands: "À nous deux," explaining through gestures 'nous' and 'deux'.

---

[28] "You can! You can cry!"
[29] Let's toast! To us two!

"À nous deux. Inye aňi bekaya nanu. Inye aňi goona nanu." My voice still sounded weak.

"What the fuck?" thought Rémi.

"Aňi," pointing to myself, "inye," pointing to Rémi, "bekaya." I took Rémi's hand in a firm grip, almost a handshake.

"Friend?"

"Friend."

"Aňi," again pointing to myself, "inye," again pointing to Rémi, "goona." I pointed to arteries on my wrist and on Rémi's and put them together.

"What's that?" Rémi wondered. "Something about blood? Together? Same?" and then "Brother!" he exclaimed.

"Brother."

We had been drinking rapidly. I refilled the wine glasses for a third time. The bottle was almost empty.

"Wait! Wait!" Rémi lifted both hands wide open, palms towards me. He took out his tobacco, papers, and ganja and started rolling a joint.

I looked on patiently. I liked that wild Rémi had taken the bottle of wine for us to share. Wild Rémi! Wild Rémi teasing his mother. Wild Rémi laughing at the serious adults. My eyes drifted away from what he was doing and eventually settled on his hair. My hand reached forward to touch it, wandering through the curls—soft to touch—which gently wrapped themselves around my fingers. Rémi was grinning at my attention and glanced up to greet my now smiling face. My hand moved slowly down, caressing his cheek and then further to run slowly down his chest. Never had anyone—a friend, a cousin—anyone touch him in that way, let alone a stranger. A sort of examination—an exploration of the new and unknown. He put it down to the fact that he was white and I had probably never seen white skin so close—blonde loose curls instead of thick black tufts. Mind you, he had touched my hair, so it could be a reciprocation of that discovering. He sat completely still allowing this getting-to-know-of-bodies to run its course.

54

For me, Rémi's skin felt like the skin of ripe mango. I let my fingers touch and examine one of his nipples. They were a different colour from his pale skin—darker—a pale reddish brown like leaves in autumn. And he had hair in his armpits darker than the hair on his head. Why didn't he cut it? Altogether I liked Rémi's body. I knew many girls would like his body also and would want to lie with him. He could make as many children as he wanted.

"Come." Rémi had finished preparing the joint and wanted to take me with him to claim another bottle of wine.

He picked up the glasses—offering me my own—and led me to the door and out into the mute and soundless corridor.

Rémi took another bottle from the cupboard near the fridge, opened it, and once again filled our emptied glasses. I immediately took him by his arm to lead him to the back door of the house.

"Wongái![30]" I insisted as we stepped out into the fresh night air.

We crossed the gravel drive and felt the dew-covered grass beneath our feet. At the far end of the lawn was a stone bench under an old Lebanese cedar. We sat with our wine while Rémi lit his joint and passed it to me.

I was feeling fairly drunk already and immediately felt its power. I looked at Rémi with a quizzical frown, twisting an open hand—palm skyward—in a gesture of asking.

"Ganja," said Rémi.

We both fell silent, looking at each other. The brilliant full moon illuminated Rémi's pale skin, his elegant form made distinct by finely pencilled black lines of shadow. Conversely, I was completely black with patches of my smooth skin reflecting blue in the moonlight. It happened often that on such occasions of the full moon, my village would have a party. Everyone would keep fires going all night to ward away the lions, hyenas, and any other big animals, and there would be roasted goat for everyone to eat and plenty of home-made beer. There was always singing, the men singing about how strong and handsome they were, how good they were at sex, and the women also singing about how

---

[30] Come!

55

beautiful they were, about making strong and beautiful children, how the men had to be careful because the girls didn't want just anyone who had no cattle and was lazy or ugly. People would make up the songs spontaneously for the occasion, and back and forth we would go improvising lines and stories and jokes, both collective and singling out individuals. The younger men, especially those who were not married and didn't have a girlfriend, would dance naked to show off their bodies, and likewise the teenage girls their beautiful young breasts. Sometimes these parties would go on until sunrise when the magical cloak of darkness was lifted.

I stood up and pointed to the moon. I wanted to sing, then hesitated, reeling slightly from the wine. I looked at my boxers and pulled them off, saying:

"Boxer a gerthi – no good. Wóhólò!" I struck a pose, putting my hands on my hips and holding my head up proudly. Then, looking at Rémi with a sweep of my hand as if on stage performing an opera, I indicated my whole body, "wóhólò chàlli!"

Pointing to the moon again, I started dancing and singing quietly:

"Wongai, duríyaye, duríyaye, shodigái a chàlli!
Duríyaye, duríyaye, shodigái a chàlli!
Shodigái wóhólò a chàlli."

I beckoned to Rémi to join me, pouring more wine into our glasses and handing him his.

"Wongái! Duríyaye."

Rémi, slightly taken aback by my brazen nakedness, knew I wanted him to dance. Should he join in and be naked as well? He was drunk enough to lose inhibitions and just enjoy the audacious moment without scruples. Would we be caught by the parents? The alcohol made it easier for him to persuade himself it was not every day you had the chance to make a tribal dance naked under the moonlight. I knew this. I saw it in his face as he looked up at the moon. The look of surrender to her temptations. That beautiful thought, naked in the moonlight, with this new and strange friend, inviting him to dance, made him laugh.

"Boxer . . ." he hesitated as he took them off.

"Gerthi," I reminded him.

"Gerthi," he repeated loudly, throwing them into the night sky in a gesture of liberation while laughing loudly.

At that precise moment, a large white bird flew above us as if in concert with our nakedness.

"Baragadúy," I said.

"Owl," Rémi replied. He watched its silent white flight as it seemed to take his boxers in its talons and disappear into the moon. "Wow! Great catch!" he giggled drunkenly.

I indicated Rémi's naked body.

"Wóhólò! Wóhólò chàlli! Rémi a wóhólò," I sang and started my dance. "Rémi a wóhólò, Rémi a chàlli! Anye wóhólò, inye wóhólò, age kan chàlli!"

"Nous nous aimons nus et libre!" Rémi joined in the singing, swaying and slightly staggering. "Ton corps nu! Mon corps nu! Nous sommes les magnifiques, au clair de la lune nue, Le clair de lune bleu et blanc!" He was high with astonishment that even he—so inhibited about singing and about his own body in front of others—had so quickly become like me. He had briefly for an ecstatic, drunken moment become Suri.

After some time, we lay down on the dewy grass and I explained some words: about tagí, the moon; shodigái, the full moon; wóhólò, naked; and chàlli, good, beautiful. When the wine was finished, I put my arm around Rémi's shoulders to return to the house. We were completely drunk, high on the ganja and our midnight dancing.

By the light of the bedside lamp, and in my intoxication, I was briefly drawn by Rémi's golden yellow hair and his autumn copper curls around his dormì (penis) and in his armpits. Why different? I wondered. We were reeling slightly as we sat next to each other giggling. I lifted one of Rémi's arms and put my face into his armpit. I had to taste the perfume of his body. After all, we were brothers, I knew, and becoming brothers more so, now and in a future I had seen. The perfume of my body was that of my birth leopard, coming from his spirit and his skin he had left me to sleep on since I was a newly born a skin which my mother would also wrap me in and I would also wrap myself on occasional cold winter mornings. Rémi's perfume was what? Maybe a slight taste of burned wood, I wondered, knowing his spirit would reveal itself to me one day in a not too distant future. Powers that bind!

"Challi!" I exclaimed laughing and clapping my hands together.

What both surprised and strangely reassured Rémi—since there had been only the two of us—was this confident, at-ease examination of his body, which he just let me get on with. It was the intimacy of careful attention any creature might make. He knew he could do the same with my body if he so wished. Perhaps it was the way bodies spoke to each other before words—something so ancient, its power bound us to all living creatures. I fell backward onto the pillow of my bed and pulled Rémi towards me. The quilt was folded at the bottom of the bed and I briefly opened my eyes to watch him sit up to pull the quilt over both of us. I looked at his back—the dorsal muscles, shoulders, and spine leading down to his buttocks. All was good. His body was good. It didn't occur to me but, of course, Rémi had slept with friends before but never completely naked; they would always at least keep their underwear—whereas I knew that I had never slept alone in my life and never been clothed. The utter foreignness to each other's customs and the evident open trust reassured us both. Before passing into sleep, I was aware of my arm around him—the heat from the top of my thighs and belly against his buttocks—and a deep purring of contentment within my chest.

*　　*　　*

"Hmm, do you think they are OK?" wondered Claudine. She was at the kitchen table with Nathalie.

"Of course, they are fine. Why?"

"Well why aren't they up?"

"They're teenage boys. What do you expect? They always sleep until midday if they can."

"But I thought Chár always woke early."

"True. He has tended to always be awake at dawn. Maybe he is happy with company. I'll put some coffee on and take them a cup each to help them wake up. Anyway, what do you want to do today? Should we go into town, do some shopping, find something nice for dinner? Maybe we could take the boys with us."

"Mmm. Maybe. Perhaps we could go alone, the two of us. I doubt Rémi will want to go."

"As you like."

Claudine got up and left the table, deciding to take a walk down the garden for a cigarette. She didn't like to pollute the kitchen. No one else smoked.

It was a beautiful morning, clear, fresh, and the sun was already warm. Even for Claudine, who had to experience this through a veil of anxiety about Rémi, about her gallery, about Robert who seemed to drink too much and never really supported her worries and the discomfort smoking gave her, including the ashtray taste in her mouth, even through all of this, Claudine was able to appreciate the beauty of this spring morning and warm sun. She walked across the lawn towards the edge of the garden deciding to sit on the bench under the cèdre de Liban[31] in the sun. It was so pleasant to let her worries be subdued by the stillness of nature, clearly getting on with being in tune with itself, the leaves with the sun, the grass with the dew, the birds with the insects. It was a mannerist poem she had going on in her head and as soon as she had acknowledged that imposition of her everyday, the veneer of beauty shattered into invisible shards around her feet. She threw her cigarette to the ground and, watching where it fell, she noticed another dog-end. It seemed unusual and as she leaned forward to examine it more closely, one foot went backwards under the bench and knocked something over. There was a clink-clink of glass. Suddenly those invisible shards had turned against her and were inflaming the wounds of her fears. She bent over and put her head between her legs to see an empty wine bottle and two glasses. She lifted them out and put them on the bench next to her. They were fresh. They looked clean and there was even a drop of wine in the bottom of the bottle and red wine stains at the bottom of the glasses. Who was going to leave these here apart from Rémi? Presumably, he had been here with Chár last night. She couldn't imagine me, Chár, only recently arrived from darkest Africa, to have

---

[31] Lebanese Cedar

organised a midnight drinking party here at the bottom of the garden. It had to have been Rémi! It was one thing to drink the wine, but it was quite another to steal it from Charles and Nathalie. She would have to tell them and make Rémi apologise. Then she looked at the butt-end next to her discarded cigarette. She picked them both up, to tidy up a bit and to put them in one of the wine glasses when she noticed the peculiar rolled card in the end of the one she had discovered. Oh, no! He's smoking drugs!

She leaned back and lit another cigarette. She was going to kill herself with these damned things, but she didn't know how to manage without them. There was too much going on without making life even more difficult.

What was that hanging from a branch in the tree? It looked like a pair of shorts. Weren't they Rémi's? Oh, my God! What on Earth? They were too far away, too high to reach. She cast her eyes about to see what else she could find and there a few metres away were another pair of shorts. This time she didn't recognise them and could only assume they were Chár's, mine. What on earth had we been up to?

*   *   *

Charles and Robert-Louis had arrived back from the village with croissants and bread. Nathalie prepared a tray with two bowls of milky coffee and a couple of croissants. She tapped on the bedroom door and slowly entered. We were still sleeping, now with Rémi's arm across my chest.

"Morning!" she called.

Both of us looked up.

"Bonjour, Nathalie," said Rémi.

"Bonjour, Nathalie," I said.

"I've brought you some coffee and croissants."

"Merçi," we both said.

"So, you have slept well together?" she asked, smiling.

Rémi looked slightly embarrassed being found in bed next to me.

"Nathalie," said Rémi, "Don't tell my mother that we slept together. Nothing happened. We were just sleeping. Chár prefers sleeping next to someone. You know. And my mother is crazy. She imagines all sorts of mad things."

"Elle est anxieuse, c'est tout. Don't worry, Rémi. I don't doubt you were simply sharing a bed. Don't worry about your mother. So, you had a good time last night, after we old people had gone to bed?"

"I stole a couple of bottles of wine. I hope you don't mind."

"So, you both have hangovers then."

"Yeh, I have a thick head. I don't know about you," Rémi said, nudging me with his shoulder.

"Ok? Good? Chàlli?" he asked.

"Chàlli. Good." I replied.

"You speak Suri now? My goodness! Drink your coffee, eat your croissants and we'll see you in the kitchen shortly."

Thirty or forty minutes later, we walked through the kitchen door and the entire kitchen fell silent as all eyes turned upon us. The empty wine bottle and glasses were standing on the kitchen table, next to our underwear from last night. Claudine had been exhorting the others to censure our conduct.

"Ah. le vin!" I said. "Le très bon vin!"[32] Suddenly hearing my deep African voice speaking French dumbfounded the grown-ups. "Merçi. Merçi, Charles."

There was a general hesitation. Then Charles, so pleased to hear me addressing him personally in French, jumped up and embraced me with even a slight tear in his eyes.

---

[32] Ah, the wine! The very good wine!

"De rien! De rien!"[33] he said. "It's nothing! You are welcome. Il a un très bon accent, eh?" he continued, turning to the rest of the room.

"Rémi, what were you doing last night that suddenly Chár is speaking?" asked Nathalie.

"We took some wine. That was my idea. I am sorry, Charles. And Chár wanted to go outside to see the . . ." he paused, "Tagí."

"What?"

"Tagí."

"La lune,[34]" I explained, as if French was now suddenly the most natural of languages for me.

Everyone looked at both Rémi and me, astonished.

"In fact the . . . Shodigái."

"Full moon," I explained again.

"And what about these?" demanded Claudine. She had been pacing back and forth, waving an unlit cigarette between her fingers, looking more and more fraught.

"Boxer a gerthi," I said.

"What?" Claudine looked exasperated.

"Boxers are no good, ugly," Rémi explained.

"Wóhólò a chàlli," I added.

"Naked is beautiful," Rémi translated. He must have been laughing inside behind that seriously humble look.

"Oh, my God! My God!" Claudine finally collapsed in a chair.

"Calm down, Claudine!" said Robert. "Of course, naked is beautiful!

---

[33] It's nothing!
[34] The moon!

Enfin!" he laughed. "Don't have your nervous breakdown again and upset everyone!"

"Rémi my brother," I said. We looked at each other and grinned. "Suri. Same me."

Everyone was still stunned !

« Alors, on va fêter tout ça, je pense, eh? » Charles declared. "Rémi, go down to the cellar with your brother to find some good bottles of wine for lunch."

Rémi took his mother's hand and said: "Don't make anything of it, mom. Everything is fine!" He leaned forward to kiss her on the cheek.

"Wóhólò Tagí!" I exclaimed, looking at Rémi with a big smile. "This is my Wóhólò Tagí! My Naked Moon!"

*   *   *

Leopards are born survivors. From the jungles of the Rift Valley they have successfully spread through Arabia into India, South East Asia, China and Eastern Russia. While other big cats have found it difficult to adapt to alien environments, not so the leopard. In that respect, they are like humans. In fact, they often live close to humans and with civilisation encroaching further into their environment, even amongst them, unseen. They know how to be invisible. Leopards try to avoid confrontations with their enemies, mostly lions and hyenas, preferring to escape and hide. This makes them no cowards, but simply more intelligent.

Black leopards are black through an anomaly of pigmentation. They still have the ghost of the natural markings faintly visible through the predominant veil of black. The black leopard, sometimes referred to as a ghost, a spirit leopard, by humans living near them, are better suited to the gloom of dark forests and jungles where they disappear into the shadows. Of course, at night they can never be seen and even during the day easily disappear, which is why, even though widely reported as existing in the wild in Britain, it is practically impossible to verify sightings. They are the illegal immigrants of the natural world.

*   *   *

Rémi, Rémi, what is on your mind? What are you thinking?

Back at school, Rémi didn't chat with his school mates about his weekend. Why? He was not really sure. His two best friends had asked him about it, since, when he was in Paris, they tended to meet up at Rémi's home and his absence had been missed. Hamid Reza was very beautiful, with black curling hair and pale brown eyes. As Robert, Rémi's father, said often about Hamid Reza, « Les Persans ont toujours les yeux perçants ![35] » His family left Iran at the time of the revolution, fearing a future under the mullahs and, maintaining family relations in Iran, had made their fortune importing carpets and caviar. Jacob had a slightly elongated face and similar doe eyes to Hamid Reza but whereas Hamid's eyes, the corners were all on the same horizontal plane, with Jacob, the exterior corners were slightly higher than the interior corners near the bridge of his nose, which gave him the appearance of always laughing. Again, as striking as Hamid's nut brown eyes, his were of a colour which seemed to fluctuate with the weather, from bluish grey to green and back again.

They were both religious, Hamid Reza Muslim and Jacob, Jewish. But neither in the sense of the obsessively, newly converted, or campaigning for rights, or Sharia, They believed and took the truths of their convictions for granted, but without arguing the superiority of one over the other. They were not interested in persuading anyone, nor angrily defending their beliefs. The little rituals and customs were just part of them. They just got on with it. But both of them were really good at using expletives and insults from their own cultures, especially to insult each other. For Jacob, anyone who annoyed him was a fucking goy, a stupid goy, for Hamid Reza, it was kuffir, dirty kuffir. For each other, Jacob was the stupid yid, and Hamid Reza a fucking sand nigger, mossy or towel head. Jacob attended the temple regularly and Hamid Reza the mosque, it was their mothers who insisted, and their mothers who would not allow them to stay overnight at weekends with each other, even though they were best friends. Meeting in the evenings to do homework was one thing, but staying over for the pleasure of it, no. The boys put up with their mothers as just fucking racists. What could they do? Their mothers loved them, did everything for them and did their best to smother any desires they might have outside the family. So, they both ended up inviting themselves to stay over at Rémi's, which was fine with both their mothers, it being perceived as neutral territory. And although Robert was perfectly capable of using racist slurs, cursing and insulting

---

[35] Persians always have piercing eyes. (Of course in French it is much more of a play on words.)

people, it seemed to both boys it was no more than with the same vulgarity that they also employed. They thought he was funny.

These three had known each other since primary school. They knew each other so well, they were practically family. During prepubescence, they had compared penises, like all boys around that age. Jacob and Hamid Reza were so pleased to discover their penises were more or less the same, circumcised, that this reaffirmed their convictions that their parents attitudes to each other's religions was stupid bigotry and racism. In fact, they continued to find similarities, ideas on hygiene, what is kosher and what is halal, a lot of the foods they enjoyed were the same, or very similar and their mothers were practically identical with their neurotic over-protective and controlling ideas, not just over them, but their sisters and fathers also. They even had a common ancestor, Abraham.

As for Rémi, he was a communist, like his father, although he didn't really understand how Robert-Louis could be communist and extremely wealthy. When he was younger, he just took it for granted, wealth. It didn't mean anything; it was just there. It was only later, as a teenager he started to have moral uncertainties about the contradictions between his father's political convictions and his material wealth. Typically, of many non-religious families in France, since state education provided no religious education whatsoever, Rémi had no knowledge at all of such significant Middle Eastern mythological characters as Abraham or Moses and certainly didn't know Mohammed from Adam. He even knew nothing about Jesus and had no interest in a vague figure to do with — a donkey and Christmas; his family, nevertheless, celebrated Christmas as a time to reaffirm family relations and affections, even though Robert as a confirmed Marxist would always find the opportunity point out the 'obscenities of capitalism' through exploiting financially the general public as much as possible over both festivities Xmas and New Year. Raised by his Marxist father who'd declared war on superstition and soup kitchens alike, Rémi had simply grown up without any of it. As well, and importantly, there was no religious education in state schools since the Revolution; in general, it had been agreed that the Catholic church had interfered far too much in political affairs during the time of kings and would always want to be the dominant force in ruling France, hence all religious teaching was excluded from state education. It wasn't that he hated religion, he just couldn't fathom why anyone would waste time thinking about it.

"God wanted to test Abraham's faith, so he told him to sacrifice his son," said Jacob, launching into a familiar debate.

"Why?" said Rémi, with a grin, knowing what was to ensue.

"It was a test, right?" Jacob shrugged.

"So he hears a voice telling him to kill his kid and goes along with it? What was he, some kind of nutcase?"

"Of course not! Then an angel shows up and tells him to sacrifice a lamb instead."

"Voices and angels? Come on. That's the kind of thing that gets you locked up these days. Heavy meds. No scissors and your shoelaces taken away."

"Look, you dumb goy," said Jacob, rolling his eyes. "The point is that it ends child sacrifice. Primitive religions used to do that. This was God saying don't. It's a step forward."

"You really are a blaspheming kafir. There's no salvation for you, Rémi. Even I, before God, although reluctantly, would have to bear witness against you," mock seriousness followed by a glance for response.

"As long as I get to keep my dick intact, that's fine by me," Rémi grinned.

"Even today, in some places, kids get accused of being witches or possessed and get killed," Jacob said, his voice tightening. "What Abraham was doing was…civilising people."

"I'm proud he's our founding father," added Hamid, nudging Jacob.

"Me too," said Jacob, both of them grinning back at Rémi.

At which point the argument trailed off into half-laughs. They'd had versions of it before. For Rémi, history didn't begin with a man about to murder his son because of a divine whisper. The whole vertical line from Abraham to the end of the world — it was all a story people told to make sense of the chaos. If people wanted to believe different stories, fine — so long as they didn't kill each other over it.

What mattered more to Rémi was what his own body was telling him: the sculptures, the paintings, the plays of ancient Greek myths, with their wine and wrath and naked gods, made more sense than voices from the sky, and a lot sexier. They didn't ask for blood. They just asked you to feel some sort of passion through the most fantastical and often hilarious stories, Hercules having to clear horse shit, for example, from some old and massive stables as one of his twelve labours.

He knew, although he could never have predicted, that Jacob and Hamid would always be his friends. They were different, yes, but not divided. Remembering his weekend with me, - now I was something else entirely, from a different world altogether with its own special and bizarre customs - Rémi decided it was best to say nothing for now. But he also sensed that the longer he stayed silent, the more of a secret it would become. Was this a good idea, such secrets from friends?

*   *   *

Leaving school, they had crossed the courtyard and were at the huge, decorated iron gate of the main entrance. Busy Parisian traffic raced along Avenue Georges Mandel not far from the school entrance, with trees and a pedestrian walkway, mostly used for parked cars, at the centre, separating the two carriageways. At the gate, Jacob took his kippah out of his pocket and sat it on the back of his head, not allowed in school, but for him, automatic out in the streets. Within a few yards, they were confronted by the Russian bully. He was a student at their same lycée, friendless, apart from a couple of thick ugly cohorts whose only quality was accusing other students of being gay.

"Got any money, Yid? Oh yeh, that's right, you Yids are good at collecting gold, in't yer? How much are you going to pay me to not smack you?"

"Haven't got any money."

Zhukov hit him across the head knocking his kippah to the ground.

"Pick it up and give it to me."

Jacob bent down to pick it up and Zhukov punched him on the back of the head. He fell to his knees. Standing slowly, with tears in his eyes, he handed over his kippah.

"OK, idiots, empty your pockets."

All three handed over what cash they had. Zhukov and his thugs left tearing the kippah to pieces and throwing it aside.

"Make sure you've got more cash tomorrow, fucking slimey Yid!"

The three friends walked slowly to Square Lamartine to sit on a bench under the trees to recover. They took the Metro a short distance, accompanying Jacob home.

*   *   *

I was lying in bed. In my own bed. This was a new idea for me. Until now, I had only ever shared things. With my family. With friends, other boys, when I was away from the village taking care of the cattle. My body also was part of my family, or part of my friends, even the cattle, each of which had special names, special characters, special needs and special love. And the jungle also, as I walked through, it was part of my body and I was part of it. I was my own body's physical experience of everything around me. I am because of you, because of that, through that other.

There were so many things here. Most things seemed only to be looked at, or of use so rarely as to be lying around like uncovered corpses. The world of things was distracting, occasionally charming even and hilariously irrelevant, but it was not possible to share it, what I mean, was to be part of it, my body and spirit becoming part of it. The idea of something belonging to me, any more than the entire world and planet being mine, was strange. I had some beads which hung around my hips and more around my neck, but after that, oh yes, my bhirɛ[36]. My father had cows. It was possible to count cows, know their names, drink their milk and their blood. The cows gave themselves into the care of my father and he cared for them. Hence, it seemed to me that all things in my life and immediate experience were mine but never exclusively so, just as everything was also Rémi's in this, our world, including me. I become responsible for him, for his well-being, and he for me.

---

[36]   Fighting stick

68

The more private something became, the less it seemed possible to share in its nature and the more its nature seemed to gain an insidious power over others. Thank goodness there was Marie Jeanne to look after the world of things, to clean them, organise them and control them before they took over. This is why I did not trust clothes and preferred to remove them at every opportunity. I couldn't help noticing how white people had lost their bodies; their bodies were just their clothes. It was impossible to know these people; they were always hidden. I was not going to let clothes do this to my body, make me disappear. I was my body and nothing but my body and I was happy for others to know me as I was. I was especially happy Rémi had easily thrown away his clothes also. In his heart he was Suri.

Of course, I loved Nathalie and Charles, but what a pity I couldn't see them.

*   *   *

So, I was lying alone in my own bed. I had understood that I couldn't climb into bed with Nathalie and Charles. But what I found now was that, sleeping alone, I was subjected to far more dreams. It was as if my body had to imagine away my being alone. On several nights, my mother had returned. . . . I felt a painful incomprehension . . . the landscape was strange, with my home and other huts unusually crowded upon each other with too many wooden fences both to keep animals in and others out, but they had become complicated . . . I had difficulty finding my way through them, through an uglified, complexified, and decomposing familiarity. My mother was at ease, unperturbed by the environment, which had tilted out of shape, and unconcerned by the fact that she had been absent for such a long time. I even asked her through my anxiety, "Where have you been for so long?", but she gave no explanation.

For a second or so, after I had woken, I felt relieved she had returned. Then there was the realization and appalling disappointment.

This particular night, I had been dreaming about the first time I had seen aranjinya. . . . I was in the country and very young, maybe six or seven, with Bongáy. We were looking after the cows. I was squatting on the shoulders of a cow that loved me with unfaltering devotion, Chooka, her name. Both Bongáy and I had just finished rubbing ash into her white and beige hide to protect her from mosquitoes and other pests. We were also covered in ash, naked apart from a string around our waists, not even beads. So, I was squatting on Chooka's shoulders while Bongáy stood on the middle of her back, leaning with both hands on my shoulders. We were looking out across open countryside with mostly grassland and clumps of bushes. It was hot. In the shimmering distance, I saw a figure walking along a path, dressed in white and red. As I watched the figure approach, it became Nathalie, smiling and waving. I turned to tell Bongáy and saw it was no longer Bongáy, but Rémi. Now, still in the dream, Rémi was lying next to me, his knees into my folded legs, hips against my buttocks and warm belly against my back, an arm around my chest.

I slipped into deep thought about Rémi. Why did he have to go back to Paris after that weekend? When people meet new friends, they stay together for a long time to make the bonds of friendship strong, to become close, as one, to share the same heart, the same spirit. It made no sense to me that only after two days some power, some invisible force was making Rémi do something he clearly didn't want to do. And why couldn't I go to Paris with Rémi? I knew something about school. I had been to a school near Beyahola for a short time, but then they wanted me to wear shorts, so I stopped going. Nathalie had promised that soon we would be going to Paris for a visit. I had to be content with that.

I curled up under my duvet. I felt warm and happy remembering Rémi, but now I couldn't sleep. My mind was racing wildly through memories and imaginings. I had not known this world of dreams or paid attention to it until coming to Europe; generally, I had slept solidly through the night until dawn.

I got up and started pacing about my room. I quickly decided to go out. I went into the kitchen and chose one of Charles' knives from amongst a collection hanging on the wall. I returned to my bedroom to find a belt to hang it from, then stepped out into the fresh night.
There was a full moon. This is what had kept me awake, causing my mind to race. I knew my excited imagination was simply a symptom of my body wanting to do other things. It was like dogs running back and forth as they waited impatiently to follow their master into the forest. As soon as I was outside, my mind immediately focused, heightening my vision and hearing. My skin intensified the sensation of the molecules of fresh oxygen swirling across its surface. I crossed the field at the end of the garden and started running. The cold stars watched in silence as the moon guided my instinct. As I met the edge of the forest, I disappeared.

70

There was an immediate change of air—straight away humid and warmer—the fetid fermentation of fallen leaves and undergrowth filled my lungs. The overhanging branches and stiff spikes of bush twigs scratched at my skin and swallowed the silver moonlight. There were different perfumes in the air: some of leaves, some of soil, some of faeces and some of death. I let my electric body follow the scents until I found a small winding path—a path which took note of surrounding trees, bushes, grasses, and stones; a path not made by humans or civilization; there were no straight lines to it; it was not measured, but responded to everything it encountered—a dark and secret path that only forest creatures could know. By now, I was floating, no longer needing to think where my feet fell; it was a sort of transcendent walking—silent, secretive, undisturbing to everything that composed the path itself—a walking which none, even the wildest of animals, would notice. At a short distance, I saw the reflections of moonlight through branches in a still pool of water and then my steps and body movement changed to lift me without a sound into the branches of the overhanging trees.

It was impossible to know how long I waited, watching small animals come and go—forest rats, des loirs[37], some ground birds. Then a cat appeared. This was not a domestic cat; it was too big—yellow with a few black spots here and there—not so dense as a leopard but nevertheless a trait of its race—not a genetic aberration. The cat leaned forward to drink and then turned to look directly at me, the exception to my conviction. Only another cat could know I was there. Only another cat could recognize me. The sky was turning a dark blue. Dawn was arriving and birds were starting their morning calls. Then I heard something much bigger and cumbersome making its way through the undergrowth. It was big and fat—maybe bigger than me—and black with coarse hair. I could hear it grunting and snorting; it didn't care about being discreet. Once its snout was in the water, the intense moment of snapping through silent stillness arrived. I fell from the branches onto its back, my right arm held high with a knife in hand; as my legs hit the animal's back, I stabbed the knife into its neck and pulled to make a wide cut. There was a loud scream and I instantly jumped back into the branches. The boar bounced around, splashing the edge of the pool and crashing into bushes and tree trunks—blood spouting from its throat. I remembered the commander—the stupid soldiers herding my people through the jungle. I knew how to hunt and kill—that black shadow— the ghost—falling from the trees—disappearing their captain's driver—

---

[37] dormice

71

arranging the corpses of two Dizi soldiers side by side—and finally blinding the captain; I was leopard; I was Chár!

And now you know me.

The trees swooned with the commotion until the boar slowed and eventually fell into the mud at the side of the pool—the final spurts of blood pulsing into the water. The dark blue of the sky was changing—lightening—and slowly the bushes and trees became more distinct. I jumped down beside the dead boar and slit open its belly to eviscerate it.

*   *   *

Charles got up and sleepily wandered in his pyjamas towards the kitchen, pausing to unbolt the back door so that Marie Jeanne would be able to enter freely when she arrived. The bolts were already open.

"Nathalie, did you open the back door earlier?" he called out.

"No," came the reply from the bedroom.

The door opened and in walked Marie Jeanne.

"Bonjour, Monsieur."

"Bonjour, Marie Jeanne." Charles returned the greeting and then again called to Nathalie, "Is Chár still in his room?"

Marie Jeanne hurried into the kitchen and started tidying up around the sink and work surfaces.

"Should I put some coffee on for you and Madame Nathalie?"

"Oui, merçi, Marie Jeanne."

"The young master has gone out already, has he?"

"I don't know. The bolts on the back door were already open when I came downstairs."

"He's not in his bed." Nathalie had just arrived in the kitchen in a dressing gown.

They sat down at the kitchen table. Charles started cutting bread.

"Where's my big knife?"

Marie Jeanne put butter, jam and honey on the table.

"Where can he be?"

"I suspect he cannot sleep at night. I've heard him a few times."

Marie Jeanne picked up the cafetière and hurried towards the table, passing the kitchen window.

Suddenly, there was a loud scream. The cafetière went flying through the air and Marie Jeanne fell backwards to the floor, leaning against a cupboard.

"Jesus Christ! Marie Jeanne, are you OK? What is it?"

"There's a monster, Monsieur! A monster on the lawn!"

Fortunately, the cafetière had not spilled on anyone but simply smashed and thrown coffee up the white wall and over the tiled floor.

Charles looked out of the window and sure enough there was a monster walking across the lawn on its hind legs, over 2 metres in height with a boar's head looking straight at the kitchen window.

"What the bloody hell!"

"What now?" said Nathalie who got up to look also. "Oh, my God! What has he done?"

"Alors, là, je ne sais pas! Incroyable! Comment a-t-il pu tuer ça ?"[38]

Charles rushed out of the kitchen, through the back door and down the steps to cross the gravel yard towards the lawn and then stopped, agog at what he was seeing. I was completely naked, of course, but now covered in blood and slime. I had eviscerated the boar and put the carcass over my head such that the boar's head was sitting on top of my head and I

---

[38] "I've no idea! Unbelievable! How on Earth has he managed to kill that?"

was inside the rib cage and belly, its back and rear legs hanging behind me. It had been the best way to carry it back to the house. I had padded the inside of the rib cage with grasses so that its bones did not hurt my scalp for the trek home. I stopped, lifted it off my head and shoulders and dropped it on the neat lawn.

Charles looked at me, speechless, grinned and started laughing.

"What have you done? Are you mad? How did you do that?" He stepped over the carcass and threw his arms around my bloodstained shoulders and back and gave me a big kiss on the cheek. He himself, his pyjamas, his face, his hair were now also covered in blood and slime.

"No! Stop!" called Nathalie from the doorstep suspecting we were about to drag blood, slime and a dead carcass into the kitchen. "You can't come in! Charles, get the hose and hose both of yourselves down before you put blood everywhere."

"Yes, of course. I didn't think. How is Marie Jeanne?"

"She's in a state of shock, obviously. You know how nervous she can be."

"Call her husband, Louis-Marie. Ask him to come. Explain that we have a boar's carcass here and we need help. Give Marie Jeanne a glass of cognac. She'll feel better," demanded Charles. "There are some of Claudine's cigarettes she left behind in the drinks cabinet if Marie Jeanne wants."

In the kitchen, Marie Jeanne was still on the floor, legs apart, and missing a shoe. She was panting heavily and fanning herself with the folds of her skirt, most of which was now around her waist. She was murmuring incomprehensibly, possibly a prayer, with every out breath as if in some religious trance and speaking in tongues.

"Here, Marie Jeanne. Drink some of this," said Nathalie, putting a large glass of cognac to her lips.

"What did I see, Madame? What horror was that? My heart! It's beating too fast! Already the Doctor is worried about my blood pressure."

"It wasn't a monster at all. It was Chár with . . ."

"Ah, non!" Marie Jeanne immediately and hysterically interrupted. "No, no , no! It wasn't the handsome young master. It was something horrible, black, hairy and covered in blood, standing on its back legs so you could see its . . . ."

"Calm down, Marie Jeanne. It was certainly young master Chár who, without anyone knowing has been out hunting and returned with his kill, a wild boar."

"No, I don't believe it! He is too young to do that. How is it possible?"

"I'm going to call your husband. . ."

"No! Don't do that! He'll think I am stupid! He'll just be angry!"

"Not for you, Marie Jeanne, for Charles. He wants help with the boar. Now come, let me help you up and you can sit more comfortably on the kitchen bench."

She seemed to be calming down and was no longer panting and moaning in tongues.

"Let me get you another cognac. In fact, I'll have one with you. Don't tell Charles what we are drinking; it's his favourite."

"Madame, you are too kind."

Nathalie took Marie Jeanne into the parlour away from the kitchen window.

"Look, Marie Jeanne, Charles is outside with Chár hosing him down. He is covered in blood from the boar so he has to get rid of that before he comes in the house. As you know in the jungle in Africa, he was naked all the time, as naked as the day he was born. He is naked now and I guess he was naked when he was out hunting. So I want you to stay here with me until they are clean and have returned to the house to get dressed. I don't want you seeing him naked and giving yourself a heart attack. We'll stay here, have another glass of cognac and smoke a cigarette."

"Oui, Madame," said Marie Jeanne with a look of exhaustion and horror on her face.

Nathalie tried to smile benignly and reassuringly and quickly lit two cigarettes passing one to Marie Jeanne.

Outside, Charles had attached the hose to a garden tap and turned it on. Water straight from the tap was icy cold and as the jet hit my chest, the shock made me shrink away with a loud howl.

"Wait! Stand still!"

I looked up at Charles with a grin and started to rub my skin to remove the blood, slime and mud, panting, and occasionally howling with the cold.

"Fuuucck!" I shouted.

"What?" Charles turned the jet away. "What did you say?"

I stopped rubbing the blood from my skin and looked at Charles.\

"What did you say?"

"Fuck."

"You said fuck?"

"Fuck," I said again grinning.

"Fucking hell! Now it is cursing that is part of his current vocabulary!" Charles lifted his arms into the air as if praising the heavens.

"Fuck, fuck, fuck, fuck!" I repeated and started dancing around the lawn.

"That's wonderful you've learned how to swear but don't repeat words like that to Nathalie! You hear me?"

Of course, Charles knew I was understanding little of his words, so with waving arms, gestures and expressions, I guess I realised the limitations of the use of this word.

Charles aimed the jet of water at me again which made me scream and run.

"OK. OK," insisted Charles. "Calm down! Now you get clean."

I finished rubbing away the blood and dirt until nothing remained but my glistening black skin.

"He's very beautiful," I saw Charles pause to look at my body, "not too muscular but clearly strong. A handsome boy." And I knew he was pleased.

His reverie was interrupted when I took the hose from his hands and indicated for him to take off his pyjamas. He was content to do so not because he wished to expose himself in front of not only me but also the birds, sky, Gods and possibly Marie Jeanne and her husband who was due to arrive. He was content because underneath he had his boxers which he could legitimately retain. I indicated with a nod and a cheeky smile towards his boxers.

"Boxers a gerthi – no good!" I laughed.

"Yes, so I've been told."

Charles declined with a shake of his head and with great delight I directed the jet at his chest.

Nathalie wondered anxiously sitting next to Marie Jeanne what all the screaming and shouting was about quickly poured two more glasses of cognac and lit two more cigarettes.

"Alors, feeling better, Marie Jeanne?" Charles had taken a warm shower was now dressed and had entered the kitchen where Marie Jeanne and Nathalie were cleaning up the coffee and broken glass.

"Yes thank you Monsieur. I am so sorry for the coffee stains on the wall."

"Don't worry it's nothing. Nathalie go see Chár who's getting out of the shower. His skin has been badly scratched in several places by I don't know what. I think they need to be attended to. Your husband still hasn't arrived Marie Jeanne? I want Chár to join in with cutting the carcass to learn how to prepare and joint the meat."

"Ah, oui! Louis has done that all his life."

Nathalie found me coming out of the bathroom and followed me to my bedroom intending to check my wounds. She had tears in her eyes to see my body damaged and scratched. I stood like a child with complete surrender in front of her, moved that she should have tears for me. She applied some hexomédine transcutanée to my abrasions and a couple of plasters where there was fresh blood.

Louis Marie stepped out of his Deux Chevaux[39], to find Charles, who was waiting at the backdoor, and I, sitting on the steps. The carcass was still on the lawn.

« Bonjour, Monsieur ! Oh là là ! Belle bête, n'est-ce pas ? Comment l'a-t-il tuée, le jeune maître ?[40] »

"Bonjour, Monsieur Morel! We don't know! No idea. He took a knife from the kitchen that's it."

"Ah oui! I see one blow to the jugular. Impressionnant!" And then Monsieur Morel, Louis Marie, turned to me, demanding directly: "How did you kill it, eh?"

We had all approached the boar's carcass. With my people on such occasions as a successful hunt, everyone wants to hear the story of the kill, and it's expected the hunter will perform the kill for the rest of the village as part of the general entertainment and excitement for the feast to come. I danced a stabbing gesture, pointed to the sky, indicated jumping onto the beast, stabbing its neck, then jumping back up, each movement performed with grace and strength, showing off my body and letting it explain itself.

"Have you seen what he is doing?" exclaimed Louis Marie. "It's like he is dancing!"

We Suri, we don't just talk with words, but with our bodies also, which was fortunate because here I didn't have any words at all!

"Have you understood what he's telling us?" Both men were a little taken aback.

---

[39] Citroen 2CV
[40] Good morning, sir! Oh my! Beautiful beast, isn't it? How did he kill it, the young master?

78

"He flew out of the sky?" The two older men laughed.

"He jumped from a tree don't you think? Stabbed it then jumped back into the tree?"

"Unbelievable! You could have died eh?" Louis Marie exclaimed, looking at me. "Boars are very dangerous." And then turning to Charles, "He's really special, the young master you've adopted, eh, Monsieur de Rochbrune?"

"How much do you think it weighs?"

"It looks like a young male adult, two years old perhaps, which could weigh in the forests nearby between seventy and a hundred kilos, 90 kilos. Now eviscerated? I don't know – fifty kilos, I guess. How was he able to carry it here?"

"On his head!"

"Quoi?!" said Louis-Marie starting to laugh, "Incroyable! He's pretty fit, isn't he, this young lad!"

When it came to deciding what to do with the boar Charles wanted to cure the two hams. The belly pork could be kept frozen likewise ribs and forelegs. The head? He didn't know what to do with it so Louis Marie suggested calling the restaurant in the village which had a wood-fired brick oven. Maybe they could use it. Very soon, the eldest son of the restaurateur, who shook my hand and introduced himself as Michel, had arrived with his own knives, ready to help.

Once the three men had finished burning off the hair, scrubbing the skin with stiff wire brushes until almost pink, then sectioning it, the young Michel left with the head to roast it, offering to bring it to our house whenever was convenient after midday. The cure for the two hind legs was a mix of salt and sugar which had to be rubbed into flesh. I had never seen any such preparation before.

Very quickly, it seemed that everyone in the village had heard the tale of the young black boy rescued and adopted by Monsieur and Madame de Rochebrune, his adventures in the forest, hunting and killing an "enormous" boar, possibly the biggest ever slaughtered in that part of La

Sologne; the rumours of simple humanity. All those who considered themselves friends of the de Rochebrunes were so excited they had to be invited to celebrate this brilliant kill, meet their wonderful adopted son who had proved himself part of the hunting community of the Sologne already.

"Charles, I have some very good bottles of Burgundy which we must open to celebrate this moment in the history of our village. It will not be forgotten for a long time!" telephoned the mayor.

"I'll arrive with the roasted head around three o'clock. my wife wants to bring a Salade Nicoise," said the restaurant owner.

"It's been too long since this boy arrived in the country. We should meet him," said the local pork butcher, "I want to know how he killed that creature!"

Nathalie insisted I wear shoes for the afternoon party, even though I couldn't stand them, plus a nice pair of jeans and beautiful white shirt which she had found in Dolce et Gabbana in Orléans. I surrendered to being dressed and requested I borrow a string of Nathalie's pearls, which was the only decoration I wanted to wear. Seeing myself beautifully dressed with my new white shirt, white pearls contrasting against my black skin filled her with admiration and pride.

"I love you Chár," she said kissing me on both cheeks.

"I love you Nathalie," I replied putting my arms around her neck.

"OK let's go meet the world. Don't forget to shake hands with each person you meet (she showed me how), say bonjour Monsieur or bonjour Madame."

« Bonjour Monsieur, Bonjour Madame, » I repeated.

« T'as un très bon accent, mon chéri »

*   *   *

"Bonjour Madame Comment allez-vous?"

"Très bien merçi," replied Madame le Maire (in fact she was not the

80

mayor simply the mayor's wife but preferred to be known as Madame le Maire), then turning towards the crowd exclaimed: "Ooh là là! Qu'est-ce qu'il parle bien le Français! How well he speaks French! He's just asked how I am with an absolutely exquisite accent!" And turning back towards me, she asked: " And what is your name?"

"Je m'appelle Chár, Madame. Et vous vous appellez comment?"

Immediately Madame le Maire launched into incomprehensible rapid French addressing the gathering, interspersed with high pitched laughs, smattered with a selection of expressions of astonishment, ecstatic joy, admiration, which she had used so often in company that she thought them quite natural. I was too polite to allow myself to react to what reminded me of the screeches of a baboon spotting a lion. This social hysteria seemed bizarre. Fortunately, my teacher intervened to distract Madame le Maire and explain the French I was starting to learn. Madame le Maire fulminated congratulations on her efforts as my teacher.

I was led away by Charles who introduced me to a group of men, who all wanted to shake my hand, Once again I managed to greet everyone politely. Louis Marie considered himself my representative, assisting in recounting the tale. Earlier, while Charles and Louis Marie were busy salting hams, cutting entire sides to barbecue and long before everyone arrived, I was with my teacher and Nathalie explaining with drawings and learning sentences to summarise predation and the hunt.

"There was a path, some water, a pond, I climbed a tree over the path, and waited. At dawn, the boar came to drink. I jumped on his back, cut his neck with my knife and jumped back into my tree." I had learned my lines.

I gestured with my hand, blood pumping from the boar's, neck, dropping my head to one side, closing my eyes, lolling out my tongue and dying. Louis Marie's daughter Juliette had left Marie Jeanne, her mother's side, where she had been assisting to prepare the table, to join the group of men around me. She was watching and laughing quietly at my gestures and face pulling.

"I can't believe this," said one "It's impossible!"

"Why? Very difficult maybe but if you're used to hunting with a knife . . . " demanded another.

'It is not possible to confront such beast on foot They're too dangerous."

"Well, yes, but even so."

"I believe him," said Juliette.

"Chár," said Louis-Marie demanding my attention "I want you meet my daughter, Juliette."

Oh là là! What had happened?!

I became very conscious Juliette had been looking at me. I could feel a heightened sense of awareness in my body as it moved from one foot to another. She was looking at the black skin of my chest beyond the open neck of my white shirt.

"I believe him also," said her father. "He was raised like that. He has met many other creatures no doubt far more dangerous than this one."

"His tribe was almost hunter-gatherers as I understand," said someone else.

"A hunter-gatherer society has a totally different view of life to us, it must be said," said another.

"Yes, a very primitive life."

"They keep cows think."

"Without writing, without art, without culture."

"Do they have a religion?"

"Well perhaps one day he'll tell you all these things when he speaks your language fluently himself," said Juliette testily "In the meantime, perhaps we should keep our ideas to ourselves. It is bad manners talking about him to his face when he doesn't understand, right? All we can say is, you French like debates!" she laughed.

"C'est vrais, Juliette. C'est très français les débats!" said Nathalie, who had just arrived amongst the little group of the opinionated. "So everyone, Bertrand Dussault, our dear neighbour and mayor has brought some very special wine for us all to taste. Please let me fill your glasses."

"Come with me," said Juliette, quietly holding out her hand towards me "we can help Monsieur Charles with the barbecue."

Suddenly time had stopped for me, but at the same time everything happened too fast.

"Juliette," I repeated, under my breath, to write it's music into my memory.

I saw this very small, white, delicate hand held out towards me. As I lifted my eyes to meet hers, I noticed a slightly quizzical smile; she had heard me repeat her name. I didn't know what to say; it seemed stupid to simply repeat those phrases I had learned for this barbeque. But more than that, Juliette had carried me back to what could have been a village party in Beyahola and just like young Suri women, finding a partner, as was our custom that the women choose and pursue a husband, rather than the men, she had revealed a future in which we would be living together, making a family. Something special, something unusual had happened. A repeat of a Suri way. It happens at stick fights and big Suri gatherings - she had chosen me! Juliette had chosen me! I understood nothing of course of the conversation around me and felt slightly uncomfortable, but now this delicate, beautiful young girl was rescuing me, holding out her hand for me to take. I watched my own hand reach out to hers, our fingers touch, and the hard dry skin of my palm reach her soft delicate hand. Juliette! Ah Juliette! Juliette! Something in my body seemed to rise up, which was going to determine my being in the world.

Chapter 3.

Friendship deepens

Ça m'amusait. (See how I was beginning to learn some French?) It amused me this difference in being invisible. For the aranginye, they clearly felt it was better to hide their bodies, whereas I wanted mine to be perfectly visible, to be me. Yet, at the same time, we Suri people put a lot of value in being able to be invisible. Sometimes a necessity in the forest. If I wanted to be invisible amongst the aranginye, I would dress like them, obviously. Nevertheless, I have discovered there is hope for these aranginye: bodies always find a way of making their presence known, in spite of the disguises.

*   *   *

Rémi had become somewhat distanced from his two friends in Paris. Jacob and Hamid Reza's sole interest recently had become looking at naked women on the internet and Rémi didn't feel exactly comfortable with that. For a start, he felt obliged to be interested, eager and excited by often bizarrely freakish images and too often, he didn't find the women at all beautiful, which, rather than making his penis swell and stand up as it should have done, it tended to make it shrink and his scrotum tighten in fear. Was he gay? He didn't want to be gay, he wanted to be . . . normal.

Jacob, who was the smartest of the three, reckoned there was no normal, just as no one nose was the same as another, just as every penis was different, so every sexuality was different. He explained all this with the dismissive tone of a superior intellect and the two others were silenced by his brilliance. Rémi was quietly unpersuaded; in some respects his friends were the same, in others quite different, but not in a way that difference became absolute. He couldn't help noticing Jacob and Hamid Reza were far more like each other than he was like them. For a start, two or three years earlier, they had both started producing sperm, and in large quantities, at least six months before him and around the same time, which had somehow put him onto the back foot in their friendships. Both had teased him because he couldn't do it. In any case, their penises were very similar. OK, when they were erect, one tended to lean one way and the other, . . . the other. But in other respects, they looked the same, were the same size, colour and both were circumcised. This made them like brothers. They even felt like brothers, even though, religiously, they were supposed to hate each other. But mind you, their balls were completely different: Jacob's were huge and hung very loosely half way down his thighs, which for Rémi seemed incredibly inelegant, and as for Hamid Reza's, first of all his fuzzy pubic hair spread uncontrollably out and down his legs, but also between his legs and, densely, between the cheeks of his arse, in fact there was so much hair you could hardly notice his scrotum at all. He had wondered about waxing, but hadn't been brave enough so far, and besides neither Rémi nor Jacob were ready to help him, especially around his arse. When he had suggested it they had both made really loud "Errghah!" noises and told him not to be so disgusting and then laughed for such a long time, without him laughing, that he had almost got up and left, such was his embarrassment.

Producing sperm was no longer a problem for Rémi and when he finally announced to the other two, six months later than them, that he could, Jacob demanded that he prove it. It had taken some time under the cold eye of observation for his penis to stand up, but finally things were working. Jacob and Hamid Reza lost interest for a while and had started to discuss their science homework when eventually they heard Rémi panting, noticed his belly pulling in and out and started watching again. Suddenly, there was a huge explosion, at least that is how it felt to Rémi and the first jet of sperm hit Jacob right in that cold eye of observation, with an accompanied cry of horror. Subsequent spurts hit his school shirt and another fell on his open science exercise book. Hamid Reza was holding his sides and rolling around with laughter.

"You asked for it!" he cried.

Rémi fell back into the armchair in the study corner of his bedroom, exhausted, his pants and trousers around his ankles.

"My book! My shirt! My fucking eye, you dirty bastard! Fucking aim somewhere else, can't you?"

The following day, when the science teacher, M. Clermontcourt, asked about the stain in Jacob's exercise book he explained that it was Rémi's fault, he had spilled some of his crême Anglaise[41] on it. There was

---

[41] direct translation: English cream, although the English would say custard.

general quiet tittering throughout the classroom, everyone knew what had happened. Clermontcourt glanced around the room from behind his wire rimmed glasses to silence them all.

"Is that true, Fontenay?"

"Yes, sir. But why did he have his science book out while I was making crême Anglaise?"

Laughter.

"Making crême Anglaise?"

More laughter.

"Is there a joke I am missing here?" he shouted out to the entire classroom.

"Sir, I was trying to revise, and I was not so close," Jacob pleaded. "I didn't know he was going to splash it everywhere. In my eye and on my shirt as well, sir."

General uproar in the classroom.

"Silence! . . . Detention for both of you, every evening for the next two weeks!" shouted Clermontcourt above the noise, angry he had somehow become part of a joke everyone understood but him.

You see, as I said, Rémi's changing body was making its mark on the world, its presence felt!

More recently, in fact several months since Rémi had returned from meeting me but the same week Zhukov had ripped up, on three different days, three of Jacob's kippahs claiming he was doing Jacob a favour because the kippah made his head look like a giant tit, both he and Hamid Reza had become obsessed with internet pictures of breasts.

Jacob had been reading Portnoy's Complaint. The hero's general sense of failure leads him into psychoanalysis during which he describes the anxieties of his teenage years and obsession with masturbation, On one occasion of desperate wanking, he manages to hit the bathroom light bulb with his jism. Jacob decided, subsequent to his eyeful from Rémi, the best way to achieve the same results, hitting the light bulb, would be to over-excite oneself looking at naked breasts. This quickly turned into a fascination with sizes and then different nipples.

"No two nipples are alike. That means that the two nipples on your body may not be a mirror image of each other. This is normal." having read this, the boys immediately opened their shirts to check and compare their own.

"The larger outer ring is your areola. For some women, the areola is light pink. For others, it can be darker and range from red to brown. For some women the areola becomes darker when they're sexually excited. As a result, some cultures have even been known to paint their nipples to darken them in the hope of inspiring passion in their mates." Jacob read out loud.

"I want to see!" shouted Hamid Reza. "I want to see them change colour!"

Rémi thought about me. He knew from photos he had seen with Nathalie and Robert, the Suri people, especially the young men, painted their bodies. But did they paint their nipples? Besides, they were black, so the description couldn't apply to them. Was this description, which seemed to apply only to pale skinned people, racist?

He still hadn't told Jacob and Hamid Reza about me. When would be the time? Why should he bother? "They'll never meet Chár, anyway," such was his thinking.

"Fucking hell! Look at those!" shouted Hamid Reza. "What are they called those things? Areola. They're as big as saucers and nearly black!"

Both him and Jacob were staring wide-eyed into the screen, most of which was filled with a pair of gigantic breasts, behind which was the grinning lipsticked face of their owner. She had no doubt paid for them at great cost. Jacob and Hamid were in total awe of these massive boobs. Rémi glanced over their shoulders at the screen and, if anything, was disturbed; he felt them slightly scary. Jacob clicked on the screen and the huge breasted woman started dancing. He and Hamid Reza were whooping with glee. The porn star turned as she danced to show her naked backside, spread her legs wide to reach between and rub her hand from her anus to her vulva, back and forth, back and forth, to the rhythm of raunchy guitars, her huge breasts swaying from side to side between her legs, as, bent in double, she feigned arousal and orgasm.

There was a knock at Rémi's bedroom door. The whooping and screaming laughter stopped immediately. There was rapid, urgent whispering. The screen was switched off and power cut to Rémi's computer. The door slowly opened and Robert stepped into the room.

"Alright, boys? Been wanking together watching porn then, have you? Good thing it was me and not your mother at the door, Rémi."

Jacob and Hamid Reza were immediately relieved. They loved Rémi's father, he could joke, tease and say things to them that their own fathers never would.

"No, of course not, M. Fontenay," said Hamid Reza with a grin, "of course we have not been masturbating, except Jacob, who does it all the time. For him it is an illness, as you know."

"He's lying, M. Fontenay. He's lying!" protested Jacob.

"Anyway, Rémi, Nathalie and Charles will be here this weekend to take you back to their place . . ."

"Yeh, I remember."

" . . . . while Claudine and I are in New York."

"How long will you be?"

"We don't know yet. It all depends on Claudine buying and selling her paintings. And what about you two? What are you doing during les grandes vacances[42]?

"Going to Israel."

"Going to Tehran."

"Visiting family then? Rémi will be in the Sologne with his friend Chár."

"He's hardly a friend. I've only met him once."

---

[42]   The long school summer holidays in France

"I thought you liked him."

"I do."

"Has he not told you about Chár?"

"No!?"

"Yes, I have!" he lied. "You were arsing around with tits on the computer and didn't listen."

Robert caught his son's eye: "And you call me a racist!"

"I did tell them!"

"Right. Anyway, he's coming here with Nathalie and Charles for the weekend before we leave. I've just spoken to him on the phone. He can speak French quite well now. Really nice. He can't wait to see us and you of course. Anyway, it's time for these boys to go home. Come on. I'll take you. The car is outside."

*   *   *

"What did your Dad mean, 'he can speak now'?" asked Jacob as school ended, only a few days before the long summer holidays. "Was he a mute and a miracle happened?"
.

"Chár? Is that his name? It's a bit weird, isn't it?"

"So, who is this friend you're keeping a secret, anyway? Is he your boyfriend?"

"No, he's not my boyfriend! I met him once. It's not that important!"

"Well, he's desperate to see you again! Come on! Tell us."

"He's this young guy. Maybe the same age as us; I don't know."

"What do you mean, you don't know? You don't know how old he is?"

"Just shut up and listen! No one knows how old he is, not even him, probably, nor very much about him. Aunt Nathalie and Uncle Charles have adopted him."

"They've adopted him and they don't know how old he is?"

"Jacob, shut up! Let me explain. He comes from Ethiopia. They smuggled him out, or something. I don't know how it happened. My Dad helped them. He comes from a tribe that was massacred while they were there on holiday. He survived, and Nathalie wanted to look after him."

"Fucking hell! Why didn't you tell us? That's fantastic! We want to meet him!"

"Is he black?"

"Of course he's black. He was part of a tribe living in the jungle. They've all died apart from him."

"Wow! Has he got a big cock?"

"Please! You two are disgusting!" Rémi was feeling more and more uncomfortable with this intrusive inquisition. But of course, his innocent and consummately curious friends wanted to know everything.

"Well has he? That's what people say, black guys have big cocks."

"That's all you think about. Tits, fannies and cock."

"Well, has he? Have you seen it?"

"Yes, I have. It seemed normal to me."

"How come you saw it?"

"I shared his bedroom."

"Did you share his bed?"

"Oh, Christ! Anyway, he has no hang-ups about his body. He is completely unselfconscious, which is good, unlike you two. Oh, by the way, he shaves his pubes. I don't know why. It's their custom. Maybe you'll meet him and if you asked him nicely, Hamid, he'd probably help you shave yours." Rémi suggested, finally putting the ball back in their court.

There was a pause, too long, while clearly Hamid was mulling over the idea. Jacob and Rémi waited with slight grins on their faces.

"Well, are you going to ask him?" Jacob asked.

"Fuck off! No! I'm going to ask him to cut your balls off instead, you arsehole, and we'll barbecue them together."

"Anyway, he hasn't had the end of his dick cut off, like you two weirdos. He is complete. He has a foreskin, like me."

There was a pause. The bright summer sunlight greeted them as they stepped outside the main school building.

"Which way are we going to avoid the Russians?"

"Zhukov had escalated his persecution recently," Rémi explained to me later; we were lying in his bed, the night after I had arrived in Paris with Nathalie and Charles to take him back to our home in the Sologne, "and we were relieved it was now almost the long summer holidays, just a few more days until the weekend. At first, we had managed to successfully avoid him for several weeks, but then it was as if he had been searching for us—one time catching us at a metro entrance, another on Avenue Victor Hugo and finally discovering the side gate we had been using each time, beating Jacob, taking his kippah and any small change we had in our pockets. Jacob was in trouble with his mother because he felt he had to lie about losing them and she was annoyed at regularly buying him new ones."

Friday lunchtime in the canteen, Rémi received a text message from his Aunt Nathalie (for me, she had become Ma Nathalie), telling him that she would drop me at the main school gate so that I could meet him as he came out of school, meet Rémi's friends also, and spend time together before returning to the apartment. It would be a great opportunity for me to see a bit of Paris. I would have money in my pocket. Maybe we could walk down to the Seine together. She also gave him my mobile phone number in case there was a problem.

91

I was speaking now! I had a mobile phone! Last time I saw Rémi, I couldn't speak even a word and had started my French with him. How long had it been since I first met him? Had I changed?

Rémi was also worried about meeting me at the main gate. What if the Russians were there? Perhaps it would be better for Hamid and Jacob to take a different exit.

"Don't be stupid! We want to meet him. Suckoff and his mates, fuck them. Maybe they won't be there."

The world was changing, especially fast for Rémi and his friends. They all looked at each other as much to say, "Let's do it!", and stepped intrepidly into the unknown.

Nathalie dropped me at the main gate of Rémi's school. I was beautifully dressed: blue jeans, bright red boat shoes, formal voluminous white Egyptian cotton shirt. I looked handsome. Nathalie, of course, had already provided me with a considerable wardrobe, mostly choosing for me but consulting slowly on my choices. How could I choose? I had never seen clothes before except on occasional tourists and certainly never worn them. Free choice is not innate; it is not a given. Of course, in the jungle, there is choice, but once again it is made by experience. It is something that has to be learned, especially the infinite choice of markets. For her, it was an enormous pleasure dressing me. I was her baby and always would be.

"The lycée Janson de Sailly, a non-fee-paying state school, the biggest school in the region of Paris, educating over three thousand students, both boys and girls, was the first Republican lycée of France (the others started as royal or imperial establishments); it aimed at training the future French scientific, literary, military, industrial, diplomatic and political male élites of the young Third Republic. Within ten years of opening in 1884, it had become a mixed school of both boys and girls. It gained a national reputation and attracted students from around the country with the possibility of boarding. It also became one of the lycées of Parisian high society, being situated in the 16th Arrondissement, where the political, cultural and financial élite of Paris live."[43]

Having grown up in the Seizième (16th), Robert had also attended

---

[43] From Wikipedia

Janson de Sailly.

Unlike in the United Kingdom where the study of foreign languages is no longer obligatory, in France students must study two foreign or regional languages. Rémi, Hamid Reza, and Jacob had all opted to study English and German and additionally Latin.

I looked up at the high Parisian buildings, the façade of pale stone of the school, decorated with sculpted figures set into the walls between the windows of the first floor, and the classic Empire style Haussmann roof with smaller windows set into it. I understood windows now. I knew what they meant. I knew that behind them were rooms and behind rooms were more rooms, often with people in them doing . . . different things. I knew that this huge building, with its pronounced central columns and more prominent statues topped by an ornate clock, synchronizing everyone inside and out, contained Rémi and hundreds more young people. Also teachers, like my teacher of French and English. I knew these buildings were old. Nathalie had told me. But seeing their solidity, their permanence gave me the first inklings of a past, a history, of time even, or aranginye time at least, which has separated itself from Nature, the seasons and Nature's cycles. Already I had started to have some idea of white man's time, but prior to coming to France, there was no permanence, unlike our house in the Sologne and this building called a school; there was no history. Nothing remained the same. Nothing remained. Even humans were no different from the leaves on the trees. I was not surprised discovering that these white people were frightened of dying.

But I was here for living, for renewing my friendship, for seeing and being with Rémi. I heard a bell sound inside the school. Slowly, children emerged and wandered off along the street in the afternoon summer sunshine.

As I was waiting, someone walked past, knocking into me and looking at me angrily. Then I saw at a distance those yellow curls. I ran, threw my arms around Rémi, and hugged him so tight he was lifted off the ground.

"Rémi! Rémi! Comment ça va?"

"Fine," he replied quietly a bit taken aback by my excitement; I was still holding on to him, wrapping my arm around his waist and kissing him on the cheek. Rémi smiled, pleased I was so happy to see him and returned the kiss.

"So, you speak French now."

"Yeh," I laughed. "I've missed you so much!"

"These are my friends, Jacob and Hamid Reza."

I offered my free right hand while still holding onto Rémi. Jacob and Hamid were a bit overwhelmed by my excitement and somewhat in awe, I could tell, of this black, handsome young man with those beautiful high cheekbones, dark eyes, and delicate enticing lips. They both took my hand and I pulled them towards me to embrace them also.

"Ah! My Rémi, my Rémi. Rémi Tagí. So, I can speak some French. Can you remember some Suri words, Tagí?"

"Tagí . . . Tagí . . . ah yes! Moon!"

Jacob could see Rémi was not so at ease with my enthusiastic embrace and whispered quietly to him:

"Are you okay, Rémi? You look a little uncomfortable with Chár, who you hadn't told us about. Don't let me think you feel uncomfortable presenting him to us. Remember, I'm the Jew!" And then he, Jacob, threw his arms around me and kissed my cheek. "Welcome to Paris, Chár!"

"Thank you, Jacob!" And then addressing both friends, "this is my brother, Tagí. You remember, Rémi, the full moon when we met? This is your Suri name. I give you this name: Tagí. Wóhólò Tagí!" I laughed.

"Wóhólò Tagí?" At first Rémi looked puzzled and then he remembered and laughed.

"We were drinking wine in the middle of the night," I explained to the other two, "and smoking ganja together. I took Rémi outside for fresh air and to feel the night. We both threw away our boxers and started dancing naked in the moon!"

Rémi Tagí put his arm around my shoulders while we both grinned at the memory. Jacob and Hamid Reza were wide-eyed with astonishment.

94

"So, what does Rémi's name mean? What is it? Wóhólò Tagí?"

"It means naked moon!" said Rémi grinning.

"Wow! I want a Suri name too!" declared Hamid.

"And when do we get to dance naked in the moonlight?" demanded Jacob. "You didn't tell us any of this, Rémi: drinking, smoking and dancing naked. How come we were not invited?"

Upon seeing Rémi, I had run through the gates along a lane separating two parts of the school. As we walked back towards the gate, Jacob noticed the Russians waiting until we were almost upon them.

"Oh, fuck! Look who it is!" said Jacob.

I watched the faces of the three young Parisians change. Zhukov swaggered towards us, surrounded by his sycophants, blocking our path. I realized this was the one who had knocked into me, and had given me that poisonous look.

"Hi, girls. Got something for me, have you?" he said. "Teacher's bitches, like you, could end up in trouble without me to protect you."

No one responded, my three friends were trying to avoid Zhukov's menacing gaze.

I could smell the poison seeping from this ugly person's vile skin. I had seen that expression of contempt before. The Dizi police captain had been the same.

"Who's your nigger boyfriend, you little prick?" Zhukov sneered at Tagí and me.

"Don't do it," Rémi said, staring straight back into Zhukov's eyes. "It's a very bad idea."

I knew bad words were directed at me like the pus of a bursting abscess, and I saw the brilliant flash of anger in Rémi's eyes.

"What? Don't tell me what to do, cocksucker," Zhukov shot back.

"You don't know what you are doing," Rémi warned, glancing at me, both of us acknowledging the terrible inevitability of the situation.

"Fuck you!" Zhukov scoffed, and turning to Jacob, smacked him across the head, knocking his kippah to the ground.

"Wóhólò Tagí," I said quietly. "Wóhólò Tagí, we must! We must…"

"What's that? Bongo bongo language, you dirty, black…"

Part of any victory is deception, being invisible. Before he could finish his sentence, lazily believing he was all powerful, his face was suddenly broken. No one really saw what happened. A lightning shadow hit him, splitting his top lip and breaking his nose. Blood poured down his shirt front and snot slid into his mouth between loosened teeth. He couldn't see—only the supernova behind his eyes.

"Whuh, huh, uh," he moaned to his little gang, who understood they were supposed to help him. One threw a kick at Rémi, who caught his foot, lifted it high, and pushed him back, causing him to fall on top of Zhukov, who was already on his knees. Another tried to grab me. Jacob jumped on his back, causing him to spin unsteadily, and Hamid punched him between the eyes. More blood and blinding tears followed. The last one stood, mouth wide open in disbelief, I leapt at him with my arms above my head and hands held out like claws, my red eyes and deep screaming growl sending him into a panic. The poor boy fell backward and turned to run. The other two staggered away—one clinging to the wall for direction and the other limping next to him. Zhukov was pinned to the ground with Hamid's foot on his neck.

"Pick it up! Pick it up, Jacob's kippah!" Hamid shouted.

Zhukov reached out and collected the kippah.

"Now give it to him and apologise."

Hamid Reza released his foot from Zhukov's neck, who struggled to his feet. His face was a mess.

"I'm sorry, Jacob," he muttered.

"And! . . . And!" Hamid Reza demanded.

"I will never do this again. I am sorry." His voice broke into whining tears.

.

"Now go home and tell your father what a cowardly little shit you are and how you got what you deserved."

Of course, the Parisians were not the only ones bullied by Zhukov and his mates. A small crowd of students quickly gathered around the fight, and loud applause broke out as they witnessed brutal justice administered.

*   *   *

Nathalie was very disappointed to see blood on my beautiful new shirt.

"It is not my blood, Nathalie. We met a very bad person with his bad friends."

"Donne-la moi," demanded Claudine. "Je la laverai toute suite.[44] You can borrow a shirt from Rémi for the restaurant tonight."

Rémi explained the history with Zhukov, his bullying especially of Jacob, taking their money and so on.

"I tried to warn him. I knew Chár would not let him bully Jacob, nor any of us. But he was stupid. And then of course, he started insulting him because he is black.

"I think his nose is broken," concluded Rémi. "That's why there is blood on the shirt." And then pointing to his mouth, "And his teeth!" He made a grimace of horror.

There were a few moments of silence and then Robert clapped his hands together and burst out laughing.

"And the others?"

"Well, we all had to join in!"

Both Charles and Robert were now laughing at further details of what

---

[44] "Give it to me," demanded Claudine. I'll wash it straightaway.

had happened. Claudine and Nathalie were horrified.

"Stop laughing, you two! It's not funny! These two in a public street fight! Enfin!"

"So, Jacob and Hamid are coming here tomorrow morning. Jacob wants to take Chár to the Musée D'Orsay, spend some time together before they go on holiday."

"Oh, Jacob is a delightful boy!" said Claudine. "He comes from a big Jewish family, related to the Greys of Grey-Poupon, so I've been led to believe. I am not sure of the detail, but that's what I've heard. You can just imagine, Nathalie!" she said, rubbing her forefingers and thumb together to indicate banknotes. "Fortunately, you two defended him."

"Ah, so you've changed your opinions now," commented Robert.

*   *   *

"When girls are about to become women and want to find a husband, they have their bottom lip pierced and slowly stretched to put a plate in it. Is that right?"

"Yeh. But not all do that."

Rémi and I were lying next to each other in his bed, that same night in Paris. It was after midnight and with the shutters closed and curtains drawn, his bedroom was completely dark. Our eyes were open but we saw nothing. Rémi had seen some of his mother's photos of the Suri people and wanted to know about them.

"Because of this, when the women speak, the words sound different, prettier."

"You mean they can't speak properly? Their speech is deformed?"

"No! It's just women's speaking. Sometimes babies try to copy their mothers, even baby boys, which is really funny."

"What about kissing?" asked Rémi. "How do they do that?"

"What do you mean?"

"Don't you know kissing? You know, when a man and woman love each other, they kiss."

"Quand Nathalie et Charles me voient le matin, on s'embrace. Comme ça, tu veux dire?"[45]

"No! I mean kissing – on the lips."

"You can show me?"

There was a pause. It was summer. The day had been very hot and the night was also too warm for sleeping comfortably. Rémi couldn't resist laughing quietly, but said nothing.

*   *   *

Claudine and Robert left for the States, and Rémi had returned with Nathalie, Charles and me to what was now home, my countryside, my forests.

It was very late at night, well after midnight. The house was sleeping deeply, except for the little candle-shaped lamp next to the bed and the hushed voices of the sleepless Rémi and me. It was summer, and the air was stiflingly hot, so the windows were open, and the shutters left ajar, hopefully to catch slightly cooler night air should it decide to waft into the room. We had showered to cool down, tried to sleep covered by only a single sheet, and finally gave up and kicked the sheet away.

"Do you want some beers? There are cold beers in the fridge."

"Good idea."

There was always a thrill, creeping through the dark and sleeping house, like thieves in the night. At times, we could see nothing, and the pressing silence filling the air pushed us closer together, in whispers, touch and excitement, at last returning to the haven of our bedroom.

"Rémi, I have a present for you. For a long time, I have wanted to give you this, but I am shy. I wait, I wait. Now I think I am stupid, eh?"

---

[45] "When Nathalie and Charles see me in the morning, we embrace. You mean like that?"

"Maybe you're stupid, I don't know," laughed Rémi, "but shy? Don't be ridiculous!"

I jumped up from the bed, opened a drawer. Rémi watched me take out my Suri beads, my sole possession from home, kick off my shorts, and fix them around my hips.

"Here." I turned to Rémi with a big smile and another string of beads in my hands. Rémi left the bed and approached.

"OK, let me do this." I hesitated, indicating Rémi's shorts.

"Please, let me look at them first," said Rémi.

"Nathalie helped me choose them and put them on a thread."

"They are beautiful! Black and white."

"You and me."

"What are they? Pearls?" he asked with some surprise.

"They are challanya. Pearls? What are pearls? I don't know."

"Beautiful! Thank you so much."

"Let me put them on you."

Rémi removed his shorts to finally be undressed like his Suri brother. I knelt down and, hanging them loosely on Rémi's hips, simply wrapped either end around each other. I leaned back, sitting on my heels. "Perfect! Now you are not just naked, you are sexy. Like me!" I laughed.

"OK. Photo! Photo! Where is my mobile?"

I started taking photos, from all directions, close-ups, front, back, sides, and at a distance with Rémi's full figure.

"OK. Now, a photo together." We put our arms around each other's shoulders and smiled.

"I want to show Nathalie."

"What?!"

"In the morning, I want to show Nathalie."

"Why?" Rémi was starting to panic. Nathalie? Charles? That's going too far. It's even beyond embarrassing. "Non, non, non! They will think we are fucking."

"What is fucking?"

Rémi started thrusting his hips with an orgasmic expression on his face. I laughed.

"Choga! Choga is good!" I insisted with enthusiasm and then frowning, "Oh! Is that bad for French people? They don't like choga?"

"Yes. . . No. . . . I don't know. . . . No, it's not bad." How could he explain to an innocent, to someone, me, who, at the time, knew nothing of sin, for example, or religion, or all the restraints and historical controls and obsessions over sexuality, bodies, nakedness, shame, for some god's sake!?

"Anyway, I want to ask Nathalie to take a photo of you and me together. My photo is no good."

"You mean naked?"

"Yeh."

"No! It's OK for you; you've been naked all your life. Nathalie and Charles have seen you naked plenty of times. They have only seen me in clothes since I was a baby. They don't see my naked body."

"You don't want them to see? Why?"

"Ils n'ont jamais vu ma bite!"

"What is "bite"?"

Rémi pointed at his penis.

"Ah, dòrmi. You think they won't like it?"

"Maybe. I don't know! They're not supposed to like it!"

"Why not? Here. Let me look." I reached forward to take Rémi's penis in my hand. Rémi automatically withdrew. "Wait. Wait! Let me look!" I took his penis gently in the palm of my hand. "It's good. Dòrmi chàllī. This is very good, beautiful. Believe me, they will like it. I do. Yes. I do. Do you like it?"

"Well . . . . yeh, I suppose so."

"You can help me, Rémi, with names. These. What are these?" I said, lifting Rémi's balls.

"Mes couilles."

"Búrrà:. One búrri, two búrrà:. Same eggs, same word. I like. You have good búrré:. Ooh, look, your dòrmi, your bite, wants to stand up!" I laughed.

"Maybe you should stop playing with it, ok? In French there are too many names for it - bite, queue, zizi, quequette, biroute, ton gourdin, pénis. Maybe pénis is better for you to use when you speak to Nathalie. Zizi, quequette, is for children. With me, with men or people the same as you, your age, you can say bite, queue or biroute."

"So look. What is this?" I said holding my own foreskin.

"Le prépuce. Hamid Reza and Jacob don't have one."

"This prépuce?" holding my foreskin, I wiggled my penis up and down again.

"Hamid and Jacob don't have? Why?" I asked, astonished.

"Cut off." said Rémi, and with a gesture of scissors closing, "Chook, chook!"

"What?" I looked horrified. "Why?"

"For God. Their God wants them to do this."

102

"What is God?"

"They think there is this super being who made everything, the sun, the sky, all the animals and plants, people, you and me. He lives forever, but he is invisible. You cannot see him."

"I can be invisible too, if I want! Where is he?"

"In heaven."

"Where is that?"

"Don't know. No one knows. Maybe he is all around us, but we don't see him. He sees everything we do. If we do good things, when we die, we can go to heaven to be with him forever."

I frowned. "How can you go to heaven if you don't know where it is, be with someone you don't know and can never see? You think this idea also? You think this is good thinking?"

"No."

"Suri people like to make stories also, especially old men. They have nothing else to do but fill the minds of little children with dreams and when the children repeat the stories to their parents or brothers and sisters, the family sometimes lie to them even more, for laughing, for fun. Sometimes the old men tell stories to make the children strong, or brave, or happy. This is good. But they are not true. Everyone knows that. When you die. That is it. Finished. Slowly you go into the earth, maybe eaten by insects or sometimes animals. Maybe Jacob and Hamid and all those people who think like that are frightened to die or they believe they are too important to die, eh?"

"I don't know. Maybe."

"So, why does their God want their prépuce?"

"Some old guy, thousands of years ago called Abraham heard God telling him to do this for himself and all the boys and young men in his family . . . forever."

"And people believed him? How many?"

"Many, many, many! Millions! Hundreds of millions, even today."

"These are the same as the Dizi, the Bume, the Nyangatom. You know Bume?"

"No. What's that?"

"Their real name is Nyangatom. They are people who live maybe, like here to Paris, away from the Suri. But we call them Bume! They can . . ." I gestured with my hand exploding open near my backside and at the same time making a fart noise with my tongue and lips. " . . . but they cannot think." I laughed.

"Fart?"

"What is that word? Fart? Yeh."

I took hold of Rémi's penis again and pulled back the foreskin, commenting: "But you are not like the Fart people."

"Good. Good." I continued. "Looks good. You have to take care of this prépuce. This is very important for . . ." I said seriously, then hesitating, trying to remember the word, "choga . . choga . . fucking. Fucking. I remember. How can you come inside without this . . . eri?? What is eri??" I asked rubbing the skin of his arm and belly.

"Skin. La peau."

"It is very important this skin, this prépuce."

"And this God," explained Rémi, "says no sex. Sex is bad. Fucking is not allowed except when you are married, like Charles and Nathalie and only for making babies."

"You don't think this, do you?"

"No."

"And what is this?" I tapped my buttocks.

104

"Les fesses."

"Sugum. And this?" parting my cheeks to show my anus.

"Le cul."

"Dolé."

Rémi laughed.

"Why do you laugh?"

"Because you are funny."

"Me? Funny?"

"Talking about bodies like this."

"I like it, talking about bodies. Suri people like bodies. They talk a lot about bodies. They like to make their bodies beautiful. They like to put paint on their bodies, like Nathalie on her face, but put colour everywhere. We can do this some time, put colour together. I can find. I know. Near the boyɛ, chaga boyɛ." He put his hand to his forehead to think, desperate to remember. "Lake! Lake, boyɛ. Chaga boyɛ, blue lake. I can find colour at the blue lake. I like your body, I want to paint it. I want to find out everything about it."

Rémi was suddenly moved, I could see. A sort of compassion. Before him was this young guy, the same as , but struggling to be French, to speak French, and at the same time struggling to remain Suri, to stay true to what he had always been all his life, even though his village had been destroyed, his family and people murdered, never able to return to that life he had had. I would have died in Ethiopia if I had stayed, he knew. Without Nathalie and Charles and living with them, I would die here, very quickly, in France. I would be lost. He, Rémi, would struggle without his parents, but at least he would have some idea how to survive, he would manage, but me, Chár . . . . The Innocent! This is how Rémi saw me, and suddenly wanted to protect me, take care of me to let me be my beautiful, so he thought, and innocent self.

He was also aware of a sort of racism. Was it really racism in him? He knew nothing with me, this strange friend from a different time and world, could be taken for granted. For a start, I came from a culture which seemed, at least to his mother, to be almost cultureless, there was no art, except painting on bodies, there was no writing, so no recorded history. It couldn't be racism because he didn't think I was less than him for these reasons, in fact maybe I was better off without the burden of history. His compassion and admiration of my innocence in his world completely eliminated momentarily any consciousness of our nakedness and, without any thought, he put his arms around me to give me a hug.

"Do you like my body? You think it is OK?"

Rémi stepped back, suddenly brought back to bare reality.

"Yes, I do! Yes, I do! Don't worry! Challi! You are very beautiful."

And what is this, when you do this?" I gestured the motion of masturbating.

Rémi laughed again. The whole situation of standing naked with this new friend from the jungles of darkest Africa and talking about wanking suddenly seemed completely absurd.

"Se branler. Tu te branles. . . . Enfin! Tu me fais rire."[46]

"Me? Je me branles[47]. And you?"

"Yeh. Ten times one day."

"What?" I wondered, looking astonished.

Rémi just laughed again.

"Oh, look! Dòrmi nunu ɓu:ɔ! Your biroute wants to stand up again! I think it likes standing up, eh? What is this word when it stands up?

"Bander. Ma bite bande."

---

[46]   "To wank. You wank . . . You make me laugh!"
[47]   I wank.

Rémi had been aware this was going on with his penis and quickly put his hands down to hide it.

"What? What are you doing? That's OK. Bander is OK. I have seen this many times, every boy, every man in my village I have seen some time. Even old men. I want to see anyway."

Rémi climbed on the bed and pulled the cotton sheet over the lower half of his body, so that his body could forget about being naked and his penis standing up. I joined him, lying down under the bedsheet.

"Let's try to sleep." I switched off the bedside lamp.

Black. Slowly light from the night started to creep in through the open shutters, but not enough to distinguish shapes, nor faces.

Silence.

"Listen. You cannot say this about my friends, fart people. They are my friends. They are not that. They are not stupid. They are your friends also. Jacob is Jewish, Hamid is Muslim. If their people have these ideas, that is okay. People have different ideas. Maybe they would think that Suri people putting a plate in their bottom lip is stupid. So long as ideas don't hurt other people, that is okay."

"Hmm. Understand. But I want to keep my prépuce."

"Me also. Some ideas are bad. For example, the ideas given to the Dizi to want to kill you, your people. These are bad ideas."

"Yeh. Wóhólò Tagì challì. I love you, Wóhólò Tagì."

Silence.

"Why did you have tears," wondered Rémi, "when you saw that sculpture at Musée D'Orsay? I was so surprised, you, Chár, so strong and brave."

Nathalie had insisted, while we were in Paris that Rémi should at least take me to the Musée d'Orsay, her favourite museum, which has the greatest collection of impressionist and post-impressionist masterpieces in the world and so was glad when Jacob had insisted we go. Mostly, we wandered around with me in silent awe, amazed at all of these beautiful paintings and sculptures, clearly made by great people, artists. Rémi or Jacob occasionally explained something or pointed something out, until we came to the sculpture Amor Fugit (love flees) by Auguste Rodin.

"You think I am strong and brave? You think I am not frightened sometimes? It was me, that little thing, that sculpture, even the colour, the same as me. It was my dream. I remember trying to hold my mother when she was dying. Then in the night I saw myself floating away," my voice started to break with emotion, "trying to hold onto her and she is holding her head in pain. My dying mother. It was me. It was the same as me. I suddenly remembered . . . ."

Rémi could hear my voice wavering, stifled by anguish. He lifted his hand up to touch my face and felt a few tears.

"Hey! Hey!" he said gently, wiping the tears and putting his arm around my shoulders.

"My Rémi. Wóhólò Tagí. You are my only brother now." I managed to whisper.

I moved closer, feeling comforted, reassured, and knowing Rémi really cared for me.

Silence. We could feel each other breathing, our faces close, and the warmth of our living breathing bodies next to each other.

What about kissing?" asked Rémi. "How can Suri men kiss their women if they have these clay plates in their bottom lip?"

"What does this mean, kissing?"

"You know, when a man and woman love each other, they kiss."

"You can show me? I asked you before about this, but you only laughed at me."

"No! I was not laughing at you, Chár. I don't laugh at you now, never!" Rémi laughed quietly and grinning took my head in his hands and putting aside a moment of self-consciousness, knowing he needn't feel any embarrassment with me especially, placed his lips on mine. They felt so soft, his lips, but at the same time firm. I could feel the many tiny muscles of his lips moving sensitively over my mouth, exploring, finding their way; they opened slightly and our bodies made a secret, whispering exchange of saliva. I felt for the first time waves of sensuous pleasure rippling through my entire body, and the taste of peaches on Rémi's tongue. Rémi's body was also electrified. It was then he wondered whether he had done the right thing.

"This is kissing."

"Good, eh? This is very good!" I whispered, my voice struggling to surface through the tingling in my body. "I like! We can try again?"

Rémi's penis was wanting to stand up again. He put his hand down between his legs to lift it, and make it more comfortable; the hot and humid night had made our bodies sticky with sweat. As his hand lifted his own penis, it inadvertently rubbed against mine, which was rigid also. I shuddered slightly and move closer. Rémi put his arm around me and let it slip slowly down my back to my buttocks as his mouth approached for our second kiss. I could feel this new sensation, at the back of my throat, as if everything, all my powers of becoming a man, had climbed up though my body to sit there, silencing me. We were losing ourselves in an overwhelming present. I did the same, moving my hands down his back feeling the soft pale down towards the bottom of his buttocks that I had long wanted to touch, and which led towards the few pubic hairs

that made a halo around his ɗolé. My dòrmi was now so strong and my búrré: were reaching up desperate to share their milk. I could feel my Rémi Wóhólò Tagí's dòrmi against mine and knew his wanted the same. Our lips touched and our bodies fell apart, melting together.

"I want you inside me when your dormì makes its . . . juice," I managed to utter, "and . . ."

"You inside me." whispered Rémi.

*   *   *

Meanwhile, in Italy, the long summer holiday for Juliette had also just begun. She had managed to escape the usual routines of the farm to visit Italy for three weeks with girlfriends, one of whom had family in Perugia. This had been a lot of fun, especially taking evening walks along the Corso Vannuci, admiring the beautiful stone buildings, the easy traffic-free surrounding streets, enjoying bars, restaurants and trattoria and being wooed by handsome young Italian men, who often wanted to flatter themselves and show off to their friends by seducing these pretty tourists. In spite of this sexy chauvinism, she had great admiration for the overwhelming surfeit of culture and especially the women of all ages who expressed brilliant good taste in dress and appearance. Italian women were glamorous and sophisticated, and no doubt knew very well how to manage the naughty young men. She did manage to spend a few days in Rome, visiting the Uffizi and Borghese galleries. She especially wanted to see the Dionysus painting, as she called it, Sick Bacchus by her artist hero, a self-portrait when he was her age, more or less, plus his other paintings, portraits and Historia Sacré.

*   *   *

Back in the jungles of the Sologne, after a night of exploring and the surrendering of our bodies to the most desperate desires to speak their own language, the language of mouths, lips, genitals, arms and legs, the reality of the rest of the world loomed:-

"Marie Jeanne, I am in such a hurry this morning. I have to go to town, and I want the boys to come with me. First, I'll go to the bank in the village and buy bread and croissants for their breakfast. Can you knock on their bedroom door and wake them up quickly? I'll take the Quatrelle (Renault 4) and leave right now."

Nathalie left the kitchen.

Innocent Marie Jeanne, always busy, bustled to the other end of the house, and up the stairs, to knock on my bedroom door to wake us two boys. In her haste, perhaps she had knocked too firmly and the door, which had not been shut completely, swung open to reveal a pair of white naked buttocks sticking up in the sweaty bedroom air, with, either side, a pair of black legs akimbo. The pyramid of teenage debauchery immediately collapsed and two heads, one black, one white, appeared from behind the mêlée of limbs.

"Marie Jeanne, come in," I invited, "Did you want something?"

Rémi fell backwards onto the pillows and pulled the bed sheet over his head. I felt a flash of annoyance towards myself because I was failing to immediately defy the silly aranjinya anxieties over bodies, especially since my Rémi Wóhòló Tagí needed to learn to stand up and, instead of embarrassed, be proud of his naked good looks.

For a few seconds Marie Jeanne, stood immobile, as grey as stone, and when she tried to speak, her mouth moved but no words came out, until:

"It's breakfast time, Master Chár."

'Merçi, Marie Jeanne. We're coming.'

I turned to Rémi.

"Now, my beautiful one, you must earn your name, Wóhólò Tagì!"

I waved my phone at him.

"No, don't! Stop! Give it to me!"

Rémi jumped at me while I was pulling on my shorts. I managed to wrestle myself free and while he was splayed out on the bedside carpet, I had a head start for the kitchen.

*   *   *

"Are the boys up?"

"I don't know, Madame." Marie Jeanne looked pale and anxious.

"What do you mean? They're still asleep?"

"No, Madame, unfortunately . ." Marie Jeanne seemed to be breaking down.

"What do you mean, unfortunately?"

"Unfortunately, the door wasn't really closed. So, I saw them." She started to wring her hands and stumble over her words.

"Marie Jeanne, are you OK?"

"No, Madame, no! I think the young men were wrestling."

"They were wrestling?" repeated Nathalie with astonishment.

"Madame, I see young master Chár's bare buttocks more often than my husband's! The world has turned upside down and I am losing my footing. Of course, I love him, the young master, but even so. And this morning I was confronted by the bare buttocks in the air of young master Rémi! I can't take it anymore, Madame. I can't take it anymore!"

"Calm down, Marie Jeanne. Sit down. I am truly sorry that I put you in this difficult and embarrassing situation. It's all my fault and I'll tell the boys to cover themselves."

I burst into the kitchen, it was a way of playing with doors, which were everywhere, and sat next to Nathalie, on the bench, pressing up against her. I had my mobile phone in my hand and straight away wanted to show her the photos I had taken the night before.

"Where is Rémi?"

"He is coming. He's just . . . "

The door burst open again. This time, it was Rémi, who dived at me to grab the phone. I had to move away from Nathalie and we ended up arms locked together, wrestling, in the middle of the kitchen floor, with Rémi shouting at me to hand over the phone. The spectacle of two near-naked (apart from shorts) young guys, one black and one white, playing at fighting, left Marie-Jeanne and Nathalie dumbfounded. I was just laughing with excitement. Soon we became aware of a rising crescendo of reprimands and prohibitions climaxing in a loud whistle.

We boys froze and both turned our heads to see Nathalie, much to our surprise, with two fingers between her lips bringing the commotion to an end.

I immediately jumped back next to her and suddenly, she found herself looking at photos of Rémi naked apart from a string of beads sitting on his hips. She felt some relief he wasn't parading an erection. And so did Rémi, unsure whether there were any photos of his penis standing up or not.

"Are they . . . let me think! Let me think! . . . pearls?" I asked.

"No. Although they are very nice quality faux pearls."

"What are faux pearls?"

"They look the same as pearls but are not." Nathalie was starting to feel a little impatient; she didn't really want to be talking about pearls but about me being naked as often as possible, and how I should try to remain covered so as not to upset Marie Jeanne or anyone else who might arrive at the house by chance, the postman, the gardener, neighbours, Claudine when she visited. But instead, she had been confronted by the evident contagion of nakedness spreading from me to Rémi.

"Il est beau, eh?"[48] I commented.

"Chár, stop it!" shouted Rémi.

"Yes," she agreed, glancing up at him, "he is very handsome. I am not surprised you two have become best friends."

"Not for long!" retorted my Wóhólò Tagì.

"Listen, Chár, darling, it is fine being naked, but not all people like it and please try to cover yourself . . for Marie Jeanne's sake. For her it is shocking. She doesn't really want to see you naked."

I stood up and turned towards Marie Jeanne, who was washing a few dishes at the sink, with a feeling of surprised disappointment.

"You don't like me, Marie Jeanne?"

Poor Marie Jeanne was so upset that she had hurt or offended me, she almost said I could be as naked as I wanted and as often as I wanted.

"Dear Chár, of course I like you. We all like you. My husband likes you and wants to go hunting with you. Juliette, my daughter, likes you."

"I agree, Marie Jeanne," Rémi joined in, "Chár should just start wearing

---

[48] "he's handsome, isn't he?"

113

clothes!"

"I am sorry, Marie Jeanne." I got up to give her a hug. Marie Jeanne froze, with her arms held tightly in front of her chest.

Rémi jumped up to embrace Marie Jeanne as well, mocking my apology.

"Juliette likes me?"

"Yes, we all do. For me it is too difficult seeing naked men. I cannot do this."

I could see Marie Jeanne was upset by her own sentiments.

"OK," said Nathalie, "Everyone is fine now and we all like each other, yes? Chár, come and sit down with me. Now, you are going to try to wear clothes a bit more often, eh?"

"Yes, Nathalie." And then whispering very closely in Nathalie's ear: "Juliette likes me!"

Nathalie closed her eyes and smiled. On balance, which was more important for me, trying to keep my clothes on, or the news that Juliette liked me?

"Rémi, come and sit down, have some croissants. Do you want coffee? You slept well? You look exhausted. Marie Jeanne, let me talk to the boys for a while."

"I'll go and sort out the bedrooms, Madame." Marie Jeanne hurried out of the kitchen.

Rémi wondered whether Nathalie had been inferring something about his night with me, looking tired.

"Nathalie," I demanded, "I told Rémi last night I wanted to ask you to take photos of us two together."

"But I said no!" insisted Rémi.

"You mean wearing just your beads?" wondered Nathalie, with as innocent an expression as she could muster.

"Yes."

"That's why I said no." said Rémi, starting to feel annoyed again.

"He is shy, you see, Nathalie. He thinks you will not like his pénis."

By now Rémi was so embarrassed he felt like climbing up the kitchen wall and through the ceiling to hide. Nathalie looked at Rémi and laughed, waiting for some response from him to explain or get out of his predicament. None came.

"Don't worry, you look very cute, very handsome," she said. "And as for your . . ." she wiggled her small finger provocatively. "Your . . . quequette, it is fine."

Rémi lifted his hands to his face in resigned humiliation.

"You see. I told you," I said. "Your dormì is very fine. And when it stands up, Nathalie, it is big!"

"Really!"

"Fucking hell, Chár!"

"So, tell me. You boys. Marie Jeanne thought you were wrestling in bed this morning. But I think different. I think maybe you were having sex together, is that right?"

Immediately, both at exactly the same time, Rémi said no and I said yes.

"Well," laughed Nathalie, "either one of you doesn't know what sex is, or one of you is lying. And what about girls? Don't you like girls? Don't you want to have sex with girls?"

Rémi was far from ready to discuss his sexual desires over coffee and croissants. In fact, did he even know what they were? What, for example, might be sexual preference? He had had no sexual experience with another person until last night with me. As for me, I didn't even know what preference might mean.

"Yes, we like. Of course. We want. But where are the girls? There are no

115

girls." I replied.

"Right."

"You white people are funny. You think either boys or girls, as if they exclude each other. Until that time when we want to make babies, what we do with each other's bodies doesn't matter. It's just fun. Practice for when a girl chooses us."

"You practise?" echoed Nathalie.

This was wrong! For Rémi, this was badly wrong!

"Practice? You mean that the first time, my very first time, you want to say it was nothing? Just practice, just . . . I don't know . . . just fooling around?"

Silence. Smiles disappeared and were replaced by furrowed brows. I realised I was expected to explain. Nathalie turned her eyes back to the phone's screen. My mind suddenly flashed seeing 'Amor Fugit', the Rodin sculpture. The air of the kitchen turned to glass.

"Now, he's lying, Nathalie!" said Rémi, demanding her attention. "He'd better be! You make it sound like it was nothing! Yeah! Only practice! Worthless! Any joy, postponed until an unknown future moment when we'll no longer be practising?" declared Rémi loudly, waving his arms in the air to exaggerate the dismissiveness of my manner, what I had said.

The anger shattered the sky of the kitchen.

"Rémi," Nathalie, addressed him with sympathy, "eat your croissants and drink your coffee. It is getting cold. And then we will go to the bottom of the garden to take these photos of you and Chár together. The two friends." She wanted to calm his anger, guessing my easy casual dismissal of whatever we had been up to during the night, was upsetting sensitive innocent Rémi whom she had known and loved since he was a baby. She understood these were first and important experiences for him. "It is a good idea, a photo of the two of you. A genuinely nice idea. And a great memory for both of you. Don't take these simple words to heart, Rémi."

"Go! Both of you! But I am not coming!" He got up and slammed his anger into the door as he left the kitchen.

What had happened? Everything had exploded!

"Chár, Rémi is angry with you. You can see. You must find out why and fix it. Claudine and Robert will be back from New York soon. Time is short for both of you."

"And they will take Rémi back to Paris?"

"Probably. I guess it depends what Rémi wants also."

There was a long silence. Nathalie left the kitchen. And I was abandoned to sink into deep and lonely thought about our intimacy, mine with my Rémi, whom she knew I loved.

*   *   *

I was suddenly alone, more alone than I had ever been since Beyahola and bathing myself in sheep's blood! There was no one. Marie Jeanne's bicycle had disappeared. Where had she gone? Home? I wandered through the house. All the rooms were empty apart from the silent solitary furnishings. Where was Nathalie? The garden? I glanced from the windows. Maybe she had gone to the village. No Charles! Maybe he was in Orléans.

Rémi had gone back to our bedroom and locked the door. I made my way through the house checking every room. No one, until eventually, upstairs, I reached the locked door. Rémi had pulled off his shorts in anger (the only bit of clothing he had slipped on before chasing me to the kitchen) and threw himself on the bed, hiding under a cotton sheet.

For me, everything had been so perfect, the evening with Rémi, so excited and happy I had been to be with him again, and then offering him his challanya. Rémi had been so pleased with them. I am sure we were both surprised how our bodies had taken over! First it was talking about and naming, especially those parts I felt more comfortable talking about with him than I could ever feel with Nathalie or Charles. And then, he had been fine with touch and hadn't hidden from it. There was so much about his body I had wanted to discover and it was clear Rémi had been happy with that. Of course, we had both thought about it, dreamt about it for a long time, dreaming of sex with different people

117

while playing with our penises until they made their milky juice. But real choga, actual choga, it had been so perfect to do this for the first time with my beautiful new friend, whom already I desperately loved, but who was now so angry with me.

"Rémi! Open the door!"

No answer.

"Rémi, open the door. I want to talk to you. Rémi, open the door. Something happened. I did something to hurt you. I want to know about it."

Still silence.

"Wóhólò Tagí, goona nanu, I am waiting outside this door. I am not going away. I can wait forever! And you know that. I am Chár. I am Suri. Aňi hídɔ Suri goona nanu! Suri goona nanu lameyɔ.[49] I am waiting. I love my Wóhólò Tagí."

"Fuck!" thought Rémi. "He speaks Suri and I know exactly what he is saying!" He felt a lump in his throat.

"I want my Suri brother, Wóhólò Tagí! I am looking for my Suri brother!"

Whilst it was entirely me, Chár, calling for him, it was also all the voices of all the Suri of Beyahola, who were in me, with me, for all time. Rémi knew this. It was far more than just anyone calling him. It was all the names in my past, my Suri past.

The door slowly opened. I stood up and stepped through the doorway. There was nothing before me but the crumpled sheets of an empty bed.

" Rémi Wóhólò Tagí, where are you?"

I took a further step into the room and Rémi jumped from behind the door to grab me with both arms.

---

[49] Aňi hídɔ Suri goona nanu! Suri goona nanu lameyɔ! Both sentences mean I want my Suri brother, but the first has the implication of desire and the second of 'to look for'.

"You have no shame, do you?"

"What is shame?"

Once again, Rémi was caring for innocence.

"Shame is when you feel bad about yourself in the eyes of others. So, for example, I feel some shame about being naked in front of Marie Jeanne. I feel bad about others seeing those photos of us."

"I don't feel this. I only feel bad when Wóhólò Tagí looks at me and is disappointed or angry. Then I feel shame." I waited. I wanted him to know I didn't care about white people's shame, only about him! "I will never feel that shame you talk about and I am also very angry you should feel that."

"Chár, do you understand? I am crazy about you! Last night was the first time I have sex, choga, with anyone. Never before! No girlfriends, no boys, nothing! "

"Same me."

"What?"

"Same me."

"No, no, no! I don't believe you! You were so good at . . . everything!"

"Me? No, not me! You knew what to do. You were good at everything!"

There was a pause. Rémi started laughing. "You're lying again! I don't believe you!"

"No, not lying!"

"Look, Chár, last night, I give you my heart and my body. This is the first time. And you said to Nathalie that this was only practice! If you want to practise you can practise with your hand! And, for me, this is so much . . . how can I say? Only you and me! It is intimate delicate, can break easily and not for everyone to hear about, joke about, or say bad things about. What we did . . . changes my life!"

"Aah! No! Not practise! These words are for the others, so that they think little of Marie Jeanne's ideas. These words are not for you. I did not tell everyone; this was Marie Jeanne. I am so sorry, Wóhólò Tagí nanu! I never want to hurt you! Choga with you was everything for me. You, my Wóhólò Tagí have changed my life! You make my life possible! I am because of you. It is better Marie Jeanne thinks what she thinks. I want her daughter, Juliette. I want to make many babies with her. This is a secret I tell you. And I want the same for you. We will do this together! We will find a beautiful woman for you also. Marie Jeanne's ideas will make it possible for me to get closer to Juliette. We are men! We will both make many babies, believe me! This is what my mother said to me. You say you are crazy about me? Hey! You are my only brother, my Suri brother! Do you know what that means for me to say this? Your heart is in my heart, my heart in yours. That will always be! We are in the world, together! Understand? I love my goona nanu, Wóhólò Tagí! We will always be Rémi Wóhólò Tagí and Chár, Chár Menenge![50]"

There was a long silence while Wóhólò Tagí stared into my eyes to see if my words were real.

"What is menenge?"

"In French, in English, I don't know. Another time! Another time we can find out. And now, I want you to do that magical thing with your lips. Free our bodies to talk to each other again, like last night. Let them love and comfort each other, our hearts inside each other. We can feel better! We can stay here . . . all day! Lock the door! Heh? Good idea? Forget the world! There is only Rémi Wóhólò Tagí and Chár!"

Rémi locked the door.

"Don't go back to Paris!" I whispered quietly after the first long, and warm embrace. I felt a pull of pain in my heart. "That would be so wrong, so bad! I think I would die!"

*　　　*　　　*

As the golden pink, winged fingers of Dawn lifted up across the sky, as they slipped into the still dark waters of Chaga Boyɛ, I was standing on a large rock, gazing intently into the furthest horizon beyond the lake and

---

[50] Chár Menenge means leopard spirit.

the deepest regions of experience and its machinations. This was now a long time and unrelated, although who can tell? Perhaps connected to that moment of revealing our love, our importance, our need, for each other. Brothers! More than brothers! I had named the lake. I had made it my own. I was waiting. The important thing in looking deeply into things was absolute stillness and attention.

In this, my favourite spot, where I felt most comfortable, the isolation I experienced when I found out Claudine and Robert were arriving to collect Rémi, even though they still didn't arrive, that reminder of loss, losing everything, family, village, universe, I was waiting for that moment when I could see through the pain of my physical stillness into the very heart of things.

My father had shown me this. It was part of my becoming a man. As soon as hair had started to appear next to my penis, we spent many days wandering together through the bush, living off the bush. My father was teaching me what it means to be a Great Heart. What it means to have so much wealth of spirit that you freely give it away through acts of generosity and compassion, not only to Suri people, but to all people, animals and things. This power was innate to my body, my father had explained; I had to tend it, take care of it and direct it, but never lose it. To do so would make me no better than the hyenas.

My father had instructed me, wherever I was, to find a place that has its own power, where I feel a connection, where I can look out beyond the horizon, looking into my heart, to the beginnings of the universe, the beginning of each moment, the eternal. The white rock of Chaga Boyɛ was such a place.

I needed to rediscover, my body, my power, my direction and responsibility. Standing here at Chaga Boyɛ felt as if I had been waiting forever. Time becomes strange on such occasions, sometimes an eternity so long, sometimes so short, to reach those horizons where I forget myself. In white time this was nearing an hour and the fingers of dawn had paused, waiting to envelope me as I came to that understanding of everything. The problem of mind states. For me, as the days became routine, so I found myself slipping back into the terror. I had said nothing to the others.

I knew dawn was waiting. I was waiting. My body was waiting and burning up. As I looked into that pain, the leopards from Dibdib appeared either side of me to sit on their haunches, gazing into the same distance. They had borne witness, too.

I loved Nathalie and Charles and knew it was my responsibility to take care of them. I knew they needed me to become complete. Of course, I knew they believed, and it was true, that they had rescued me and taken care of me, but I also knew the opposite to be true, that I had rescued them and it was for me to care for them, protect them, as any Great Heart would. Likewise, it was for me to watch over Rémi, my Wóhólò Tagí. I had wanted to guide him, help him to become strong, become a man, become Suri. Maybe he needed to learn how to hunt and fight. I had wanted this summer, for both of us, to find girlfriends. How? How? Now it seemed nothing would happen. Rémi was going back to Paris soon and my plans, my dearest wishes, just a rippling mirage beyond the limit of my horizon.

For myself, I had seen Juliette, touched her fingers, felt that spirit pass from my body to hers and from hers to mine. Waiting. Waiting. Something has to give. Rivers have to burst their banks. How? How? Any Great Heart has to learn about waiting, waiting for moments to meet, for questions to meet answers, grasping when universes collide.

Beyahola village, lost somewhere out there in a universe of space/time where only the present existed eternally. I and my home had been ripped apart by brutal stupidities. I knew I was now completely alone. I would never share my language with others again. Sometimes young men would go off into the forests alone, living on what they could find and what they could hunt. They had to test themselves, learn their strength and courage. Some would never return. What had happened? Had they died, eaten by hyenas? Had they made a new life in a new place? Maybe in this new world where I found myself, I would remain separated, detached, resolutely going nowhere. I had caught glimpses, moments when I saw that Rémi also was a Great Heart, but how could I help him to understand that, to know it and to learn how to help it to grow. I knew I was condemned to never finding Beyahola again, condemned to always be wandering the surface of the Earth, outside of home, outside of my people, any people. Was this my fate, always outside? Is that where my spirit leopard was leading me?

At this moment of concentrated pain, the image of the Great Heart started to slip and nobility weaken. I was just a small black directionless little being, alone and lost. That crack in my heart had opened into a bitter emptiness, a void, lacking the completeness I had lost, of which I had been robbed. My will and hope slowly being replaced by a hollowness, corners of which held a bitterness waiting to infect all my sentiment.

The sun cracked the horizon and the fingers of pink and gold lost their wings and faded to nothing as the light solidified the air.

*　　　*　　　*

"Where is he?"

Rémi had rolled over in that semi-conscious state of dreams when imaginings are perceived and deceive as real. His body, accustomed now to my black warmth next to him, was disturbed by emptiness and called his brain to consciousness. He propped himself up on his elbows and glanced around the room.

There was early pre-dawn light creeping through the shutters. He lay back and waited a couple of minutes. Total quiet imposed. Impatiently, he got up from the bed and left the room to search the silent house. Just as I had suddenly appeared in his life, was I just as suddenly going to disappear? He wondered if this unease had pushed the empty space in the bed next to him to wake him up. Bathroom, empty. Not in the kitchen. He tapped on the door of Nathalie and Charles' room and looked in.

"Sorry. Where is Chár? I can't find him. He's disappeared."

"Rémi, it's the middle of the night," Charles quietly reproached. "Go back to bed. He's probably not far."

Rémi quietly shut the door and returned to the kitchen to pace his anxieties. The back door to the yard was unlocked. He stepped outside. The fresh morning air caressed his naked body. It was only when he had reached the limit of the garden beyond which were open fields that his feet told him he had no shoes and looking down, his genitals reminded him he was completely naked. He was not going to care. Wóhólò Tagí, Naked Moon was going to have the courage of his new body, his new name.

There was barely sufficient light to see clearly the ground beneath his

123

feet and certainly not in the gloom of the forest, but trusting in some strange unknown, he started to run, fighting off that false need to consciously choose where he put his feet. An ancient instinct would choose for him, keep him safe, free to enjoy the wild grasses whipping his skin as he started to fly. Slowly, the gap inside him left by my disappearance, was filling with a strange ecstasy, knowing his body would take him to where I was. Why had he been so concerned? Had he felt my pain, my loneliness? He was running faster now. He hardly needed to think, "river, lake," he was already in a new present in which his feet understood where to best put themselves and his body moved spontaneously through bushes and trees. He was Wóhólò Tagí.[51]

The piercing light at the bang of dawn had knocked me back and loosened my muscles, for me to slip slowly down, my spirit broken, until I was squatting on my haunches, my arms outstretched before me, the palms of my hands turned towards the sky in supplication.

Like any leopard, I knew someone was running towards me, perhaps a kilometre, or slightly more, away. As they got closer, I tasted the air. It was Rémi, I knew. I continued squatting, unmoved, looking out over the lake. Almost silently, Rémi stepped onto the rock behind me and leaned with his hands on my shoulders to look out over the lake also. After a few moments of silence, I stood up and turned to look coldly at Rémi smiling back at me. I looked him up and down noticing the dusty green and brown brushstrokes on his legs and torso from the grasses, bushes and dry earth.

"Where are your clothes?"

Rémi's smile dropped and a puzzled frown replaced it. Worryingly for him, I looked wounded, my pained faced with reddened tearful eyes seemed distant, lost.

"Where are your clothes?"

"I forgot them," whispered Rémi, looking away, "I was in a hurry."

"What are you doing here?" I could feel a strange pressure in my stomach. Was I sick, about to vomit?

---

[51]What had been a game of names was becoming a reality. The more Suri he learned, and he was learning quickly, the more he felt close to that nature. He had not spoken to anyone about it, not even Chár. Did he need to?

"I came looking for you. Don't be angry with me, I've done nothing!"

"Go home and put on some clothes." There was an electric sensation throughout my body which detached me from my words. "You are not Suri. You are aranji. White boy. French white boy. What do I do here? In the land of aranjinya?" I couldn't even recognise my own voice.

With an expression full of fear, I looked at Rémi, who was bursting with hot anger at being treated with such contempt. I could see his anger mounting and suddenly that anger burst from his skin as terrifying red and yellow flames.

I knew nothing of the myths and stories, nor their representations in Buddhist paintings and sculptures, but now I had come face to face with the most terrifying of Bodhisattvas, the wrathful Mahakala, the fierce and powerful emanation of Avalokiteshvara, the Bodhisattva of harsh compassion, who was about to cut out the fears and dark thoughts which were suffocating me. It was Wóhólò Tagí. The Yellow-Haired. The yellow leopard I had slept on as a child, slept with even now. The Bodhisattva returning to the world out of compassion for my lost spirit! The anger on Rémi's face, the flames surrounding his arms, shoulders and bursting from his yellow hair struck terror in my heart as the Bodhisattva stepped towards me, eyes wide and staring wildly. Rémi lifted his hand to strike me across my cheek and break the petty bitterness. At the crack of his hand, the knot of fear in my stomach unwound into a beatific euphoria, as I arched my spine and fell backwards onto my white rock and into unconsciousness. I had suddenly understood everything. Wóhólò Tagí, Nathalie, Juliette and many more spirits I had not yet known suddenly rushed through my vision and into a glimpse of possible futures.

"What the fuck?" shouted Rémi. He looked up at the sky and howled, frightening the birds who had been watching this battle of spirits.

He bent down next to me, trying to revive my shaking body.

"Why is he shaking like that?" And then the shaking stopped and still I could not be revived.

He decided the only thing to do was carry me back to the house.

He had to stop his general panic, move it into action, translate the pain of effort into energy. His body was on fire. The flames I had seen were now burning throughout his own body to envelope both of us as the two leopards ran beside us to the edge of the forest.

* * *

"Madame, Madame! Venez vite!"[52]

"What is it now, Marie Jeanne?" asked Nathalie without moving.

"Les garçons, Madame! Les garçons! Maître Rémi porte notre jeune maître dans ses bras, qui me paraît inconscient."[53]

Nathalie jumped up to look.

"Go and find my husband. I think he is in his office." she demanded and rushed outside.

Rémi fell to his knees and, exhausted, placed me carefully on the fresh grass of the lawn.

"Rémi, we have to carry him to his bedroom."

Just as they were picking me up together, Charles arrived.

"Give him to me. Give him to me!" he said, taking me in his arms and carrying me inside.

"Appelle le médecin, Marie Jeanne. Dis-lui que c'est très urgent, qu'il arrive tout de suite."[54] demanded Nathalie and then to Rémi: "What happened?"

"I don't know. When I found him he was squatting on a rock near the lake . . ."

"Get me a flannel and some water. Is he hurt? Hit his head, maybe? No, there are no bumps. So, you found him near the lake . . . and . . ."

---

[52] "Madame! Madame! Come quickly!"
[53] 'The boys, Madame! The boys! Master Rémi is carrying our young master in his arms, who seems unconscious to me.'
[54] 'Call the doctor, Marie Jeanne. Tell him it is very urgent, that he comes immediately.'

"He stood up, looked at me and told me to find some clothes . . ."

Nathalie smiled at the thought of me telling Rémi to get dressed.

"No, it wasn't funny. He was being horrible. He wanted to hurt me."

"Alors là, je te crois pas. Personne est aussi gentil que lui."[55]

"I know, but . . . . I don't know . . . he seemed sad, depressed, lost, as if he had suddenly found himself abandoned, alone. He said I was a white French boy; I was not Suri. Why was I naked? What was he doing here in the land of aranjinya?"

"What's aranjinya?"

"White foreigners."

"He's depressed, then. Oh, my God, my poor baby! What happened?"

"I wanted to slap him, to bring him out of it, I was so angry."

"And?"

"As my hand hit his cheek . . . not hard . . . okay, quite hard, his eyes rolled back inside his head and he fell backwards to the ground, shaking. After some time, he stopped shaking, but didn't wake up, so I carried him here."

"All the way from the lake?!!"

"Yeh."

"Whatever he said to you was wrong and he will know that. You are Suri! Well, as good as, anyway! You have learned his language, adopted his customs. You are his brother, and he loves you!"

Tears came to Rémi's eyes, his body shaking.

"Look at you now! You're still completely naked and you're not even aware of it! Go and put on some clothes before the doctor arrives. You promised not to run around the house naked again and embarrass Marie

---

[55] "That, I don't believe. No one is as kind and gentle as him."

Jeanne."

"Don't worry, Madame." Marie Jeanne had just re-entered Chár's bedroom. "For young Master Chár, it is his custom at home in Africa. And young master Rémi wants to make him welcome, comfortable, and a bit like he's at home with family and friends."

"Vous êtes trop sage, Marie Jeanne, et merçi."

"Le médecin arrive en deux minutes."[56]

*   *   *

"So, Doctor Bonnet, please, we want to invite you to dine with us this evening," I remember hearing Charles' voice.

"Thank you so much, Monsieur de Rochebrune," replied Bonnet. "I want you to bring Chár to the surgery after the weekend so that I can give him a general physical examination, make sure he has had all his vaccinations. And I want to arrange for him to have an electroencephalogram. From what the young gentleman—Rémi?—has said, it seems that Chár has had an epileptic seizure. After the crisis of muscle tension and then shaking, it takes quite a long time for the brain to recover, and this is often a period of profound sleep, if you can call it that, which was when—somehow—Rémi carried him back."

I had woken briefly while Doctor Bonnet was examining me and felt confused and distressed, barely able to grasp what was happening.

"I have given him some diazepam in the form of a suppository," Bonnet said. "He may well have a severe migraine, and I want to avoid another seizure. Diazepam will help him relax. It's a type of sedative, in fact, and really, I want him to sleep more. Has he suffered this sort of crisis before?"

"Not as far as we know," Charles answered. "Eh, Nathalie?"

"There is no need to hospitalize him now, which would be traumatic for him. He seems fine, but perhaps someone should be in attendance next to him. Call me if you are at all worried, but otherwise, I will come to

---

[56] "You are too wise and understanding, Marie Jeanne, and thank you."
"The doctor arrives in two minutes."

check on him tomorrow."

I heard everyone leaving the room, except for my Tagí. He slid under the bed sheet next to me, exhausted. He lay on his side facing me, his friend, who had seemed so strong, but now possessed the fragility of what it means to be human. Even in my disoriented state, I felt his presence and his gaze on me. I turned toward him, slipping my arm around his back. In my dazed state, I could still feel the fine golden down that many times had amazed me whenever it refracted trapped sunlight and briefly flashed into visible existence. Rémi lifted his leg to wrap around mine. My hand drifted down to the smooth skin of his buttocks, to the aureole

of pubic hair around his ɗolé. The drug was taking effect. We were floating, floating with the naked moon across the Dibdib jungle, two leopards toward the dawn.

Several hours later, as a descending moon seemed to chase the sun towards the horizon, I opened eyes eyes to see my beautiful brother, his head propped on one hand, his expression intent.

"What happened?" he murmured. "I want to know what happened."

"Not now," I replied. "I'm too tired."

I closed my eyes, put my arm around his back, and pulled him closer.

"No! You can't do that! I have to know!"

"When you found me, I was far away," I said. "Far away in my mind. You interrupted that, and I was angry. Then I saw flames jumping from your skin…"

I stopped and turned away.

"Hey! Stop it! I didn't mean that, and you know it," he said, grabbing my shoulder and turning me back toward him. "I mean, what happened in your village, in Ethiopia."

I was not going to say anything. It was the past. Perhaps I could have spoken about it when I had first arrived in France, but no one spoke Suri and I didn't speak French. Also, there was the shock of everything in this aranjinya world, toilets, for example, showers, machines for everything, cooking, washing. The world of things! Sleeping alone! Hidden bodies!

129

What had they done, these aranjinya? The overwhelming speed of the encounter with the new, the strange, the foreign, had helped me to block out that terrible event. Especially Rémi, he had helped me so much in that respect, turning complications with the new into games of hilarity. We had done everything together, learning about showers, shampoo, soap, shitting, pissing in the right place! We had spent so much time together on such intimacies, laughing all the time, that now I knew every hair on Rémi's body, and he on mine.

That moment of understanding everything and then absolute forgetting. Had a crack started to appear? A crack where the dark gets in? Had it happened when I offended Rémi out near the lake? At the moment he had leaned on my shoulders, a dark crack had appeared in the blue sky and a thousand ghosts had flown in. The fragile invisible orb we had wrapped around ourselves, the profound and special closeness we had found, now, Rémi was demanding that everything be dismantled, to go back to where it had all begun, and where the world had ended.

"No!"

Rémi grabbed my shoulders to shake me.

"If you don't tell me now, first I will beat you, then I will go back to Paris this evening!"

Opening my eyes, I could still just make out the translucent flames flickering around his shoulders.

"You want to beat me?" I asked with a simple smile of innocence.

"Yeh!"

"Okay, good. You must! What I did to you was very bad!" I paused. "And then you go back to Paris?"

"Yes! Look, stop fooling around! I am serious! Tell me about that day you were with Nathalie et ma mère[57] and the shooting started."

I felt a tightness in my chest, like a knife twisting upward into my throat. I sat up, hoping to dissipate the pain. Rémi watched as words choked and stifled me as I struggled to breathe. Exasperated, he took me by the

---

[57] My mother

shoulders to shake me, frightened I was going to die again, and kissed me on the lips, then eyes and cheeks. I watched my fingers slip through the flames leaping from Rémi's back as I slid my arms around him.

"Sometimes I feel I am standing outside myself," I whispered, "like a leopard watching its own shadow move through the grass. I speak words I do not know, meanings I don't recognise. My body, before mine alone, is now a field, like for the Donga, where wild spirits and ghosts perform without end. Their midnight stories slip through my fingers like smoke, as I chase them deeper into the dark. Am I just names crying out in endless night? If I lose myself, will I find my true voice beneath the silence? Worlds are calling out to me, constant chatter is always there. That horrible thing I said to you . . . "

"You mean my not being Suri, just a naked white boy."

"What ghost was that?" I really wondered. "I could never think that. I love you too much! You are my Wóhólò Tagí, my real brother! You, Nathalie, Charles, Juliette are now mine to take care of, yet all the voices from the past are still clamouring for a future."

Rémi looked at me, saying nothing, his silent stillness turned to perfect alabaster. Was he wondering if I had gone mad? Was he questioning the power of the diazepam's dreamlike intoxications? Did he wonder whether my madness was induced by those opposing forces of a life as part of nature and the dead hand (Rémi's words) of so-called civilisation?

"It was chaos," I said at last, my voice trembling. "Guns. Firing. No one knew what was happening. Maybe it was the young men from my village, showing off to impress the girls. People ran everywhere, shouting, screaming…"

Rémi was pushing, I could feel it in my heart, pushing me back to where everything ends, and all begins.

"I told you before! My mother died!" My fists clenched as I fought the memories. "The tighter I held her, the more she seemed to slip away!"

"I know, and I'm sorry to make you remember," Rémi said quietly. "It wasn't until the next day that Nathalie and Dieter came to find you. But what did you do after the chaos and shooting at the Donga, after you took them to their car? After you had been with your mother?"

131

"She told me to go with Nathalie," I said, meeting his eyes. "How did she know that was possible, that it could happen?"

Rémi shook his head. "I don't know. I believe women are different from us. They are interested in other things to men. Of course, it is not so clear as that, and for us all, those differences often get blurred, mixed up: your mother's voice, her heart, is in you as much as your father's; there is something of being-woman in all of us, both you and me and all men. What I want to say is, they understand things we can't, or cannot see so clearly. Your mother knew Nathalie was special, like her. She knew Nathalie would take care of you and give you the chance to make your people live again."

"You are so wise, Rémi, as well as handsome! No wonder I love you and have made you my brother!"

"So? Come on! Tell me!"

"I went back to where the shooting had started. There were already many bodies. People I knew. I followed where the Dizi were leading everyone…"

"I wanted to be with them, to die with them," I said, my voice dropping to a whisper. "But I couldn't. I was too weak, too scared."

Rémi sat up sharply, his eyes blazing. "Stop it! Stop saying that! You're not a coward. I know you're not!"

"The cries of the babies… the screaming of the children… it's all in my head, even now!" I clenched my fists and began hitting my forehead, as though I could beat the memories out of myself. "And you—you force me to see it all again? The howling and barking of the Dizi, jumping up and down like baboons. I saw them grab babies by their ankles, swinging them over their heads and smashing them against rocks before throwing them into the Akobo. The bigger children—they beat them with stones or slit their throats." I turned to look at Rémi, my eyes burning with accusation. "Now, you can remember it too!"

The crack in repressed memory had loosened, the worst was over, a gash had opened up and words, memories and pain were able to flow like a river bursting its banks.

"The Dizi baboons all rushed forward to watch, until only their captain's truck and its driver were left behind. . . "

"And?" Rémi prompted, his voice barely above a whisper.

"I jumped on the driver's back," I said, the words bitter on my tongue. "I pushed my fingers and teeth into his neck and dragged him into the bush."

Rémi was frozen, white, he felt he had stopped breathing. Already the horror of babies being swung by their ankles and smashed against rocks was enough to bring stunned tears to his eyes.

"I have tried here in France being happy, forgetting, while I learn French, find you, my brother, but . . . . You really want to know all this, eh?" I cried, as if I was accusing him for asking. "Some of the older children escaped. I saw. As it got darker, the Dizi became scared. I waited. I know I killed two more also. It was easy. I could see them in their stupid uniforms, but none could see me. And their captain, like for the wild boar I first killed in the forest here, I waited for that pig.. Eventually, he was under the tree I was waiting in. I fell on his back, pushed my fingernails deep into his eyes, tore them out and then jumped away."

And for the first time, Rémi had at last seen me for what I had become.

"He was blinded. They were all lost now. He bounced off two or three trees, tripped and fell into a giant ant's nest. It was funny!" I was almost laughing now, the feeling of horror and victory in his death was overwhelming. "His screams echoed through the trees, twisting the branches. None of the Dizi were prepared to rescue him. They watched the nightmare, as did I, the ants crawling over his neck and face tasting his blood as, very slowly, their attack pushed him deeper into torture. It took a long time for him to die. When his cries stopped, all the Dizi murderers had run off in all directions, not knowing where their terror was taking them. His body would slowly disappear, buried and eaten! I was happy. I was so happy, I had to stop myself laughing and howling with rapture."

"Rapture!?" said Rémi, astonished. "Where did you get that from?"

"My teacher. This is what I feel in my body just before I die."

Rémi was silent. I put my arm across his belly and rested my head upon his chest. I opened my eyes to look up at his face, pensive, turned towards the ceiling. I could still see the flames of the Bodhisattva around his shoulders and head.

"Out at the lake, at that White Rock – did you know that is what Beyahola, the name of my village, means? - my misery, my feeling of being alone were crushing me. It was as if I was the village of Beyahola itself, in ruins. And when you, my Rémi, found me and struck me, it was then I knew I would never be lost, I would never be alone, I would never suffer that torment of a life in desolation."

I rested my head against his chest, hearing his heart pounding beneath me.

"Dying first time was in Dibdib, when everything ended," I whispered. "Then, as the sun's fingers crept above the trees the next morning, my leopards woke me, licking my face and everything began again. The second time was at our white rock next to the lake, when I fell into the arms of forever. Your arms, Wóhólò Tagí nanu."

I felt Rémi's arm tighten around me as the flames of the Bodhisattva wrapped around us both.

*   *   *

Chapter 4.

Juliette.

Back at home, after Italy, Juliette had invited girlfriends from the lycée in
Blois to stay for a few days, or sometimes she would visit them in town,
but generally the preoccupations of the everyday seemed somewhat
restricting. She would sometimes help look after the family fruit and
vegetable gardens, or sometimes help her father around the farm,
milking the cows or preparing cheeses; they had a small production
making des fromages cendrés artisanale[58], not a huge production but
sufficient to sell to stall holders in local markets, Now, during the
summer months the busy period of harvesting had begun.

At dinner times, her father tended to be fairly silent with occasional one-
word answers to her mother. It was as if his soul was made up of the
events of nature, demanding during the day and now in the evening
reaching a restful peace. It was her mother Marie Jeanne who did all the
talking, in fact too often without even a pause, as if to make up for her
father's silence.

"I want to go and see him," said Juliette.

Marie Jeanne had just been recounting how us two boys had returned to
the house mid-morning, both naked, with the young Rémi, from Paris
(what would his mother think of these goings on?) carrying the young
master Chár in his arms. Madame Nathalie seemed to have no control
over them and just let them run wild like primitive tribesmen in the
jungle, before they'd learned about Our Lord and discovered their
nakedness. In fact, the village priest had alluded to it in his sermon only
the other Sunday. "Don't you remember?"

"I don't go to church, Maman."

"I was talking to your father."

"Papa always goes to sleep in church, which I think is a good idea. It's

---

[58]   artisan cheeses covered in wood ash

supposed to be the Day of Rest anyway."

"Well the priest was talking about Adam and Eve being kicked out of paradise after eating from the tree of knowledge, even though God had told them not to, and then realising they were naked."

"Sounds like those boys have rediscovered paradise, if you ask me," said Louis Marie.

"Discovered each other, more like. Last Sunday, Father Jacques was saying we should learn from our Muslim brothers and sisters a little about modesty and cover up more, although, as he said, if you cover up too much then modesty itself becomes immodest in how it flaunts itself in the eyes of others. Really interesting it was."

"Was it interesting, Papa?"

Louis Marie just looked at his daughter and said nothing.

"Look, mother. Are you telling us about Chár or the priest? What's your story?"

"So, Madame Nathalie was really worried. God knows what those boys had been doing in the forests! I had to call Doctor Bonnet who reckoned he had had a fit and would have to rest for a few days."

"A what?"

"A seizure, a fit, epileptic fit, he was not sure. He gave him some sort of sedative and is coming tomorrow to give him more to help prevent it from happening again."

"Is he OK?"

"I don't know. Madame Nathalie said he seemed a bit better after he had slept."

"I want to visit him."

"What? Why?" said Marie Jeanne, with astonishment. "You don't know him. You met him once a long time ago. Why should he want to see you? He is not interested in girls. He's got his boyfriend, the young

136

master Rémi."

"Mother, how come you've got the world so perfectly worked out? He has had a terrible time losing his family and home. I just want him to know others care for him also, that he is welcome here in France."

"That's very nice of you but is it such a good thing all these black Africans flooding into Europe and France? I mean, they are just not like us, are they? And no one really knows what caused his illness. I mean it could be . . . anything."

Juliette stood up from the table, her eyes black with anger, cleaned her plate and left the room. Marie Jeanne looked at her husband for support, who looked back with disgust and then turned away.

*   *   *

The following morning, Marie Jeanne left early on her bike and, shortly after, she arrived at the de Rochebrune's house.

"Bonjour madame. How is the young master?"

"He's still in bed. He's sleeping more or less. I think that's fine. The doctor has already seen him"

"What about master Rémi?"

"He's coming for breakfast."

There was the sound of a vehicle on the gravel pulling into the yard.

"Well, who's that, I wonder?"

Marie Jeanne glanced out of the window.

"It's my husband, Madame." Marie Jeanne looked worried.

"Do you want to let them in? Is there a problem, Marie Jeanne?"

"He is with my daughter who wants to see the young master Chár." She seemed slightly anxious.

137

"I'm sorry, Madame. I said not to come. Master Chár is sick. He shouldn't be troubled. Why would he want to see my daughter, anyway? I've already told them."

"Go and open! Go and open! Of course, he wants to see them both. That's very kind of them."

Earlier, Juliette, still feeling annoyed with her mother, found her father cleaning the milking shed.

"Papa, I want you to take me to the De Rochebrune's."

"Ah, bon?"

"Now!"

"Right!" he sighed, knowing he had no choice.

"You know very well, Maman is being ridiculous. I just want to say hello, bring him some flowers from the garden and wish him well."

"Quite right, sweetheart. Your mother is daft sometimes. She doesn't know when to shut up." He put his fork down and followed his daughter to the truck.

When Marie Jeanne opened the door, she was greeted by an expression of annoyance on her husband's face and a scowl from Juliette.

Rémi arrived in the kitchen for his breakfast in his favourite loose cotton T-shirt and baggy cotton shorts, announcing that I was still half asleep, probably because of the Diazepam the doctor had pushed up my arse.

"Rémi, enfin! Ta langue!"[59] said Nathalie with a frown.

"Ah, Monsieur Morel, come in," said Nathalie as Louis Marie removed his cloth cap and entered the kitchen. "And the beautiful Juliette too. What a pleasure! What can I do for you?"

"We are sorry to disturb you, Madame…"

"Not at all! Not at all!"

---

[59] "Rémi, really! Your language!"

"…but my daughter, Juliette, and I too, wanted to wish young Master Chár a speedy recovery of his health. Juliette has brought him some flowers."

"You're too kind, both of you," said Nathalie. "It'll make him very happy to see you! Follow me."

There was a gentle knock. Nathalie put her head around the door and quietly announced: "You have visitors."

I stirred, unsure whether I was dreaming. Language suggests we are either asleep or awake, either conscious or unconscious. To remember something, you have to be conscious of it happening. Hence, rationally, you cannot have been asleep if you remember a dream, you must have been conscious, you must have been awake while the dream unfolded.. This is an example of how language and rationality can simply be misleading. From experience, there are clearly varying states of consciousness between absolute forgetting, which is death itself, a hyper-alert state in the conscious present, and varying states of mind, sloshing back and forth between memories, imaginings, dreams, fantasies, and realities. In my sedated state, I was unsure whether the present was calling me or it was a continuation of my dream-wishes.

I felt myself turn to look, my brain and body still opiated and strangely separated from each other, such that for a brief few seconds, my mind was observing what my body was doing as if by itself. Opening my eyes, I saw Juliette sitting on the side of my bed, looking at me with a small bunch of flowers in her hands on her lap. Behind her stood Louis Marie, her father.

"So, Master Chár, Marie Jeanne has told us about your accident yesterday," said Louis Marie. "What happened? You passed out, fainted?"

"I… I don't know." I wondered if my words were slipping and sliding. Did they sound okay? Were they the right words?

"Anyway, we are so sorry. Juliette wanted to come to see you… and me also, I wanted to know how you are."

The diazepam was swimming through my brain, and I was feeling

139

slightly woozy. Yesterday was difficult to remember. I said nothing. Juliette could see I was struggling.

"Well, Master Chár, I have to get back to the farm; my cows cannot wait. I hope when you feel better, you can visit us and some time we can go hunting together," he said with a smile. "Juliette wants to stay a little longer, if that is okay."

He left the bedroom, and in the passage leading to the kitchen, encountered Marie Jeanne who was hurrying towards the bedroom with a flower vase full of water.

"What are you doing?"

"Bringing a vase for Juliette's flowers."

"Leave them alone. And stop being nosey and interfering. I know what you are like, Marie Jeanne. You can't let them get to know each other without sticking your nose in. If I find out you've been bothering them, there'll be trouble."

"But it's my daughter in the bedroom of this young African…"

Their whispered dispute bounced off the walls to incite Louis Marie's frustration.

"And so what? They are both adults. Besides, you accuse him of… I don't know what!"

"Yes, but we don't know. We know nothing about his… people, except they run around naked in the jungle all the time."

"Get back to the kitchen and get on with your work. I'll speak to you later."

Marie Jeanne's anxiety was hardly allayed by her impatient husband. Who could she turn to for support? Father Jacques? At the same time, in spite of her desperate need to poke her nose around the door, to interfere and to impose, disrupting any friendship, any affection which was unsupervised, especially by her, she knew not only Louis Marie, but Madame Nathalie would also be annoyed by her intrusions. She turned and walked back to the kitchen, followed by her husband who excused himself to Nathalie and left.

"Marie Jeanne, could you prepare onion soup for lunch? I'll ask Juliette to have lunch with Chár."

"Oui, Madame, but I…"

"I know you're going home for lunch with your husband. I'll bring Juliette back later. Chár will be very happy to spend the morning with her, and I think Juliette with him too. Okay? In fact, give me the vase and I'll ask."

"Of course, Madame. Certainly."

Juliette and I could hear the dispute of her parents. She looked at me and smiled in the silence of my room. Soon the voices disappeared, and Juliette dropped her eyes, waiting for words to arise between us. I also waited.

"I've brought you some flowers from our garden," she said.

I sat up and held out my hand to take them, lifting them to my nose to taste their perfume, my eyes smiling at Juliette from behind blue cornflowers and pinks. Examining the bunch, I chose one and then a second to lodge behind my ears. I noticed Juliette smiling at my self-adornment.

"Juliette, can you help me?"

"Of course."

"Can you push some flowers into my hair? It is very strong and will easily hold them."

Choosing carefully, she pushed the stems through my hair, giving me a floral coronet.

"Does it look good? I want to see."

Standing up—with her help, as I was still weak—we approached the mirror.

"Do you think I look… good? Chàlli?"

"Yes, very! Don't worry. You are very handsome," she laughed.

We stood looking at each other in silence.

"Do you want me to do the same for you," I asked, "with these others?"

I waited. She was simply looking and smiling.

"Of course!"

We sat next to each other on the bed. I carefully moved her long brown hair back behind her ears before gently pushing two flowers into place. I was sitting cross-legged and only wearing shorts, which I'd had to put on for the doctor, of course. Juliette seemed conscious of my black torso in front of her. She was sitting close to my legs on the side of the bed, the remaining flowers on her lap. She offered the next for me to arrange and her empty hand descended to touch my nearest knee.

My eyes dropped to meet hers. There was a moment of hesitation.

She watched, aware of what was happening between us, and leaned forward to kiss me on the cheek. Her lips lingered too long for it to be a casual embrace, her cheek resting on mine, gentle and warm, and I could sense her special perfume, meant for me alone. Slowly, I slid my cheek across hers until our lips met.

Juliette moved back slightly so that we might contemplate each other, secrets behind our eyes. Letting my head slip back onto the pillow, I watched as she stood to put the flowers aside before sitting down beside me. She placed her arm behind my head and around my shoulders. I could feel the electricity in her fingers as she touched my skin. I slipped closer so that my head rested upon her breast. As I turned to look up at her delicate smile, I could hear her heartbeat.

There was a tap on the door, and suddenly, both of us became conscious of what had happened—conscious of ourselves instead of wrapped in the bliss offered by the other. Juliette moved away and sat in a chair near the window. I sat on the bed and put a pillow between my legs.

"Yes?" I whispered, my voice surrendering to my heart.

Nathalie opened the door.

"I brought a vase for the flowers… but I see you have already decided what to do with them. Juliette, would you like to stay for lunch? We can take you home later."

Juliette hesitated. "Well, I…"

"Yes, she would," I insisted.

"Chár, put some clothes on, please," said Nathalie, and then smiling at Juliette: "He always forgets to do that! And take it easy, Chár. Remember, you are supposed to be resting."

With that, she left us. Turning away from the bedroom door, I imagined her throwing her eyes wide open and exhaling a deep breath of stunned consternation. Clearly, she had interrupted a very intimate little occasion. "May all go well for them both," I could hear her thinking.

There were a few moments of silent embarrassment, during which Juliette seemed to wonder what she had done—what was happening.

"What is it, Juliette?"

"Nothing, nothing! Slowly, Chár, slowly."

"I love you, Juliette. Truly, I love you. Ever since I first saw you. I wanted to tell you at the time, but I couldn't speak."

"But you don't know me! How many other girls have you said that to?"

"Don't say that, Juliette. I have only said this to you! Of course, I love Nathalie and Charles, who are like parents to me—they saved me and gave me a home and give me everything. And, of course, I love Rémi very much. He is my best friend, the same as a brother, better than a brother. I will always love him. But you…

"That first time…

"Our fingers met…

"There were sparks in that touch…

"They lit my heart… I knew then… I know now…

"You…

"You kissed me… lips on lips, more than a perfect wish…

"Yesterday, I was thinking of you, and so strong was it, my heart even stopped… and today, you are here. You have picked flowers for me… you…"

"Chár, stop! You don't know me. This talk of…" she dared not even say the word. "It's too much."

She quickly looked around for something to do. "Here, let me show you something." She took out her mobile phone and opened a photo file.

"I'm sorry. I make you feel uncomfortable. I shouldn't say these things. Maybe it's the medicine. Maybe because yesterday I… my head is…"

"Stop. Stop talking. Look."

She sat next to me again and started to show me photos of the barbecue. There were many, and mostly of me. Then she showed me photos of her friends and visits to Blois. We sat on the bed, side by side, leaning back against the headboard. The diazepam was imposing its weight, and I started to feel tired—exhausted by the events of yesterday and the overwhelming feelings of the day. I felt I had won my Juliette. It was as though I could finally relax, as the photos slowly slipped past on the screen of her phone.

"Juliette," I asked quietly, "may I lay my head here on your shoulder? Nathalie says I must rest."

She let me lean my head against her shoulder, and as the screen faded, I began to close my eyes. My head slipped lower onto her breast, and as her one hand rested on my side, reaching toward my belly, her other caressed my forehead and hair.

The purity of innocence fell around us.

She looked down at me, her eyes soft and thoughtful. My eyes were heavy, exhausted.

"So, tell me stories, Juliette. Tell me about Juliette! About Juliette as a little girl, playing. About your farm, your family. Tell me about your cows. Which is your favourite? Let me lie and listen, be filled with flowers and… mangoes… and… bo:ni-kabaré… anye inye kidi-kari…[60]" I smiled faintly up at her, my voice deep and quiet.

Juliette stroked my tired forehead, her touch soothing.

"When I was three," she began, "I followed a cat over a wall…"

And slowly, I drifted into that perfect sleep that heals all ills of the heart.

*   *   *

It took several days for me to properly recover from my seizure, days which were quite busy with medical checks, scans, and a few vaccinations. Nathalie and Rémi accompanied me on these visits. Rationalizing and accepting with a measure of equanimity a syringe penetrating my skin and leaving behind a strange liquid was not yet part of my way of seeing the world, and my expression of horror and fear made Rémi double up with laughter.

"Why are you laughing at me? You want the same?" I asked, quite disconcerted.

"Because you are such a baby! Look at you worrying about a tiny pinprick, you can't even see a mark on your skin where it happened."

"Yes, I can! Here!"

As far as all other medical examinations were concerned, no problem was identified, and my seizure was put down to just that, a single epileptic crisis.

Days passed, and still, Claudine and Robert did not arrive, and in fact, we both forgot that they were expected, spending our days fishing,

---

[60] . . . figs . . . you and me together . . .

swimming, making adventures, sometimes shopping with Nathalie, sometimes going to the cinema, making barbecues of whatever we had caught, trapped, or fished and with Nathalie, spending days searching the forests for mushrooms and wild fruit. We each made our own pike,

or in Suri, bhirɛ, which we used for hunting boar; the first kill of Rémi's, we celebrated with a big party, with much wine and ganja. And I started to instruct Rémi in stick fighting.

"Why don't you go fencing together?" said Nathalie. "There must be classes at a sports centre not far, somewhere in the region."

"Does Juliette go fencing?"

"I don't know!" replied Nathalie, slightly impatiently. She wanted us to go out, meet other young people, instead of just running around in the forests.

"Enfin, Nathalie, soit gentille avec lui!" said Charles.

"He even called me Juliette in his sleep the other night!" laughed Rémi.

I glanced at him with a frown.

"But you were speaking in French, which is really good!"

"Qu'est-ce qu'il parle bien le Français maintenant," said Nathalie.

"Ben, il faut bien," I commented, throwing myself onto the bench in the kitchen. Nathalie looked at my face, which seemed downcast.

"Oh là là, il est déprimé! Pourquoi t'es triste, mon bébé ?"

I just shrugged.

"Would you like to peel potatoes with me?" Nathalie was preparing dinner. "On va faire des frites, eh? Tu aimes les frites, n'est pas?"

"Oui, merçi."

"What's this issue with Juliette? I thought you and Rémi were . . . . ." Charles hesitated.

"What? Boyfriends?" Rémi said, annoyed.

Rémi began to redden. "He thinks we are gay. He thinks you don't need a girlfriend because of me."

I shook my head, exasperated. "Sometimes I don't understand you white people, you old white people. I understand Rémi—he's the same as me. But you old people, I don't know . . ."

"We are not so old!" insisted Nathalie.

"You have a problem with sex, with bodies. I think you don't like them. So, when you were young, like Rémi and me," I said, addressing Charles, "you and Robert didn't look at each other's penises, didn't play with each other? Maybe sometimes vous vous êtes branlés ensemble (you masturbated together)?"

Charles's reply didn't come as quickly as it should have. Everyone turned their eyes toward him.

"Charles!" Nathalie exclaimed. "Really? I knew nothing of that. Don't be embarrassed. I'm sure at least half of all men have had some sort of gay activity at some point in their lives."

"You and my father?! Wanking together?!" Rémi burst into uncontrollable laughter. In fact, everyone was enjoying Charles's embarrassment.

"Ok! Ok!" Charles declared. "Anyway, what is it about this Juliette?"

"I want her to be my wife. I have decided."

"What?! You don't even know her," Nathalie said.

"I know enough. I want to make babies with her. Many! You can be grandparents."

"Well? What are you going to do about that problem? I mean, hey, she has no idea of this plan of yours!" said Charles.

"I need your help, Charles."

"Me?"

"Please, I need you to sweeten her parents, especially her father, Louis Marie. I need you to offer him . . . some cows. For us Suri people, it is usually up to the girl to choose the one she loves at the stick fighting festivals. Then her family offers cows to the young man's family. But here, you don't have stick fights, and I think Marie Jeanne and her husband are not so rich. It could help them to have more cows."

"I haven't got any cows!"

"I know! Why not? Sometimes I see you, and you look worried, too many problems. You should have cows. They would make you feel good."

"So, how big is my dad's dick, then?" Rémi asked, grinning.

"Far bigger than yours will ever be, I am sure!".

"Charles, please," I added, "don't say bad about my Wóhólò Tagí's dormì! He has a very good dormì, I know! Nathalie has seen. I like it. He can make any woman happy."

"Thank you, Chár!"

"Stop it now, all of you," Nathalie demanded. "The conversation is veering into vulgarity. Listen, Chár, here it doesn't work like that. You can't buy a wife with cows. You have to charm her yourself, and if she loves you, then you can become man and wife and have babies."

"It's not buying; it's just warming Monsieur Morel's heart toward us and me coming closer to him, to his family. He will know I am serious."

"Looks like buying to me," commented Rémi.

I slumped back into the cushions of the kitchen bench.

"Here, mon enfant, cut these potatoes into chips for me," Nathalie said.

"Anyway, she already loves me."

148

"How do you know?"

"After I died . . . ."

"You didn't die!"

"I died. I know."

"Did your heart stop?"

"Yes. And it started again when Rémi picked me up."

"This is nonsense!"

"No. The same happened in Dibdib."

"I don't want to think about that, Chár!" Nathalie said sharply.

"I died in Dibdib. And two leopards found me and started my heart again. One black and one the colour of gold, like my Rémi. This is how I know he is my brother—the same leopard spirit in him as me."

Rémi put his arm around me and hugged me. "I believe you," he said.

When Juliette came to see me . . . . Why did she come to see me if she does not love me? When she came, my mind was still confused, like a baby. I didn't know if what was happening was true or if I was dreaming. She sat next to me on the bed, and I felt so happy and safe next to her. I leaned my head on her chest . . . ."

"What?!" Rémi interjected.

"I put my head between her breasts . . ."

"Christ! Only you could do that! What did she do? Didn't she think you were crazy?"

"There, I could hear her heart speaking. And it told me she loved me."

"Right! Well, that explains everything!" declared Rémi.

"What I cannot understand is Suri men like big breasts. I am sure

149

Juliette's breasts are very beautiful, but they are not so big as Suri men prefer. Ever since that moment, I cannot stop thinking about her. Her perfume is in my nostrils, her breasts next to my face. What can I do?"

There was a general silence, and clearly, no one had a solution.

*　　*　　*

"So what did you do while you were alone together?" Rémi asked. It was the middle of the night, and we were lying in bed talking.

"I felt bad because my mind was still confused, and I didn't feel strong," I admitted. "I worry that maybe she thought I was stupid or no good."

"Don't worry. Everyone feels like that when they want to make a good impression. But, hey, did you kiss her?"

"Only once! She wouldn't let me kiss her more."

"What was it like? Was it good?"

"I wanted to do it over and over again. My body was pushing me. Again! Again! Even now, that's all I want to do!"

"You want to know what I think? I think she wants to catch you. She wants to make you wait so that you feel more and more hungry. She wants exactly what has happened—that all you can do is think about her."

"Really? You think so? You think she wants me?"

"Sure! Next time you see her, be cool. Don't show her your heart straight away."

"I showed her the photos," I said.

"What photos?"

"She showed me photos, so I showed her photos also."

"What photos?"

"Of you and me, of course."

"You mean of you and me naked?!"

"Yeh."

"Are you fucking crazy? So now she knows what my dick looks like! Maybe that's why you haven't seen her. She knows what your dick is like!"

"You think? . . . . Non! Believe me, girls like to see that."

"Did you give her a copy?"

" . . . . . I told you, my mind was confused because of that medicine . . . . ."

"You did, didn't you? She's probably shown them to all her friends in Blois by now!"

"So what? Don't worry! All those girls in Blois will be happy. Your dick is fine, and mine is even better."

"Oh, yeah?!"

We started fighting, both of us trying to push the other off the bed.

"Shh! Shh! You'll wake everyone!"

Then kisses, and finally, we fell asleep, arms and legs wrapped around each other like the kittens of big cats.

*   *   *

Angeline was Juliette's best friend. According to everyone who met her, she had the facial type and skin quality to be on the cover of Vogue - peerless skin. She was exceptionally beautiful in the classic sense. She enjoyed sport and consequently was strong, physically well proportioned, not the skinny shape of too many fashion models. She loved outdoor activities, taking long walks, swimming, working in the garden. At home in the apartment of her parents in Blois, there was little opportunity for such activities which is why she always appreciated staying at the farm

151

with Juliette and joining in with whatever jobs needed doing at the time. Juliette also enjoyed the physical demands of the farm, but was a lot smaller than Angeline, small delicate hands, as yet unblemished by the hard work around the farm, a slighter frame, smaller shoulders and smaller breasts.

They had both of them been interested in boys for a couple of years until about a year ago and then they'd given up. They couldn't go to bars: they were not old enough And in any case, the older boys, of eighteen or more, simply wanted to take advantage of their innocence for the purely selfish reasons of augmenting their standing amongst their mates, being able to boast of their sexual adventures and conquests. Even though these boys were older, the two girls felt their manner was simply immature.

Juliette had wanted to tell Angeline about meeting me and what were after all quite newsworthy events within the village, first of all my rescue from Ethiopia and secondly my hunting prowess and reputation.

"He gave me some photos."

"Let's have a look."

"He was really ill at the time. No one knows exactly what happened. Some sort of epileptic fit. The doctor gave him some really strong sedatives."

"So, where are the photos?"

"It's just to say, he possibly didn't really know what he was doing." she hesitated.

"Is he okay now?"

"Well, yes, I think so."

"So, the photos?"

Juliette was still feeling unsure about showing them.

"They're of him and his friend, Rémi. . . . Okay, look, I'll show you."

Juliette opened the file on her phone.

"Oh, là là! . . . Oh, là là ! . . . Oh, my God! . . . He has no shame, eh? . . . Oh, là là!"

"I think his accident . . . the medication . . . "

Angeline had no time for all those possible excuses: "Have you seen him since?"

"No."

"Why not? Qu'est-ce qu'ils sont beaux, tous les deux, eh[61]?"

"I don't know why I haven't! Too shy!"

"Are you crazy, or what?"

"He said he was in love with me."

"And? All the more reason, for crying out loud!"

"And then there's my mother! You know what she is like. . . Anyway!"

"T'as vu? Between their legs?"

"I know."

"I bet you look at these photos every night, eh? Well, I want to meet them!"

"Non! Non, non!"

"Why not?"

"What are we going to say? We wanted to see you . . . "

"Your naked bodies in the flesh! . . . Yes! Why not?" Angeline was laughing. "This has to stop! Shyness? Non! . . . You have to see him again! And I want to meet his friend! Hey!"

---

[61] How handsome they are, both of them!

And then suddenly, everything slipped out of control. Louis Marie arrived, distressed.

"Juliette, phone your mother! Tell her to come back here at once. Pâcquerette is about to give birth and the calf is in breach. I've tried calling the vet but there's no reply.

"Who's Pâcquerette?" wondered Angeline.

"One of the cows."

*　　*　　*

"Madame, that was Juliette. Mon mari's alone with Juliette and her friend Angeline, at the farm, and a cow is giving birth. She's having trouble—he thinks it's a breach. He's asking me to help him."

Everyone could see Marie Jeanne was very upset.

"What can I do?" she said, her characteristic hysteria unmistakable. The vet didn't answer the phone!"

"Breach? What's that?" I asked.

"It is when the calf is badly positioned for the birth, perhaps coming out backwards and getting stuck," Nathalie explained. "The calf could die, and maybe the mother also."

Straight away, I knew what to do.

"Don't worry, Marie Jeanne. Rémi and I will help you. I've seen this before with my father's cows. I know how to fix this. Louis Marie and I, we'll manage together."

"Me? What can I do?" Rémi demanded, somewhat nervously.
"
I whispered something in his ear. He looked at me as if I were crazy but knew he must do as I asked.

Nathalie immediately offered to drive us all to the farm.

When we arrived, we found Louis Marie in the barn with Juliette and

Angeline. Louis Marie was pale with anxiety, and the two girls seemed despairing and upset. Lying in front of them was the cow, Pâquerette. I put myself next to Juliette, who was almost in tears.

"It's okay, Juliette. I'm here," I said quietly, putting an arm around her shoulders. There was a moment's pause as everyone looked on.

"Monsieur Morel—" I began.

"Please. Louis."

"Louis, let me help. I've seen this many times. My father had many cows, and I had to help him when they gave birth."

"Thank you, Chár. Usually, if there's a problem, I can call on the local vet. But . . ."

Pâquerette was looking exhausted.

"Is the calf alive?" I asked, pulling off my T-shirt. "Let me check. Rémi, get that medicine ready!"

"Where's the kitchen?" Rémi demanded, looking at the girls, who seemed frozen. "Come on! Where?" They quickly disappeared in the direction of the house.

"I need a pestle and mortar and some hot water!" he was almost shouting.

"What are you doing?" Juliette demanded.

"It's ganja! He wants me to make a paste to give to the cow!"

The girls looked stunned.

"How much ganja do you give to a cow?! Fuck! He's mad! I'm not giving all of it away, am I?"

"Don't worry! I'll get you some more tomorrow," Angeline said.

"You just have to trust him, okay? Fuck! Fucking hell!" Rémi was panicking under the weight of responsibility thrust on him. "Why does he do this? Nothing is straightforward with him!"

"Calm down," Angeline said, putting her hand on his back. "Nothing straightforward? That's why you love him. That's why he's your friend."

I bent down, stroked Pâquerette's haunches, and pushed my hand into her vulva and vagina up to my elbow, where I felt the backside of the calf jammed against the pelvic bone. I found its anus, pushed a couple of fingers into it, and immediately felt the anus muscles tighten and withdraw.

"The calf is alive. We need to get the mother to stand up. Does she have a name?"

"Marie Jeanne, there's a rope behind the barn door. We can try to hoist her on the beam."

"Her name is Pâquerette. C'était moi qui l'a baptisée," Marie Jeanne said, handing the rope to her husband.

"Joli nom!" Nathalie said.

Louis Marie threw the rope over the beam. I pushed it under the ribs, and Louis tied it, ready to hoist her to her feet.

"Here's your paste," Rémi said, staring wide-eyed at me. My naked torso and right arm were already covered in slime and cow shit. "You know what you're doing, eh?"

"Don't worry. Before we're finished, you'll be like me, covered in shit as well."

"Wait, wait!" Louis Marie demanded. "What is this green paste?"

"It's medicine for Pâquerette. It will ease the pain and help her relax. Don't worry, I know. Now, can you open her mouth? I'll put it inside, then we'll lift her up."

Louis Marie knelt beside Pâquerette, placing her head on his lap and firmly grasping her top and lower jaw to force them open. I pushed half the ganja paste as far down her throat as I could and said, "Hold her mouth closed for a short time," as I stroked her throat to encourage her to swallow. The other half, I pushed up her anus.

"It goes into her blood quicker like that," I explained. "Now, Rémi and I will pull the rope slowly, while you, Louis, help her up. Marie Jeanne and Nathalie, can you help to steady her backside as she gets up?"

Juliette and her friend, Angeline, were transfixed. Both of our bodies were glistening with sweat in the humid, warm barn. The smell of straw, Pâquerette, and young male pheromones filled their nostrils. Rémi's golden curls were sticking to his forehead, and I noticed Juliette following a drop of sweat trickling from my armpit down my ribs. The muscles in our arms, chests, and backs tightened as we leaned back to pull on the rope.

"Let her relax five minutes," said Louis Marie, as Pâquerette steadied herself, standing. "Chár, have you done this before? The arse of the calf is presenting first."

"Yes, I have."

"We have to push it back inside the uterus and get the rear legs so that the hooves are coming out first," Louis Marie continued.

"Yeh."

"Are you sure you have done this before?"

"Yeh. Have you?"

"With the vet. Not really."

I grinned at Louis Marie. "Don't worry, we will both have our arms inside her."

Louis Marie smiled back, a more serious smile.

"I can push the backside back in," I said, "and then you can move the first leg into position. After that, the second should be easier."

"Ok."

Marie Jeanne and Nathalie were holding Pâquerette's head.

"Don't let her move forward when I push," I said with a raised voice. Rémi, Juliette, and Angeline watched, astounded, in awe as I pushed until my arm had disappeared almost up to my armpit.

Louis Marie had also pushed his arm inside Pâquerette. The peculiarity of blind seeing inside the warm and wet vagina, both of our hands aware of each other as we attempted to coordinate our effort, was surpassed by the intense need to save both cow and calf. After such concentrated seconds of blind manipulation, seeing only with hands, we managed to push one knee up against the body wall and retrieve the hock, pulling it towards the cervix.

"I'll push the second knee this time, while you grab the hock," said Louis Marie.

"Ok."

"Juliette, ma chérie, bring the rope from around Pâquerette, for us to tie to the calf's feet."

The hooves had now appeared at the mouth of the vulva.

"Rémi, come here to pull!" I called. "Like that, Louis can help the baby out."

Rémi was astonished at how much strength was needed, gradually, slowly increasing, until with a wet, sloppy sucking sound the calf slipped out. Rémi and I fell backwards into the straw, the calf slipped through Louis's hands and fell on top of both of us. We laughed. Everyone laughed.

"Ooh, c'est une bébé vache. Qu'est-ce qu'elle est jolie!" Marie Jeanne and Nathalie both had tears in their eyes.

"Tickle her nostrils with some straw."

Rémi, who was holding the baby and felt a bit like a father himself, tickled her nose and immediately she sneezed on his chest.

"Put her down and let Pâquerette look after her now."

"What about the umbilical cord?"

"It is fine. It's already broken. Pâquerette will take care of her."

"And the afterbirth?"

"Pacquerette will deal with that."

The enormous sense of relief gave Louis Marie a wonderful lightness of being as if he was floating through every movement, every spoken word, every thought with the most natural ease.

"Alors, on va fêter tout ça," he said.

Nathalie returned to the house to find clean clothes for us, and Marie Jeanne went into the kitchen to prepare snacks—des plats de rillettes, jambon, salades, fromages, et pain. Sans doute, Louis Marie would find some good wines from the cellar and aperitifs.

All of a sudden, it was just Rémi and me with Juliette and Angeline.

"What you have done for my father is so . . . what can I say? . . . wonderful," Juliette said.

"Juliette, do you have an outside tap and hose? We cannot go in the house like this."

"Of course, of course, follow me," she said.

She led us to a corner of the yard, which was cobbled, with a drain at the centre. There was a tap against the wall of the house with a hose attached.

"Is this ok for you?"

"Yeh, it's fine."

I started to undo my trouser, bloodied with the sticky mess from the birth. Rémi followed suit, even though he was conscious that perhaps he should not be dropping his trousers in front of the girls. In any case, we both kept our boxers.

I watched Juliette crouch gracefully, bending her knees until her heels touched the back of her thighs, her back straight with one knee almost on the ground and the other just under her chin as she collected our dirtied clothes.

"I'll put these in the washing machine," she said.

Both girls, Juliette and Angeline, were wide-eyed and exchanged knowing glances as they entered the house.

"I think they like us! I think she loves you!" chanted Rémi in a teasing, singsong voice, grinning at me.

"What about Juliette's friend? You like her?"

"You mean Angeline?"

"Ah, you know her name already!"

The girls returned with shampoo and large towels.

"Can you hold the hose for us?" Rémi asked Angeline, offering it to her, while I took the shampoo from Juliette. I tried to catch her eye, which she quickly averted. Rémi and I began applying the shampoo, in fact, shampooing each other, as was our custom, anyway.

"Enough of the suds and rubbing each other down," declared Angeline, aiming the hose at both of us.

"Okay! Okay! Thanks! Finished!" shouted Rémi. "Enough! It's too cold!"

"What? I can't hear you!" replied Angeline with a naughty grin. That was enough invitation for Rémi, who ran at her to grab the hose. Angeline dropped it quickly and ran towards the house, screaming.

Juliette turned off the water and approached me with a large white towel, wrapping it around my shoulders and vigorously rubbing my back, as you might a small child quitting a cold swimming pool.

"Ah, nice!" declared Rémi. "You have someone to take care of you, wrap you in a warm towel! And me? Where is Angeline? She just wanted to make trouble!"

How is it possible to feel both strong and weak, both confident and vulnerable? But that's exactly how I felt. I turned towards Juliette so she could dry my chest. She smiled up at me.

"Here, put the towel around your waist and come in. Madame de Rochebrune has gone to find clothes for you, I am sure. Come!"

I dropped my wet and dirty boxers, retrieving them to take to be washed, and tightened the towel. This seemed okay as far as I could tell, for Juliette. She took my hand to lead me towards the house.

A peaceful evening light was cast over the darkening forests of my Sologne and in that quiet, beneath the fading twilight, amongst the grasses, marsh reeds, dark roots and dying branches, timid and fearful creatures started their silent scavenging. For many humans, at this hour especially, the forests were sinister, haunted by the fetid breeding of rotting death. Turn over the mud at the edge of any marsh and you can smell it fermenting and consuming itself. No wonder witches lived deep in forests; the only ones who truly understood the dark character of those places, where it could take only seconds for the innocent to lose their way, and worse, lose their minds, like the Dizi murderers, in awful damp imaginings that never see sunlight. Countless numbers had lost themselves in the penumbra of my forests and jungles and died of terror when only a few hundred metres from salvation, spinning around the eye of meaningless indifference and the drab interior of their dark hearts.

But we did not feel this, Juliette and I, nor Rémi and Angeline who were following at a short distance. For us, there was nothing sinister. It was simply nature itself, conceiving and consuming, growing and pursuing its own fertility. Our desires also, individual but indistinct. Juliette slipped her arm through mine as we strolled into the cooling evening air and ripening pink and distant clouds.

Juliette and I walked in silence for a while, linked arm in arm. Occasionally, I would look down at her and Juliette back up at me. We smiled, understanding the private language roused between our bodies. Now, I was a man. I was responsible for taking care of Juliette. That proud uplift in my heart told me so. That smile in her eyes told me

Juliette knew I was now a man, and, in that moment, I was her man, her refuge, her haven. From here, next to me, she could contemplate the world's beauty without having to be on guard against its dangers. Her eyes spoke of wonder.

She noticed a lingering oaken fragrance, or maybe chestnut. It was like some aged red wines.

"Is there a hint of acorns or chestnuts or dry grass to your skin?" she wondered and leaned her face into my neck to better taste.

"What?"

"Have you put a perfume?"

"No, why?"

"It smells like my father's hay ricks."

"My skin? Maybe because I was in the barn."

"You've showered since then." she pointed out.

"Okay," I surrendered to her questioning. "I'll tell you. But you won't believe me. You'll think I am crazy."

"Chár, just tell me!"

"It begins with my name. Everything begins with my name!"

"What do you mean, your name?"

"My name means Leopard. From when I was a baby, my father carried me in a leopard skin. I slept on it from when I was born. Leopards have the same perfume. That is my name. . . . I am Leopard." I looked at her matter-of-factly, with a smile and shrugged.

There was a long silence. I could see she was wondering how to deal with this idea.

"How do you know this?!" She was looking straight into my eyes with a piercing seriousness. "Have you met any leopards to check?"

"Of course!"

This brought a big smile to her face.

"The first time I died, two leopards found me. They knew I was the same as them because of my skin. They could smell leopard. I lay next to them until I was strong enough to walk again. I could smell their skin. The same as me. They stayed with me to keep me safe until the edge of the jungle."

Juliette fell silent, scrutinising my face for any expression which might betray my words, neither believing nor disbelieving what I was saying, astonished at the gap between her understanding of the world and the spirits that seemed to populate mine.

She leaned in towards me, I lifted my arm to wrap around her shoulders; she could feel my warm and slightly moist armpit against the bare skin of her shoulder.

"You have just said, the first time you died. . . ." she was surprised by her own words.

"Souvent la revanche vient des ombres, inattendue[62]. It was when my people were murdered. The Dizi were dressed up as police and with their captain, they took my people into the Dibdib forest. I followed, but they could not see me. We Suri people know how to be invisible. First, they cracked the heads of the children and threw them in the Akobo."

"Akobo?"

"The Akobo river. Then they started shooting everyone."

"And? . . What did you do?"

"First I killed the captain's driver and dragged him into the jungle." I was surprised by my own matter-of-factness, but since those memories had been forced out of me by Wóhólò Tagì, my Bodhisattva, I had been able to overcome their power. "Then I blinded . . . I blinded the captain. No one saw me. He stumbled into an ant's nest. The Dizi just left him to die. It took a long time. The roof of the sky was no longer black but dark

---

[62] Often revenge comes from the shadows, unexpected.

163

blue, the stars disappearing before his screams, his pleading and despairing moans ended. And then, I could die also, with my people, until my two leopards found me."

There was a long silence again. she didn't know how to think about what I had just told her. She had to stop herself thinking. What does it mean to kill people? It wasn't even open conflict of one fighting another. I was more like a secret assassin who hunts down his prey and murders without being seen. Was it murder?

"What do you mean, my leopards?"

"Sometimes I see them. Those same leopards. When I go hunting. They are running in front of me, beside me."

"You said the first time . . ." Juliette was struggling to understand all this.

"Yeh. The next time was here. I was near the blue lake, not far from the Beuvron."

"I know it."

"It was as if every idea - I was thinking of you, also - every idea wanted to come together . . . to explain themselves, to assemble themselves, to resemble a meaning. To make a story, a history. You know the English word, remember? Well, a member is a part of something, a group, a family, to re-member is to join parts together to make a meaning. This is what my mind, all those different parts were trying to do. Maybe the weight was too heavy. And then my Rémi broke their spell and saved me. . . And finally, there you were, sitting on the end of my bed!"

"You didn't die! That was an epileptic fit! Maybe the same in the Dibdib."

"That is your idea, not mine. Rémi was explaining to me about ideas, bad ideas, ideas that kill. Perhaps I have to find where those ideas are from, the ideas that killed my people. Then I can be free."

There was a long silence again. Perhaps the ideas, the experience, the horror were too much for Juliette; I knew I would have to wait. She had heard tales of the massacre of my village from her mother but to hear more directly, thanks to Rémi breaking open my suffocated

164

memories . . . Besides, killing Mihret and the Dizi and being saved by my leopards were memories of victory over pain. I looked down at her and smiled kindly, realising the shock my history had brought to her, I put my arm around her pulling her closer so that her shoulder sat in my warm armpit.

"Can I kiss you?" I asked, opening up once again my pierced heart. "Tu . . . . m'a embrassé, une fois . . . . et ma vie a recommencé.[63] Juliette, I want my life to start again with you."

She lifted her head up towards mine and at last, again, our lips touched as our spirits reached that high plateau beyond the blue mountains.

At a distance behind us, Rémi put his arm around Angeline and with his head next to hers, whispered: "Chár is in love."

"Juliette also."

"How do you know?"

She looked at him with a big smile, their faces next to each other.

"She talks about him all the time."

Their faces were so close Rémi could taste her warm breath and before they were even aware of it, their lips met also and sent a tingling vibration along Rémi's spine to weaken his knees.

*   *   *

My teacher had great difficulty explaining certain words to me, which were in common enough usage and had to be part of my vocabulary, but which clearly bore no relation to any of my life experience so far. So, for example, "society," what is French society? Or "rules" or "the law" and especially "civilisation."

Money was not quite so difficult. After all, it was possible to show me banknotes and coins. I still had difficulty understanding the value of it. It was something to do with numbers and counting. You could give money in shops or supermarkets and then take...things that you wanted. Nathalie had opened a bank account for me. In fact, she took me to the

---

[63]   You . . . kissed me, once . . . and my life began again.

bank with her so that I could understand what was going on. She put a thousand Euros into my account and then showed me how to use my bank card to draw money at a machine and also how to use it to pay in shops.

"Usually, people have to work for money," she explained.

"What?"

"Work!" repeated Rémi, with a peculiar emphasis.

"What is that?"

"For example, Marie Jeanne comes to the house to help with the cleaning and sometimes some cooking. And I pay her money because she does those things. And these people in the supermarket. You see? They are all wearing the same clothes. They are working here. They fill the shelves, they help you if you cannot find something, they take your money when you have finished shopping." Nathalie explained.

"They look like the Dizi, all wearing the same clothes. Do they have a leader who thinks for them and tells them what to do?"

"Er...yeh." Rémi agreed.

"And perhaps . . . They don't know how to think?"

"No, not at all! But it is like that in the world of work. There are workers and there are people called managers who tell them what to do." said Nathalie. And I could see that Rémi's agreeing with me was, in part, teasing her.

"This is not the same for Suri people. We don't have managers. No one could stand it. When we do things together, everyone can speak their idea and we all must at first agree. Suri people are proud. They stand up straight. Not like the Dizi people. So, these people, they are like the Dizi people, eh? Do they live here in the supermarket?"

I had the strange impression of them sleeping under the shelves and crawling out in the middle of the night to eat whatever ordinary people hadn't wanted during the day.

"Yeh, they do," said Rémi, with a grin and similar thoughts in mind. "They live in the cracks in the floor with the worms and insects."

"Arrête, Rémi!" said Nathalie. "Don't listen to him. No. They come here in the day and go home in the evening."

"And what about their children and families?" I asked, astonished. "And their gardens? Do they have cows?"

"No cows. No gardens, or maybe small. Their children go to school."

"When do they help their children learn about…hunting and fishing and cooking…eh?"

"My parents are not here," said Rémi, "to teach me those things. So what?"

"Yeh, well, you are lucky because I show you," I responded. "Hm, I don't like it, work. Why do they do this?"

"For money to buy food and clothes and so on." Explained Nathalie

"But be honest, they don't get very much. Not even enough to live," said Rémi.

"Rémi will go back to Paris soon to go to school," said Nathalie.

I looked at Rémi for confirmation, who, silent, had an expression of resigned agreement.

"And Juliette?"

"Juliette also, but in Blois."

I felt shocked, suddenly having to absorb this news.

"And what about me? I can go to school with Rémi or Juliette?"

"I don't think so, mon chou. You are not really ready. Better you study at home. You need to read books. Read everything. Learn. Understand."

"Hmm. Blois is not so far."

"Juliette comes home at the weekend, so you can see her then."

"And Rémi?"

"Don't worry!" urged Rémi. "You can come to Paris. I can come here."

This all seemed quite strange to me. Working all day in places which were not beautiful, inside giant metal boxes, not able to come and go as they pleased, not with their children, because the "law" said the children had to sit down on chairs at tables all day doing what their teacher told them. No one was free. And what if you didn't do as the "law" said? If you decided to be free, to do what you wanted? Then the police would put you in prison, which was like many rooms where you were locked in all the time, never to see the light of day! Either you gave away your freedom or it was taken away!

None of this particularly worried me at the moment. I was happy with Nathalie and Charles and for the time being, at least, I was with Rémi, although I was aware that at the end of the summer Rémi would go back to Paris. I needed to allow my understanding, the coming together of thoughts and impressions, to gestate. This was a strange place, a strange country. There was no tribe, no community. These people seemed to do little together, only occasional comings together, parties. Where was the dancing? And singing? I was lucky. Most people didn't hunt, so it seemed, so at least where I was, I could do that, alone a lot of the time, which suited me, but also with Charles and Louis Marie, and of course, Rémi. I was not so keen on…"la haute bourgeoisie," as Nathalie called them, who would occasionally arrive for a hunt. I didn't really know what that meant, la haute bourgeoisie, except that, so I was told by Rémi, they had a lot of money. They certainly had big cars. The men talked loudly, and the women laughed very loudly. They seemed to walk around the house, yard, and garden as if it were theirs. Rémi would mock them, sometimes in front of them, which made me laugh uncontrollably. What was absurd was that they would pretend not to notice he was mocking them. If children did that to older people in my village, they would get shouted at and chased away. I just couldn't understand their pretence. As for hunting, they were a disaster. They had no understanding of the forest. They were so loud and clumsy that I was persuaded all the animals were laughing at them, which meant that I, Rémi, and the animals all shared a common spirit. I did not go

168

hunting with them.

"Rémi."

"Mm. What?"

"Are you sleeping?"

"Nearly. What? What do you want?"

"Am I civilised?"

"What the fuck! What sort of question is that at one in the morning?"

"I heard two of those visitors here for the hunt whispering that I couldn't possibly be civilised."

"What?"

"They asked me how old I was. I said I didn't know; birthdays were not important for my people. Then they said to each other, I couldn't be civilised because all my life I had lived in a tribe."

"Show me who they are tomorrow. Civilised! You remember Zhukov?"

"Yeh."

"They are like him! Fucking idiots! Now, here, come close."

"But what is 'civilised'?"

"Oh, fucking hell! It is so late. It means being able to live in…this…a country like France, follow the laws, the rules, know how to work, be part of millions of people so that they can do things together to make their lives better. Ask your teacher Françoise, or Charles and Nathalie. They can explain it better than me."

"Am I civilised?"

"I fucking hope not!"

"Are you civilised?"

"I fucking hope not! Let's go to sleep, eh?"

The room was as black as I am. Very soon, I heard Rémi's breathing change and become the breath of sleep. I sensed the muscles of his chest and shoulders relax and knew his face had assumed the expression of innocence. My head was lying next to Rémi's open armpit, his arm stretched above his head across the pillow. I could taste the perfume drifting through the air from the damp red hairs clinging to the white, moist, and delicate axillary skin. The sweet musky smell widened my nostrils. I knew I could always turn to him in all circumstances.

The troubles in my mind over the clear condescension and disdain for my African past that I had sensed from the bad smells and ugly body movements of the two haut bourgeois still concerned me. What was this "being civilised"? I would discuss it with Nathalie and Charles, with Rémi again, and with Françoise, my teacher. Why, for example, did these old men value it and Rémi reject it? I needed to learn all about this place, this country, the strange ideas, God, money, work, managers, civilised, always hiding their bodies. The list was endless.

I had to read; everyone was telling me this.

"I will ask Françoise to help me to read. I read too slowly, as if my eyes are reading out loud to me. I need to read much faster if I want to understand all these crazy aranjinya ideas," I decided.

*　　*　　*

The morning after the birth of Pâquerette's calf, I kicked Rémi's naked butt out of the bed.

"What? Hey! What's going on?"

"We have to go to Chaga Boyɛ, to the lake."

"Why? Why the hurry?"

"We are going to meet the girls there."

"What? No one told me," he said, falling back on the bed.

170

I returned from the bathroom with a couple of thin cotton towels, toothbrush, soap, and razor blade.

"Come on! Hurry up! I want you to help me shave. My head. My armpits," I said, pointing. "And here also. When I make love to Juliette the first time, I want my body to be clean and beautiful."

"And when are you planning to make love to her?"

"Today."

"Ah! Right!"

The first time Juliette saw my naked body was on the shores of our lake, Blue Lake, as I had named it. Rémi and I arrived long before the girls with a very early pink morning sun. When we undressed, we both had goosebumps; the air was so fresh.

"I hope for you the girls aren't coming right away," said Rémi.

"Why?"

"Have you seen your dick? It has shrunk with the cold!"

"And yours! Go fast! Shave me before they arrive."

I soaped between my buttocks and legs and all the small curls tight around my penis. Delicately, Rémi applied the blade of the hairdresser's razor we had found in a drawer in the bathroom and claimed as our own.

"Ah, merde! As soon as I start to shave you, see what happens!" Rémi complained with a laugh. "At least we'll no longer be embarrassed when the girls arrive!"

We were both laughing excitedly with anticipation, which made it difficult for me to focus my attention on changes in sounds and movements in the air, of the trees, the birds and the grasses to know when the girls were arriving.

"Shh, shh! Wait!"

My right leg was raised and propped on a large rock next to the water's edge. Rémi was checking between my legs to make sure he had shaved all the hair.

"What?"

"I think they are here," I murmured.

Rémi was still bending forward to check his work, and at a distance, we must have looked a bizarre pair. We looked around but saw nothing but distant bushes across a fairly open terrain leading to the shores of the lake. Suddenly, everything became extremely still. There were a few seconds when even the birds stopped chattering, the breeze no longer moved through the leaves, and the water lapping at the shore of the lake paused. As far as we could see, everything had become our ears.

Juliette and Angeline had spent the night together after the birth of the calf. They were both partially undressed, with only their pants and bras remaining. Juliette was plaiting her hair, and Angeline was looking in the mirror and frowning.

"My butt is too big, don't you think?" she demanded.

"Of course not."

"Generally, boys have smaller butts than girls, right? They're lucky. At least they are not bothered by these problems."

"Your arse is perfect!"

"It's okay for you. You're smaller than me everywhere."

"What about my breasts? My breasts are too small!"

"Have you seen Rémi and Chár's butts?"

"No!"

"I mean this afternoon in shorts. They're beautiful, eh?"

"I don't know. I didn't pay attention."

"I don't believe you!"

"You know Chár is in love with you."

"Stop!"

"Rémi told me."

"Really?"

"Yes. He said that Chár does not stop speaking about you, that he is often lost in his thoughts, a little bit sad maybe, and he wonders when he can see you again. Today was his great chance! And as well, you, you complain about your breasts, but he, he adores them!"

"Rémi told you that?"

"Yes. For Chár, your breasts are perfect!"

Angeline had started blow-drying her hair and turned to Juliette with a big grin.

"And how does he know that your breasts are perfect? You let him touch them?"

"Of course not!" said Juliette, feeling slightly cornered by her friend's cheeky questioning.

"When he was sick, I went to see him, and he was so tired he fell asleep, his head on my breast."

"Wow! You let yourself be had like that?" Angeline was laughing at Juliette's embarrassment.

"He is not like that! He is honest, kind, and gentle."

"Ah! You are in love a little bit also, I see! It's going to be so funny tomorrow! You really think they'll turn up? Personally, I find Rémi very sexy. You think that he fancies me? I wonder if he is a virgin. It's sure Chár has eyes only for you."

"You're completely over the top, as usual!"

"I saw him when we were out for the walk. He adores you! When you put your arm through his, he grew by several centimetres."

The next morning, the girls descended to find Louis Marie pacing about the kitchen looking distraught.

"What's wrong, papa?"

"It is my brother, Julien. He had a crisis of ... I do not know what. He is in hospital in Chinon. The doctors are making different tests. Your aunt Elizabeth phoned. She wants us to go. She doesn't know yet what is going on. He fainted suddenly. Then . ."

"Oh, là là! That's terrible! Poor uncle Julien. You have to go, you two. Mom will comfort Aunt Elizabeth and you will see the doctors and decide what you can do for them."

" How can I do that? I can't! I have cows to take care of, especially the small calf. "

" Of course, you can! I know very well how to milk cows. "

" No. It's not so straightforward. I don't want . . ."

" OK. If you don't trust me, phone Madame de Rochebrune and ask if Chár can help keep them. "

Louis Marie hesitated.

"He knows better that you how to look after them!"

"Is that so? Thanks!"

"I didn't mean it, Dad. But you know he is more than capable and you can absolutely depend on him."

"No, no, no! I don't want to leave you girls here with both those boys! "interrupted Marie Jeanne.

"Mom! We are perfectly capable of being responsible! And anyway, according to you, they are gay both of them!"

Marie Jeanne puckered her lips in stifled silence and Angeline tried to hide her smirk. Louis Marie picked up the phone.

"What's the number? "

"I'll see Chár this morning. We intended to picnic together."

"Really? And why didn't we know about it?" demanded Marie Jeanne.

"There are things in life, Mom, which escape even you!"

"Anyway, it's only good manners to ask Madame de Rochebrune also," concluded Louis Marie.

Rémi and I had turned to swimming and then fishing to fill our time. The moment I thought the girls were arriving had passed, and luckily so, since this gave us time to bathe, clean our teeth, and make ourselves presentable for the occasion.

The sun had climbed to a much higher point in the sky. The marsh grasses and reeds in the flat wetlands leading up to the shores of the lake were now stoically brittle and dry, the land itself desiccated by the long dry summer heat, their only movement, a shimmer. Fortunately, Rémi, on leaving the house at ridiculous o'clock in the early morning, had thought to put several bottles of wine into his backpack along with what remained of his ganja, while I was unable to think of any preparations at all.

"I am so stupid! My body is now perfect, and you are as beautiful as ever, but that is all we have to offer. Where will they sit? How can they be comfortable?"

"You were in too much of a hurry! I don't think they are going to turn up. What makes you think they are coming? We can smoke a couple of joints, catch some fish and make a barbecue, eh?" which is what we did, except…

"The wine is in the water keeping cool. We have two fish, which is good, but we can save them for when they arrive. At least we have that to offer."

"Stop pacing about! I've never seen you like this! Calm down! Come for a swim, cool down, your head is hot, and I am going to open a bottle of wine."

"Ok, ok!"

We entered the water, and slipping beneath the surface, it was true, my brain felt a lot better.

"Have you seen that?" Rémi asked.

"What?"

"I noticed a minute ago. Over there, on the horizon, two floating discs. A mirage? They're getting bigger."

As we both stood looking into the distance along the water's edge, the two black discs eventually grew stalks that reached the ground, like two strange mushrooms.

"It's them! It's them! What's wrong with me? How come you noticed but not me?"

"Ok, good! Calm down! We'll pretend we haven't seen them, as if we are surprised. You want them to see us naked? That's what you have said before, they want to see our bodies. So, fine, let them."

"But Juliette... I don't know... I don't want to..."

"Stop! You're getting on my nerves!"

Slowly the hazy mushrooms on the horizon became two figures with large hats and slowly the hats became pale straw hats, and the figures became Juliette and Angeline, and just as they had become distinguishable so had our silhouettes against the brilliant blue of the lake become the figures of Rémi and me.

"Have you seen? They're completely naked," Angeline remarked quietly.

"Oh là là! What should we do?"

"Well, nothing! It's Chár's African custom, no doubt, and Rémi has

176

become a savage as well," she said, laughing. "Thank goodness!"

"Don't speak like that."

"No, but it's wonderful! With such weather, everyone wants to throw off their clothes."

"Not me!"

"Don't be such a prude!"

Putting aside Juliette's hesitation, Angeline called out to us.

"Hé ho!"

Rémi and I looked up.

"Hi! Can we join you?"

"Of course!" said Rémi. We were both standing in the water.

Both girls, still at a short distance, were each carrying a basket and had bags on their shoulders. I saw that Juliette was burdened down, and her cheeks flushed by the heat. I immediately stepped out of the water to take her bags and greet her, my eager impulse sparkled with droplets of water, clinging like stars to the cool black skin of night.

"Juliette! Juliette, let me take your bags. You are hot. How are you?"

I put my arms around her shoulders and kissed her on the cheek as I knew French people to do. She could feel the fresh of my wet body pressed against her and my cheek next to hers.

Rémi followed my guileless welcome and stepped out of the water to greet Angeline.

"So, when you come fishing, you do a bit of nudism at the same time, I see," commented Angeline with a grin.

"Er... yeh," replied Rémi, "we do. Please, don't feel we are naked to try to impress or anything. We throw away our clothes every time we come here. It's Chár's influence, really."

"Don't worry! It takes a lot to impress us, doesn't it, Juliette?"

"I am sorry," I murmured, leaning towards Juliette, "I forgot to cover myself."

I had taken the bags in one hand and with my other around her shoulders was leading Juliette to where we had been sitting.

"That's ok." she smiled.

"My people, we don't really like clothes. You can see, Rémi, also, has become Suri now."

"Yes, we noticed!" Angeline interjected.

"I forget that French people like to wear clothes all the time."

"Not all the time!" Juliette wanted to reassure me.

"You're so kind, Juliette." I picked up the two thin cotton towels, offered one to Rémi, and put the other around my waist.

"They hardly hide too much, anyway, your wet towels," laughed Angeline. "I like your beads, by the way, Rémi."

The girls produced a couple of blankets from their bags, which they placed at a slight distance from each other.

"May I sit with you, Juliette?"

"Of course."

I sat carefully in front of her on one side of her blanket, I could feel Juliette's look tasting, assessing my every movement, my every gesture, making me strangely self-conscious, proud even.

"Rémi, come and sit with me. Leave the two lovebirds to each other. You can be my paramour for the day." suggested Angeline.

Rémi was being charmed, and he knew it. He liked the provocative edge to whatever Angeline said. Moreover, he was awestruck by Angeline's

178

immaculate beauty. There was not a blemish to be seen on her face, her shoulders, arms, legs, whichever part of her body was exposed, nor would a blemish dare to appear.

"I want to lie down and relax after that long walk. Could you serve me a glass of wine?" invited Angeline, "Juliette has glasses in the wicker basket. You see? We have thought of everything."

Rémi dutifully rose and went to retrieve the glasses, the wicker basket, and the wine. Angeline stretched luxuriatingly on the blanket, her movements measured and fluid, also aware she was always in the spotlight. She propped herself up on one elbow, observing Rémi's actions and gestures with a faint, knowing smile.

When he turned back towards Angeline with the glass of wine, she had removed her blouse and was slipping off her bra. She turned to lie on her stomach, propped on her elbows. Rémi knew he lived in a world in which it was perfectly fine for women to be bare breasted at the beach or at lakesides. He had been at the beach and seen many times, at a comfortable distance, the bare breasts of all shapes, sizes and qualities of women of all ages, including his mother. But he had never been so close! The proximity wreaked of enticing passion and the overwhelming desire to touch. He had to sit down and feign a cool, casual acceptance, as if this was the most natural thing in the world, which, he reassured himself, it was, even though, secretly he knew Angeline was doing this for him, just as he had remained naked for her. What might she be thinking or feeling about his penis and his testicles lying loosely on his leg, he wondered, as he stretched out on one side propping his head with one hand? The perfume of eroticism filled the air.

"I have some sunscreen lotion. Could you put some on my back?"

He almost choked on his wine, but managed to maintain his cool, emptying his glass.

Beautifully soft and cushioned skin, already lightly tanned, met his hands. He realised at that moment, only sentient beings can touch. A touch that heightens awareness, sensation, humanity and desire. The desire to touch. Perhaps it was that, the between-of-bodies which was the affirmation of existence, its raison d'être. I am because of you!

After a short while, Angeline rolled over and suddenly Rémi was confronted by her very close breasts. He was amazed by the nipples, deep pink, much bigger than his. He immediately felt a need to put his lips to them, kiss them, hold the breasts in his hands.

Angeline could see he was completely awestruck. She smiled.

"You can touch," she whispered.

Rémi had completely lost his voice.

"Put some more sunscreen, can you?"

He started to apply the creamy lotion, his hands exploring the firm breasts. The soft nipples slowly becoming erect.

He was aware his penis was swelling and starting to push against the thin cotton towel. Angeline sat up and leaned forward putting her lips next to Rémi's ear, resting one hand on the high inside of his thigh, only the thinnest of muslin cotton separating her hand from the delicate, softest skin high up near his testicles and hot penis.

"I think it is pleased to see me," she whispered, looking pointedly at what was happening between his legs. "Here. Let's go for a swim. I want to see what is beyond that part of the shoreline jutting out into the lake."

She took his hand and pulled him to his feet. As they ran towards the warm waters of the lake, his towel slipped from his hips and fluttered to the ground.

I stood up to collect it from the dry dirt, folded it with an anxious frown and placed it on Rémi's bag. I glanced at Juliette who smiled back, reassuringly. There was this strange feeling of uncertainty which had overtaken me.

"I love you, Chár," Juliette wanted to say. She had noticed my shyness, and wanted to reassure me.

"Chár, come and sit with me. Let's relax."

I immediately came to sit close to her.

"I think Rémi and Angeline have disappeared for a while, so we can leave the picnic for later. Let's have some more wine."

I quickly, nervously, picked up the bottle of wine and filled the glasses.

"Are you ok, Chár? You seem . . ."

I looked at the ground, unable to confront her.

"I don't know what is wrong with me, Juliette. I am not normally like this. It is a wound."

"What?! What are you talking about?"

"We Suri people, we call this feeling the wounding of the bright. I think Rémi starts to understand this. Sometimes, especially and often, for young men, it is like a fog descends around their heads and they can't think, they can't react. Sometimes they get completely lost in their thoughts. Sometimes, they disappear into the jungle and don't come back. Or they think their happiness is somewhere else, in the city, with another people."

"Don't think this problem is especially with young men," said Juliette, "girls can feel like this also. Maybe they hide it better. I don't know. Look at Angeline, she knows exactly what she wants. She sees clearly. Today she wants Rémi. Tomorrow, we don't know."

"Lucky! . . . . And you, Juliette, what do you want? Do you know?"

Her shoulders fell down and she turned her eyes to the ground. The wounding of the bright, I had said. She had always thought she knew until recently. Everything had been clear, at least for the next few years. She would finish her baccalaureate and then attend an art school at one of several universities she had already considered.

"Your life here is new. There is much you do not understand. Before, everything was simple, a happy life in the forest with your people and cattle. Here, life is much more complicated with too many difficult choices."

"You know what I think, Juliette?. I think you are talking about yourself."

181

It was as if the tip of an obsidian arrowhead, straight from the plains of Ethiopia, had pierced her forehead.

"It is true everything is new for me. But everything is new for you, also, now you are here with me. Before everything was simple for me and for you, but now everything is complicated." And to herself only she was wondering:- "What do I do with this Suri boy seeking my heart? This Suri boy who saves Pâcquerette, who has lost his family and home? This Suri boy, whom my father thinks is a great huntsman and understands his cattle as much as him. This Suri boy, who is so handsome and runs around with nothing on, what do I do?"

She looked up at me and laughed.

"Don't ask me what I want. Ask me what I like."

"I am sorry," I said, smiling at her self-doubt and my own, "Do you like Chár?"

She looked straight into my black eyes.

"Of course, I do!" she smiled.

It was now. It had to be now. I leaned forward and kissed her on the lips. She could taste the perfume of wine mixed with my own spicy sweetness as a strange dizzying vapour was filling my head making me feel I was about to swoon. I leaned forward as Juliette fell back into my arms. She could feel their strength and the tautness of my stomach and chest pressing against hers. For me, the delicate softness of her lips and face against my own and the gentle suppleness of her femininity melted my uncertainties and liberated my heart.

"I want to show you something I like."

She opened her shoulder bag and took out a book. I quickly moved to sit next to her, one arm behind her back and my body pressing against hers.

"Cara . . Carava . . . ."

"Caravaggio." she completed the name I was attempting to read.

"Caravaggio." I repeated. "Already I can read a lot. But sometimes . . ."

"No, I think you are really good! Already speaking French and some English, reading, everything."

"Thank you. Thank you."

Our faces were close, side by side. I pressed my cheek next to hers.

"Caravaggio is a painter. He was a painter. He is dead now, four hundred years ago."

She flicked through the pages of religious images.

"He makes these pictures with paint?"

"Yeh? You can see he understands a lot about people. Oh!"

Juliette had turned the page to reveal the young St. John the Baptist portrait.

"He is like me. He understands animals. See all the animal spirits around him? He is naked and handsome, like me." I laughed and at the same time felt assured that being naked was not only good, but beautiful. Artists made paintings of naked bodies, paintings so many valued and had valued for hundreds of years.

Juliette smiled and turned the page.

"Oh! He is Suri!" It was the image of Sick Bacchus.[64] "Ok, he is white, but he is Suri! He has vine leaves in his hair. You remember those flowers you brought for me and we put them in each other's hair? He is the same as me. Same as Suri people."

"This painting is a self-portrait. Caravaggio did this painting of himself as Dionysus, as Bacchus."

"You mean he looks exactly like that? Hmm. Handsome. Who is this Bacchus?"

---

[64]
https://commons.wikimedia.org/w/index.php?search=sick+bacchus&title=Special%3ASearch&go=Go&ns0=1&ns6=1&ns12=1&ns14=1&ns100=1&ns106=1#/media/File:Self-portrait_as_the_Sick_Bacchus_by_Caravaggio.jpg

"He was a Greek God thousands of years ago . . ."

"Greek?"

"Ask your teacher about all that, those stories about Gods and heroes, but Dionysus was the God of wine, getting drunk, parties, also drama, music, art. You remember talking about your leopards? He had leopards with him wherever he went."

"You think I am like him?" I laughed. "He sounds more like Rémi with his wine and ganja." But already I was being infused with that power, that name, by the power of names and naming, becoming Juliette's Dionysus. A power I recognised since being named by my father. I would always be my father's Chár, the Leopard. But now, slowly, with a new name, Juliette's Chár Dionysus.

"I am so glad you like them anyway, these pictures."

"You see, Chár," she hesitated, "I want to paint like this, like Caravaggio. In a year's time, when I have finished school, I want to go to a University to study painting."

"Oh." A frown fell across my face. "Some young people in my village wanted to go to school to learn to read and write, me also. Some, especially the old people, didn't like it. They wanted them to look after the cows as our people have always done. Where will you go?"

"I don't know, maybe Paris, Nantes, or Bordeaux."

"And me? What can I do?"

She looked at me and smiled. There was no real answer.

"What I want to do . . ." she started. In her mind was drawing and painting. For her, my body was beautiful, I was the perfect model for figure drawing, figure painting, even portraits.

"What I want to do? No!" I interrupted, turning away from the books and towards her, holding her cheeks between my hands, demanding her look and attention.

"Juliette, what are we doing? What do we want? My body is longing for yours, for you. You know that." I pressed my lips to hers and as I felt a brief surrender: "I think your body feels the same, your body also longs for mine. I think. I believe."

She lifted my hands away from her face, kissing the palms as she placed them in her lap.

"I want to make love, Juliette. You know that."

"I know! I know! Slowly, slowly! Not now, not here."

"Why not? My body is going crazy for you. My heart will burst!" I paused, then, "Listen! Can you hear? Even the birds – you listen – are shouting their disappointment!"

Juliette laughed quietly:" This is the second time you tease me. But listen, Chár. I need your help."

She explained about her uncle falling sick and her parents having to travel to Chinon to visit and how they would not return until tomorrow at the earliest and that her father wanted me, Chár, to look after the cows.

"Of course!"

"So . . . can you stay at the farm with me tonight?"

I jumped up and started whooping and dancing.

"Juliette, I love you!"

I pulled her to her feet to give her a huge hug and swing her around in my arms and the birds truly did burst into choruses and various librettos telling each other how beautiful and strong I was and how delicate and pretty Juliette was and how perfectly we seemed to belong to each other.

"I am sorry, my towel has gone again."

"You are beautiful just as you are, Chár. But when Angeline and Rémi return, I want you to cover yourself. Your body is mine to see, not for everyone."

"Rémi sees me naked all the time."

"But not Angeline."

"Ok, fine." I smiled. "So, what can we do until tonight?" I spread my arms out either side of my torso, palms face up to the sky, and with my feet in a T-shape, bent my knees, as if in a curtsey, and then threw myself into a series of cartwheels and leaps along the bank of the lake.

"Chár! Chár! Come back!"

I ran back towards her, threw my arms around her and kissed her face over and over.

"Wait! Wait! Stop!"

Once I had calmed down, she explained:

"I want to draw and paint pictures of you, like the Bacchus picture."

"Yeh, the one that looks like Suri people. But what about the cows? I think we should go now."

"The cows are in their meadow and the baby is with Pâquerette in the barn. They are fine for a while."

"But I am worried. Suri people never leave their cows alone. We should go."

"As soon as Angeline and Rémi come back, we can go."

"I have fish! I can cook for you tonight."

"Where? Where?"

"I tied them in long grasses and kept them at the water's edge."

"What are they?"

"Trout? Maybe."

"Here. Let's find flowers again for your hair. When I start drawing, I want you to look just like Dionysus in the painting." She took out her sketch pad and pencils.

Juliette watched millennia of being Suri, of being young Greek gods, athletes, bodies in rapture over their sexuality, desires and passions unfold before her as I wove with centuries of skill a wreath-crown for my head. The naked nobility of simply being the joyous human that I had become at that very moment, was now fixed in her mind. When might she reproduce it on canvas?

I returned my attention to Juliette. Her gaze was soft, curious, and yet laced with a shyness that charmed me. I could feel the tentative threads of connection between us beginning to weave themselves into something delicate but unmistakable.

"You are very quiet, Juliette,"

She smiled, her cheeks flushing slightly. "I'm just taking it all in. You, the place, the... power of it all."

"Power?" I repeated.

"Yes. It's different here. Free, in a way. Like nothing can hold you down."

I nodded. "That's what I love about this place, the lake, the rock. There is no time here, it has been here, like this, with occasional lovers like you and me, since before time. A place where the world, its madness, cannot intrude."

Juliette looked out at the water, her fingers brushing absently at the edge of the blanket. "I think I understand why you and Rémi feel so at home here."

"It's a place where you can feel the same as in ancient times, like being next to the river, playing in Mother Kibish near my village," I said. "But today, more special, with you."

We sat in comfortable silence for a moment, the breeze carrying with it the scent of wildflowers and the faint rustle of leaves.

"Chár," she said softly, breaking the silence.

"Yes?"

"Do you ever miss… home? Your people?"

The question caught me off guard. I looked down at my hands for a moment, collecting my thoughts.

"Yes. Of course. But they are always with me even now. In my heart, in my memories. And it is my intention, my will, to carry them wherever I go."

She nodded, her expression thoughtful. "That's beautiful. To stay connected like that."

"Rémi is Suri now, my brother, my friend, my family and you also whose heart is open and loving. It tells me what is good and beautiful in life is not just in one place. Nathalie also, she is so much the same as my mother. How else could my mother know I would find my life here?"

Juliette smiled.

When Rémi and Angeline returned, it was as if Rémi was walking on water, and reaching the shore, he was floating ten centimetres above the ground.

I hurried them to dress and leave for the farm.

"Rémi, you carry the fish."

"Oh, right, thanks!"

"I am carrying all these bags."

"What's happening?"

"We are going back to the farm. I have to look after the cows. We can barbecue the fish there. You can play at being rabbits all night if you want. Juliette's parents are away."

"Wow!"

"I am shy."

"You, shy? I don't believe it!"

"Yes, I am. There you are, just looking, looking and I . . . I am just lying here."

The fading light of nightfall hardly penetrated Juliette's bedroom. She needed to put on some lamps to better see me. At the lake she had barely had time to take but a few photos and start a couple of sketches when the others had turned up and I had insisted on returning to the farm.

"How long for your painting?"

"I don't know. I am not going to start painting proper tonight, just a few outlines. Maybe another hour. It's only a start, you understand? It will take a long time for me to finish."

She had spent some time arranging lights, mostly spots in the penumbra of her bedroom.

"Ah, Juliette! You know how to keep me waiting! Do you know how long, how many days, weeks?"

She grinned.

"Er, I don't know."

"For months now! Ever since you first took my hand!"

"When was that?"

"When I first met you at that party; the barbecue of the boar I killed"

She smiled.

"Hmm. That's a long time."

"Very long! But that is when you chose me. Did you know?"

189

"Look at a book! Look at the Caravaggio book while you are waiting."

I picked it up and started to flick through the pages

"He likes young men, doesn't he? Young men like Rémi."

"Yeh. Women also. He had his favourites, women and men who appear regularly in his many paintings. And you?"

"Yes, of course! I guess I am like Caravaggio. Maybe he was my brother at one time. You think that is possible? Perhaps we share the same menenge."

"What is menenge?"

"In your language, I don't know. Something that is part of us that we cannot see, touch, nor hear, but sometimes we can feel it inside. It can be something we share with others. For, example me, menenge nanu, my menenge, I share with leopards. How many, I don't know, but I think every leopard knows me, would recognise me. I am lucky, because sometimes I see my menenge. Usually, people do not.

"And Rémi?"   ·

"I love Rémi. He is my brother. Menenge nayo, our menenge is different, not leopard, although probably close. Menenge nayo is fire! In Rémi this is very strong. I have seen!" I paused, my eyes wide open and drew in a sharp deep breath to express a sense of awe. "I was frightened, very frightened! And then I died! Remember? You came to see me after when I was sick in bed."

"You didn't die."

"I don't want to talk about that! You think I don't know? I said bad things to him and then I saw my mistake! There were flames coming from his hair, his face!" I paused again, drawing in breath through a wide-open mouth of terror. "Flames around his shoulders and arms, every part of his skin! Then he struck me across my face and all those bad things died. We share this menenge of fire, but also we share this same menenge as Caravaggio, as . . . ." I turned the pages of the book to find the Caravaggio self-portrait as Bacchus/Dionysus. "This! This is

190

also our shared spirit. The same menenge as your Greek God, as Caravaggio. Understand?"

"Yeh, I understand very well! Menenge means spirit! But what about . . . sex?"

"Yeh, of course."

I paused seeing her moment of concern.

"Look. You see this?" I pointed to my penis. "Dòrmi. Biroute. We, Rémi and I, we each have a penis. They are out of control. They do what they want. With Rémi, his penis stands up all the time! What can I do? He is crazy! Of course, we have to do something."

Juliette smiled, amused.

"I joke a little and I must not. When Marie Jeanne told everyone about us making choga, I said it was only practice for when we meet girls. Rémi was truly angry and he was right. Many people cannot understand when two men love each other. I know it is difficult for white people, for many Suri also. But I am Chár and Rémi is my Wóhólò Tagí, he is mine and I am his. My body is his body and his, mine. When I am in him, or he in me, it is because of this. I will always love him. This is how our bodies speak to each other. Sometimes I worry for white people. Have their bodies forgotten this? What do you think they are doing now, Rémi and Angeline? Choga! Their bodies are speaking to each other! Eh? Of course! Lucky!"

Juliette was quietly smiling at my frustration, I could see.

"Go and get some more wine."

"I don't even know where to find your cellar."

"You'll find it soon enough, the door under the stairs."

My black body crept through the house like a cat, quickly finding the latch of the door leading to the cellar. The slightly damp cool air embraced my skin. The mud floor had little gullies dug into it for drainage and at the end of the house was a small room where Louis Marie kept his wine. I looked at the labels and chose a wine I had seen

before, and tasted with Rémi. I was becoming French, I knew, and liked
it.

Of course, I was already surrounded by paintings, living now with
Charles and Nathalie. They had paintings all over the sitting room and
dining room walls. Charles liked occasionally buying something, often by
modern French artists who were beginning to acquire a reputation.
Claudine regularly organised exhibitions at her gallery to which Charles
and Nathalie were automatically invited. And, they had many books to
look through and many prints throughout the house. One thing I found
confusing was that it was acceptable even highly valued, respected and
admired to display the naked human body in paintings and sculpture,
but wrong to be naked, or be seen naked in the real world. Apparently in
Renaissance paintings these naked people were Gods, so that made it
okay, so Rémi had said. Then later about one hundred and fifty years
ago the naked women in these paintings were prostitutes. These were
people who had sex with others for money. Another equally strange
thing! Both Gods and money were strange ideas for me. Both Gods and
prostitutes seemed a very peculiar way of dealing with that human desire
to look at and admire naked bodies. Didn't everyone want to discover
each other in this way? As for money, it was no more real than their
Gods, it was just a belief that everyone stuck to and trusted. It amazed
me that these white people could be so easily fooled.

Juliette was puzzled. It was interesting, no, more than interesting,
exciting and profound, finding out about what I called menenge, not just
ideas but actual experience, not only of my own menenge, but menenge,
spirit, in others, how it could be so different. I had even noticed and been
quite intimately aware of a certain spirit, as she called it, in Caravaggio.
We had become connected in some way, Michelange de Caravaggio and
I, just as we both had with Bacchus/Dionysus. It was as if I were more
familiar with them, his paintings, his spirit, than even her, who had read
so much and gazed so often at my Caravaggio's works. And, where was
her spirit, she wondered.

While I was choosing wine, Juliette's mind raced with thoughts on how
to approach painting such a portrait. It was an overwhelming but
exhilarating challenge, blending her art with her deepest admiration for
her Chár. This portrait would not just be a representation of him; it was
her chance to spend hours immersed in the essence of the person who
had captivated her completely—her beautiful, kind, and handsome
Chár. He was utterly unique, so foreign yet profoundly human to her,

more so than anyone she had ever encountered.

Sketching him in pencil or charcoal would be straightforward enough, but painting? That was another matter entirely. Especially if she wanted to honour the style of her artistic hero, Caravaggio. His mastery of chiaroscuro—those powerful contrasts of light and shadow that imbued his figures with an almost divine presence—seemed almost beyond reach. Caravaggio had elevated chiaroscuro into something even more dramatic: tenebrism, where the light illuminating the scene appeared to radiate from the very figure itself.

Juliette pictured Caravaggio's St. John the Baptist—naked, sitting on a rock, an arm draped around a ram's neck. The figure glowed as though lit from within, the light emanating from his shoulders and torso, transforming the body of the naked teenager, young St. John, into a vessel of divine light. For her, it was a great improvement on Michelangelo's Ignudo, a work she knew Caravaggio had drawn upon. But could this technique, this tenebrism, ever transcend its cultural and racial constraints, she demanded of herself.

Historically, the sacred figures in such paintings—Caravaggio's and many others that followed—were always white. Did tenebrism inherently require its subjects to be ethnically white to achieve that divine glow? Could this technique, so revered in Historia Sacre art, be turned on its head to portray a black Dionysus, or a black John the Baptist? Juliette felt the weight of centuries of racism embedded in sacred history through art, and the injustice of it stirred something deep within her.

If she were to paint her Chár, me, the black one, in this style, she would have to subvert its traditional message, to reclaim and redefine it. Already, ideas were beginning to form in her mind, taking shape like shadows shifting into light.

Dieter had sent Nathalie a print of the 'Judgement of Paris' photo he had taken of her with me, Bongáy and his brother Golε next to the river near my village. She had been careful asking if I wanted to see the photo and perhaps put it in my room, but I had seemed happy to have this souvenir of my past there with me. With Rémi, we had also chosen a couple of Manet prints of Déjeuner sur l'herbe and Olympia. Nathalie put our choice down to teenage boys being fascinated by pictures of naked women. We both liked Olympia so much. She was so obviously our age, her perfect firm young breasts, standing invitingly above her smooth, flat stomach and small hips.

So when I walked into Juliette's bedroom with the wine, my vision was both clouded and enriched by the paintings I had seen and were surrounded by. That experience had somehow bled into my conscious mind. Juliette was lying naked on the bed. Suddenly, the bed, the curtains, the furnishings and pictures became complete, with Juliette naked on the bed, it had become her boudoir. Boudoir or inner sanctum. I approached through beams of golden light and sat beside her, the

reality of her naked breasts (wáy), her stomach (kwengɔ) and hips (sugum) far greater than any imaginings. I leaned forward to place the bottle beside the bed and at the same time pressed my lips against hers. Both of us felt our heads filling with a giddy perfumed vapour, which left us spinning above the bedsheets. She wanted to hold my penis, to know what she had longed to feel inside her, to feel and to hold in the soft walls of her vagina. She had already seen it and admired it, along with my couilles[65] as part of how the body's simple physicality decorates itself, how desire becomes its own thing of beauty, to be worshipped and wished for. Desire desiring nothing more than desire itself. Now that it had changed, become bigger, stronger, she needed to explore its new nature. Through the vapours in my head, I began to distinguish Juliette's breasts (wáy), her waya-tugó (nipples), and nyangí (vulva).

"Aňi huya inye,[66]" I looked deep into Juliette's eyes as I quietly sang these words, "way-tugó nunu tugo nanu ahuya,[67]" and each time my purring voice stopped I completed long exploring moments over each intimate

part of her body, "nyábí-l:tenì nunu búttɔ, guidú nunu huya, nyangí

búttɔ, lésshuí chàlli aňi chobbosa[68]"

She had almost asked what I was singing, as my I slipped and moved across her body. Juliette followed what I was doing, each gesture, each kiss, caress and taste of my tongue, bringing new and unknown sensations, new ways of knowing, experiencing her own body. It was as if the quiet purring of my voice, as I chanted, was inviting those waiting parts of her body out of their dormant state. Between the words and phrases, I repeated the deep melody of my love song; Juliette found herself joining in with my song, our bodies singing together. We were

---

[65]   testicles
[66]   I kiss you
[67]   my mouth sucks your nipple
[68]   I lick you earlobe, kiss your navel, lick your vulva and kiss your perfect clitoris.

being organised towards, being led by our hands, lips, caresses, by the music arising from deep inside us, into the magical world of two becoming one.

Tender, tentative efforts we were taking to let my dormì enter, but slowly we reached a point where I was now completely inside. Both of us sighed, looking at each other, smiling. Juliette felt the strength and watched in wonder at the taut muscles floating above her. She let her body follow its own will, her hands reaching down my back to grasp my buttocks and pull me further inside, inside as far as possible. Folding higher with her knees up towards her shoulders, her legs wrapped themselves around my waist with her feet pulling me deeper and deeper. Her hands felt my buttocks tighten and relax as I moved back and forth, my búrrà falling against her vulva. The walls of her vagina, were tightening, grasping my dormì as it swelled even bigger. My genitals, my body felt hotter as I became aware I would soon empty and surrender myself. There was a frown of great physical effort on my face and then a vast pulsating thrust burst inside Juliette, with each throbbing surge I felt the walls of her vagina tighten as if pulling at the head of my dormì; the muscle inside, tightening in surges like the swell of the ocean, as my biroute throbbed and filled her with semen. A wave of heat rushed through her spine to the top of her head. My perfect body quivered and fell against her.

Her one hand held the back of my neck as I lay against her, while the other slipped slowly down my back. Her legs relaxed downwards but still remaining open as I moved one leg higher up so that her hand could reach between my buttocks to find the delicate skin surrounding my búrrà. We rested like that, Juliette gently playing with my búrrà as my biroute continued to occasionally throb. Slowly, I slipped to one side, remaining between her legs and still inside, her vagina clinging tightly even still: Nyangí dormì kidi-kari.[69]

*   *   *

Now that we were sharing our bodies, I pictured a happy future in La Sologne, Juliette had chosen me as partner and future father to her children. Her own father, Louis-Marie would eventually cede responsibility for his cattle to me, Chár, the devoted partner of his daughter. It was simple.

---

[69] Vulva and penis together, Lingam resting in the Yoni.

Not so for Juliette. She would soon be going to Bordeaux to develop her painting skills, away from the cows, the farm and her overbearing mother. But now that I had entered her life and the more time we spent together, the stronger the knots and threads and loops wrapped around us both, coloured, bloodied even by frightening tales from my Suri past, My people had been murdered, I had killed several Dizi tribesmen, including their police/army captain. She persuaded herself I was not murderer as such, because the situation was a massacre, a war over land. But I had killed people and was glad! But then again, her hero, Caravaggio had killed someone in a fight and been banished from Rome. I had happily adopted him as a Suri brother. As for Dionysus, the more she thought about me in that painting, the more he seemed to invade her consciousness and paint himself onto me, her new-found lover. Things were becoming not simply extremely beautiful, but there was a hidden, lurking disquiet behind these dangerous complexities. Sometimes, gazing at me, she saw not just multiples of Chár, in many guises, but multiples of her own imaginings. Fearful intoxications! What might the future hold?

Chapter 5.

England

"So, where's our Chár?"

"He's out. He likes to go to the lake first thing, have a swim. He'll be back soon." Nathalie was preparing coffee for breakfast.

"And probably with something for a barbecue this afternoon!" commented Charles.

"Which is very nice of him!" Nathalie reminded Charles.

"Of course it is! By the way, we have a freezer full of game to consume," Charles explained. "take whatever you want back to Germany with you, Dieter, we're already supplying the local butcher!"

"It's his nature!" said Nathalie. "So, how was your trip, Dieter? You decided to go b
ack again."

"I – er – yeah. I felt I had to."

"You can show us your photos later."

"I didn't take any this time. I haven't taken any for a while. I met up with Joseph. I decided to contact him before going. He's in Arba Minch now, in a shack along the road to the university. He's become a complete alcoholic, drinking Tej and running a Tej house. At least, that's what he calls his shack."

"What's Tej?"

"Local alcohol brewed from honey." he explained. "He reckons he still works as a guide also, but I didn't believe him. He was either too drunk or raving. He never goes back to where we were, where the village used to be. He's frightened, kept jabbering on about ghosts. The Dizis won't go anywhere near it either, nor into the forest where they took them, for the same reason. At least I got a better idea of what had happened, although considering his alcohol consumption, that cannot be certain.

They were in the kitchen of Charles and Nathalie's house in the Sologne and Dieter, eager to see me again, had just arrived.

"I think the world needs to know about what happened to Beyahola. That's why I'm here. I've been in touch with Survival International. I wanted to talk about it with you. And, of course, Chár." Dieter suggested, knowing nothing of how I had avoided being murdered myself nor how I had arrived back at the river near the burned out village, covered in sheep's blood.

"He's coming, said Nathalie. "Look. You can see from the window. He's just coming up the yard."

Dieter got up from the table to watch as I walked across the lawn towards the back door of the house, in one hand my bhirɛ and the other the corpse of my kill, a sanglier[70]piglet. I was no longer naked, but wearing red shorts, white T-shirt and rubber flip-flops. It was a clear spring morning.

The kitchen door pushed open. Seeing Dieter, I dropped the sanglier, ran the few steps towards him and, wrapping my arms around him, kissed him on both cheeks. It was now two years since I had last seen him and I was bigger, stronger, but still with my youthful good looks (no beard!).

"Chár! How are you?"

"Well. Very well! It is so good to see you!"

I picked up the baby boar, and put it on the wooden work surface.

Dieter found his chair and sat down.

"Go and take a shower," said Nathalie, "change your clothes and make sure you are clean before you sit down for breakfast."

---

[70] wild boar

"I had a bath in the river. "

"Never mind. I prefer you to take a shower."

"See! My clothes are clean."

"Chár, please!"

Was I really that same difficult teenager as we all knew Claudine believed my Rémi to have become?

I left and returned in five minutes, fresh, with new T-shirt and shorts and pushed my way between Nathalie and Charles on the bench at the kitchen table, as was now my custom.

As the morning progressed Dieter was increasingly astonished at how I had grown into this "confident, young man, intelligent, speaking French fluently and English also", although he had had no opportunity to hear it yet.

"So, Chár, would you like to go to England with me, to London?"

Marie Jeanne had arrived and I was standing with her next to a work surface, sectioning the small piglet. Dieter watched on. I had become completely at ease and at home with Charles and Nathalie and clearly the house and countryside had become mine also. Dieter spent some time explaining about Survival International and Amnesty while I stood in silence working on the corpse of the piglet.

The outside world and its demands had crashed in on my tiny cosy little family where everything was perfect, safe and loving. Not that I felt that this outside foreign unknown was a threat, but certainly, Nathalie felt it. She had by chance found her son. Her, Charles and I had become complete together. Who knew what risks and dangers might await me were I to leave them, even though she absolutely trusted Dieter? She had willed time to be frozen in a perfect moment. For her, I had learned so much about France, I now spoke two aranjinye languages as well as my own, I had a best friend who loved me and a beautiful girlfriend, Juliette, who clearly thought I was wonderful and why disrupt all that?

Even Marie Jeanne, who had found it very difficult accepting me, this strange black and foreign teenager, not just foreign as in the sense of

199

from another country but foreign as in utterly different and challenging to her well sorted out and rigid values, even Marie Jeanne had softened and warmed to me. She had felt somehow side-lined, the great passion her daughter and I felt for each other (she excluded from her mind what we might get up to privately), the obvious affection her husband, Louis Marie also felt towards me; since saving Pacquerette and the calf and then going hunting together, he treated me as a friend and equal; now, even Marie Jeanne was obliged to loosen her attitudes and allow herself to perceive me in a more generous light, especially since I had asked her to help me understand the village, its people, all about them and how best to flatter or manage them; she had become my confidante in that respect, my ears and eyes into the little world of the Sologne.

"Let things just stay as they are, mon chou. No need to look for complications."

"But they cannot, Nathalie," I finally insisted, "Things cannot stay the same. Rémi and Juliette are at university. I didn't want that! Why did Dieter go back to Beyahola? It is the past! The past is calling him to act. Maybe he doesn't even know clearly yet, what he must do."

"You are an innocent, Chár! You are already a young man, but money makes no sense to you!" insisted Charles. "You only feel contempt for work! So much of modern life, for you, is absurd. You will be lost out there!"

"But, Charles, he will be with me!" insisted Dieter.

"Chas[71], Natha, it is true. I will be with Dieter. He saved me; he is my brother. I will be fine; it is only a few days. And I must go! It is my Komoro who made him Suri and who calls him now, and all the young men who welcomed him at the time of the donga[72], they are calling him also."

"They even gave me a bhirɛ[73], which I have in my bedroom."

"And it speaks to you every night, eh?"

"Yeh. True." A short 'ha' accompanied his words, acknowledging my

---

[71] Chas, pronounced Shaz
[72] Stick fight
[73] Fighting stick

understanding of the strange and special powers drawing him into action. "That is true."

"And all that past, with its ghosts," I continued explaining, turning to Charles and Nathalie, all the time acknowledging their scepticism, "has sent him here to find me."

"Okay, fine! Do what you must do," said Charles.

"I don't want this," said Nathalie regretfully, "but if you need, if you feel you should, then go."

"Before I decide, I want to talk about it with my Wóhólò Tagí."

"Claudine's son," explained Nathalie. "Rémi. His best friend. They have been an enormous influence on each other. No one knows Chár better than Rémi."

"I love him. I know everything about him, and he knows everything about me. We are the same. He is Suri now."

"Chár, I want to know what happened before I found you at the river."

"I will not speak about it. I have not told Nathalie and Charles, only Rémi and Juliette. Juliette only a little, mostly I have spoken about it with Rémi Wóhólò Tagí, and why? Because he loves me and saved me from myself, from those terrible memories. If you want to know, you can ask him. But don't be surprised if he tells you nothing."

"It is better we don't know," said Charles. "He is protecting us with his silence."

I put my arm around Charles' shoulders and kissed him on the cheek.

There was a long silence as Dieter tried to accommodate to my determined views.

"So, what's this, Chas and Natha?" wondered Dieter, with a smile.

"He's changed our names!" explained Nathalie. "He doesn't use them all the time; usually when he wants to persuade us of something. He's changed everyone's name! What is your name, Marie Jeanne?"

201

Marie Jeanne was standing next to me, assisting the cleaning of the piglet.

"I can't pronounce it, Madame. Too difficult for me."

"Nyábí, or plus intimement, Nyábí nanu[74]," I revealed.

"And what does it mean?"

"Ah, it's a secret!" I asserted, grinning at Marie Jeanne, who blushed.

"I surprise myself how much I am in awe of this Suri leopard," reflected Dieter silently, "who has grown into a confident young man, intelligent, fluent in three languages and clearly loved by all around him. His friend, Rémi, is arriving at the weekend. Who is this famous Rémi who knows more about Chár than anyone?"

*   *   *

Dieter and the Leopard, he enjoyed referring to me in that way, giving my name an English translation, we were attending the Survival International meeting, co-hosted by Amnesty International at their Human Rights Action Centre. Dieter had been invited to make a presentation about the massacre at Beyahola and the murder of its people in Dibdib. We had both spoken to Rémi Wóhólò Tagí. Between us, Wóhólò Tagí and I had decided not to tell Dieter about my actions and the details of what had happened to my people, but Tagí was happy for me to attend this meeting.

"It is better you are free, Chár, without any opinion or advice from Dieter. If he is right about anyone, a politician or government department, from anywhere, Ethiopia, England, France, the US, instigating this clearly organised massacre, giving guns and uniforms to the Dizi, they will show themselves when it is made public. You will not have to look for them; stupidly, they will find you, not knowing what they are doing. And I want you to say exactly what you think you must say. They are like Zhukov, whoever they might be. I was a coward and I feel shame over that. But you were not. And you are never a coward. Stand up to them. Show them your courage. Be yourself! You are

---

[74] Ear, or more intimately My Ear.

leopard! You are Chár! You are Suri! Remember, I am always with you! Whenever you want, you must send for me. Send your leopards to call me. Now is the time to act. Nothing can stay the same. I love you!"

Now, in Shoreditch, the centre of London, Ray Ferrier stood at the back of the hall with his erstwhile partner, Jack DeLange. He said that was his name, but who knew? Everyone in their covert world had a multitude of false names, identities and personalities. Everyone was pretending to be what they were not. Mind you, such occasions as these were fairly straightforward. They were here to watch what was going on, hear what was being said, make a note of those whose ideas seemed troublesome, look out for known activists, photograph everyone . . . That was the easy bit, constantly arsing around with his mobile, like everyone else in the hall. How more invisible could you get?

Jack DeLange sidled over from the entrance to the side wall where Ray was standing. Slowly, the hall was filling.

"What's going on tonight? What are we supposed to be doing?"

He was looking sallow and drawn, the skin of his prematurely aged faced seemed covered with a thin film of slimy sweat. His intestines were twisting in knots. He had tried to eat something to find the energy for the evening, but his belly, so used to being empty was finding it too difficult to handle solid food. He would have to find a toilet to regurgitate his futile attempt at nourishment.

"Didn't you get the directive?" and then looking at him with a frown, "Are you ok? You look really rough?" commented Ferrier.

"Coming to another of these do-gooder get-togethers – it pisses me off. What happened to good honest assassinations? Don't we do that anymore? You know, James Bond shit!" His mouth twisted with another stabbing pain in his abdomen.

Ray smiled to himself at the straightforward hatred for the tedium of these moments.

You're not wearing the right clothes! In fact, you look like a down and out!" said Ray. "Amnesty wants to implicate Overseas Development in the disappearance of a village in Ethiopia. There's more to this than just tea and biscuits."

"Oh, right! Great! So, what do we do? A bit of disruption? Shouting abuse, stuff like that?"

"Don't be fucking ridiculous. We're just hear to watch. I'll be taking advice, anyway."

"You're wired up, eh?"

"Look, they're about to start. Who the fuck's that at the front there? There's the German photographer making the presentation, but who's that with him, the black kid?"

"What did Overseas Development do?" Jack was shivering and breaking out into a cold sweat. Starvation was having its toll. Since his wife had left the country with the children for somewhere in Canada, he had slowly become anorexic if not bulimic, the modern disease of control. His family never contacted him.

"That's Dieter Schliemeyer, photographer, even published some collections, East German communist and of course eco-campaigner. Overseas development? What did they do? They funded the freeing up of land for international development. What do you think?" Ray laughed at treating Jack as an idiot.

"Fuck! Fuck you, you fucking smart-arse!"

"And? " demanded Ray.

"Got rid of the tribals."

"And in Africa?" Ferrier was being objectionably patronising.

"Just fucking murdered them, eh?"

"That's about right! But not in England. You can't just murder people here!"

"Ooh, I don't know!" Jack tried to laugh.

"So far, the ministry has been able to counter the rumours that

International Development was involved with accusations of the usual bullshit in the Daily Mail - Communists, Marxists, etc." he started laughing cynically, "People believe that bollocks, let's face it! But if the black kid is a survivor, or even a witness, the Minister and Department are in deep shit."

"Right!" Jack's imagination started to fill with violence. "Take control before the shit hits the fan!"

For Jack, things had been spinning out of control for a long time now. Losing his wife and children, he couldn't remember whether he had been drinking too much before they left or whether their leaving had caused him to drink more. He'd tried health, as if it were a dress code for making himself feel at ease in other's company. But whenever he checked, looking in a mirror, he only ever saw a void of disconnected anxieties. Then, everything went, the mortgage, the house, family, credit cards. He continued drinking heavily, to bring the days to a conclusion, to blunt the sharp edge to every tedium. Not eating was both the remedy for his failure and his punishment for failing. He didn't, like some, moralise it into a series of prohibitions to save the planet, for example: not eating fish, because the oceans were being depleted, not eating red meat, or any meat for that matter, because cattle fart methane. In fact, he ate everything, hoping the planet would fucking die. Then, eventually, he would force himself to vomit as a punishment. His hatred now extended way beyond his own body. Even control over his own body had slipped out of control. Wet shit was seeping regularly from his anus. The soreness and frustrated anger it generated, further incited, not just a personal death wish, but one that had been globalised to encompass all of humanity, or any random victim he might wish to pick on. It would be the final, ultimate act of control, his own death; the closer you come to absolute control, the more out of control absolute control becomes. Ugly life, ugly fucking England.

This was not how I felt. In fact, I had quite liked what I had seen of London. Dieter and I had arrived a couple of days before the event to meet some of the organisers. Shoreditch, I had liked; all the slightly anarchic wall paintings, little shops and cafés. And I loved some of the English pubs and the choice of beers, with so many different people of all different colours, languages, features and smiles. It was an adventure speaking English with whoever we met. On both evenings I had got drunk with locals and sent photos to Rémi of all my new friends. One afternoon we had visited the New Tate and on another . . . . was it Tate

Britain? Juliette would have loved it, I knew.

For Ray, the issue of Ethiopia could be dealt with through honest racism. He didn't give a shit about black Africa. These tribals, running around naked with spears! What the fuck? Over the entire history of humanity, they had failed to make any progress. As far as any civilisation was concerned, forget it! They hadn't invented anything; they had no written language. Honestly! The West had been trying to help them out for centuries with education, farming, simple industry. It was fucking hopeless! So, for him, black women were sex objects. Like most women, this was the first and immediate judgement he would pass on them. Black men were at most a sexual threat. It was easy for him to despise the young black guy with the German communist. As far as he was concerned, his racism was the norm. It was natural. Everyone generalised. Without generalising, no one would make any sense of the world at all. Everyone he knew thought like him. Look after your own. Ethnic nationalism, that was his logical perspective.

He looked around the room and laughed with a short contemptuous snort. Everyone with all their different skins, hair, dress, religions, beliefs, pretending they were all the same, all equal, all decent, intelligent, compassionate, kind, considerate, educated caring members of humanity. They were woke! And how wonderful it was to be their type of human! His contemptuous mockery reduced thinking to its most obvious.

If International Development had blundered into assisting a massacre with a nod and a wink . . . what the fuck! Who cares? Cabinet ministers, Secretaries of State who had been around long enough knew the agency would clear it up. They would take on the dirty stuff. And since operations had been partially privatised, which suited him and Jack just fine, there was a lot more money in it, him and his addled partner would benefit. Violence pays well when you're selling it. Besides, nothing happens out of national interest any longer. You can lie about it if you want, but not really. Doffing your cap to authority, loving the Queen and shedding a tear when singing the national anthem, forget that shit! It's all about cash in hand, now. No one respects or admires anyone else anymore. It was just a globalised white man's free for all out there, mate. These people in here were just the deluded herd and quite right they should remain so.

The meeting took the form of an interview. The interviewer was Peter

Manson, well known to middle class intelligentsia, writer, left wing independent journalist, TV commentator and reporter. His intention was to film the meeting as part of a possible documentary project. The usual approach. Everything he did was going to be recorded, both by him and plenty of others, he was sure.

It started with Dieter Schliemeyer presenting what he was doing in the region of Beyahola that January. He mentioned with whom he had met and visited the region. And the unfolding of events as he experienced them, with his photographic presentation. Already the smoke of righteous indignation was rising amongst the chattering classes.

"So, Chár, tell us, what is it like for you living in France after this terrible incident?" asked Manson.

"I have been incredibly lucky, now I am a French citizen. Claudine's husband, Robert, s'est occupé de ça. Robert took care of that. I feel good. Nathalie decided to take care of me. She is like my mother and Charles also, a father."

"And what does that mean for you, being a French citizen?"

"I like it. I like the spirit of their Revolution very much, Liberté, Egalité, Fraternité; these are ideas my people, the Suri people of Beyahola, would have liked. In fact, these ideas are our instinct, so natural to us we don't even have to think about them. They are your instinct also, which is why you have to think about them all the time." I was doing the English thing.

A hushed attentiveness fell over the Hall.

"So, what do you do, in France?"

"I hunt . . . . and take care of the cows of Juliette's family. They are neighbours . . . . . and I study. I learn a lot from Nathalie and my tutor."

"You speak both English and French fluently . . . ."

"Yeh, quite good. With French it was very quick, because I needed to learn, and I was hearing it all the time. I also found, and my teacher told me, at some point learning a language, you must read books, all the time. I remember when I read the adventures of Tom Sawyer and Huck

207

Finn, I noticed how at the time, I started to use the same words as them, even whole sentences. It was as if their spirit had entered into me. I became Tom and Huck. Even at night, they would come to me in my sleep, talking to me. It was exciting!"

I paused to sense the response to my words. From what I could judge people were happy and amused by my reading experience.

"This was when I decided I had to read as much as possible. In that way, I can become . . . many. Maybe only names stay the same. First I am Suri, then I am French, hunting in the forests, now I am English. And each time, I am different, someone new. When I take the cows out for a walk in winter, I take a book. I build a fire to keep us all warm and we stay until the sun gets low, or the cows get restless. I have learned to read fast. I think you call it speed reading, lire à vitesse. My tutor in France helped me with this. I have too much reading to do. Especially for Rémi, he pushes me really hard."

I could see this man questioning me, Peter Manson, was struggling. My multiplicity confused him. I was unconditioned, untamed by this world of lazy thinking that wants to hammer everyone, especially the unknown, the unidentified into a single entity. That I should refuse it, stand up, tall, and say 'No!' to this reduction, upset a lazy habit he had never questioned. It was the same stupidity as saying foreigners have made the English poor! I felt some pity for him. The laziness was not his alone, but something all-pervading.

The pinks and blues and browns of the hall were closing in on everyone.

"So, you have been able to keep some of your customs as a Suri man, looking after cattle. Where are you living now?"

"La Sologne. It's like a jungle, a lot of it is like that, but not so hot . . ."

There were clearly a few radical strong-minded activists present who wanted to ally themselves to my people. According to one Amnesty activist who had listened to a voice inside and needed to speak out, money from the Department of International Development had funded the massacre, pressuring the Ethiopian government to free up land for international exploitation. Euphemistically, this was called 'development', in spite of all the bloodshed.

"The only thing that would be developing," the activist concluded loudly and angrily, "was not the land nor the people, but its financial exploitation!"

There was a murmuring, a rumble as of distant thunder which rippled through the room. I had already been made aware of this deeply political and contentious issue by Dieter, but at the time, it had hardly made any sense to me. Now with it being repeated and even affirmed by others in the room, I started to realise that the Dizi were just stupid, cheated out of their lives by something or someone unknown. Even their captain, was as bad as them, maybe worse; he had been arrogantly stupid. Maybe, even the government in Ethiopia were stupid also, acquiescing to some strange power which offered to empty the land for them; after all, they don't get development cash unless they clear the land and then who benefits from that? Did they even know about the spilling of blood until it was too late? I had started to notice, even see and smell this strange body which hovered over all white people, sucking their strength, organising them, telling them how to think. And I was beginning to realise what it was, this strange thing which made no sense to me.

 "And what about friends in France? You have friends there?" Peter Manson wanted to cool things down by pretending the world could be simple and happy.

"Of course! Rémi. That is his French name. But I call him Wóhólò Tagí. This is his Suri name."

"And does it have a meaning?"

"We Suri give names to people by what we see at the time of first meeting, for example, when a new-born comes into the world. When I was born, a small child ran to tell my father who was caring for the cattle. The boy surprised a leopard sleeping nearby on the branch of a tree. The leopard fell, terrified, right in front of the small boy. My father had to defend the child and drove his Bhirɛ, which you might call a spear, through its heart. Out of respect, he gave me the name Chár, meaning leopard, and I grew up sleeping on the skin of that leopard who died as a consequence of my birth. Rémi's name is Wóholò Tagì, Naked Moon. The first time we met and danced together in the night, we were naked. And there he was, his name was obvious to me, my naked moon, Wóhólò Tagí."

I couldn't help feeling secretly amused at how the crowd responded to this information.

"And then of course, I have my beautiful Juliette. I decided a long time ago just after I arrived in France, she would be my wife one day. What amazed me was Juliette, just like the custom of young Suri women, chose me! We will make a new Suri tribe together, a new people. This is what my mother asked me to do when she was dying."

"Do you want to tell us about that day? Dieter has already told us about the shooting at the stick fight. Perhaps you could tell us what happened after you had taken Dieter, Nathalie and Claudine to safety."

"I went to our village to find my mother, knowing something terrible was happening. The village was in flames and she was bleeding from her side, already dying. I had already seen the bodies of the Komoro and Chagdo."

"Who are these?"

"The Komoro is like a wise leader."

"You mean like a king."

"No! Not like your kings and queens! He was just a wise old man everyone respected, and turned to for advice."

My tone had seemed indignant, offended, and Peter Manson, found himself, to his astonishment, suddenly reddening with embarrassment and apologising.

"And the Chagdo can sometimes understand the future." I continued, "I stayed with my mother until she died. At that moment, I knew I was also dying, but still I needed to see what had happened to the rest of my people.

"When their captain threw the children into the Akobo river, hitting them over the head to make sure they were either dead or would drown, I decided to kill him. . ." I paused.

No one spoke. Who readily talks about murder?

"Do you feel ready to continue?" asked Manson, his eyes wide with the cold horror of incredulity.

There was a long silence, but a silence so deafening, it created its own subterranean shudder.

"A storm was approaching and the forest of Dibdib was becoming darker. The captain's driver was left behind in his truck while everyone rushed forward to watch the children being slaughtered, so he was the first whose neck I ripped, dragging him into the bush for hyenas to consume." I paused again.

I had decided before attending this meeting that I wanted to wear my favourite costume that Nathalie had first bought for me and which I had worn at the barbeque when Juliette had chosen me. I wanted to dress to kill, as the English say. I was wearing my white Egyptian cotton shirt, perfectly fitting dark blue jeans, my dark leather belt with brass buckle, my red boat shoes and Nathalie's white pearls, which I had practically claimed as my own. The striking contrast of my white shirt and white pearls against my black skin added to the tension between my admitting killing and my relaxed, guiltless, guileless manner. I became aware of a possible danger in the room, my leopards had felt it also, and wanted that threat and whomever it came from, to be aware of the danger attendant within me and my accompanying leopard spirits.

"Then I killed two of the Dizi murderers." I waited for the weight of my words to sink into the hearts of all present. "The captain? I blinded him, quickly jumping on his back to tear his eyes out. When you know how to hunt, it is not difficult to do these things unseen. He stumbled, bouncing from one tree to the next, futilely trying to escape the bleeding blindness of the two empty sockets in his face. Finally, he fell into an ant's nest. The ants slowly killed him with their vicious attack, and no doubt consumed him. The Dizi were too scared of the ants to rescue him, and very soon they scattered, leaderless and lost, many, most even, to never find their way out of that madness and home to their families. I stayed the night in Dibdib. In the morning, my leopards woke me and led me to the edge of the jungle."

I paused again. And then, with a grin:- "But since the Ethiopian government denies the massacre took place, I must be either a liar or a madman. You can choose."

211

Manson had difficulty responding to this cold, wry sense of humour over the Ethiopian government's denials: "It is true, the Ethiopian government is not pursuing charges against anyone and your status in Europe has been legitimised by the French authorities, but as a refugee . . . ."

"I am not that word, your English word. I am not refugee!" My voice was raised. "I am Chár. I am Leopard. My two leopards who take care of me since Dibdib, my brother, Wóhólò Tagí, they are with me now and all the dead people of Beyahola village, my village, are in me and they will be with me until they are finally appeased through what is to come. I am many! I am Chár!"

Again, a stunned silence. What did he mean, appeasement, everyone wondered. I, this young man from a prehistory, before recorded time, before so-called civilisation, with the startling madness of what I had expressed, I, Chár, had silenced their minds and focused everyone's attention. Perhaps I was mad, or driven mad by history. My intimacy with my people, my relationships in France, my current friend, my moral decisions entirely and assertively my own, which theirs never were, nor had ever been, humbled and highlighted their inadequacies in human endeavour. At the same time, my fearlessness was a challenge, a challenge to anyone who may have encouraged, or profited from the elimination of my people.

Dieter was white with fear and anguish at what I had said. As for Peter Manson, he knew that what he had just recorded was completely explosive. Was it naivety? A sort of ridiculous innocence? The values of primitive culture without any imposing laws? Was it guilt without any feeling of guilt?

"May I ask a question?" I asked.

"Of course."

"I have already asked my Rémi, but it was difficult for him to explain. What is civilisation? Am I civilised? Did white man's civilisation kill my people? Who in that civilisation is responsible?"

There was no answer.

212

"It seems to me in white man's civilisation everyone is good at talking but they have lost their freedom to act." It was just coming out! So much of what Tagì and I had talked about. "Who did you give it to, your freedom? To your God? To Money? Your king? Maybe I am not like you! Maybe I am not civilised. Your civilisation want me to write myself into its own fate, to fix my story in ink for all the machinery of power to nail me to your cross of servility, to sign its forms, to speak its own truths and accepted lies. But I come from a world where words live only as long as breath. We don't write our stories—we sing them, dance them, cut them into the earth with our feet. Our language changes like the river, like the wind on cattle skin, like the red dust after the rain. It lives in the body. In the mouth. In the scars. In the silence between things. You say your writing is civilisation. But the first writing wasn't song—it was counting. Grain. Taxes. Debts. Guilt. Who owes what. Who belongs to whom. Manhours. Slave wages. Weakness and submission instead of strength and freedom. All carved in clay, chiselled in stone, so no one could forget—so no one could escape. Your language doesn't move. It locks. It binds. It freezes. It says: you are this. It says: you belong here. But my people don't belong. We move. We vanish. We return. We have no alphabet. But we have the wind. We have the stars. We have the songs of the elders and the names we give when we see something being born. They fear that, your high-priests of morality, because our language cannot be owned. They fear our ambiguity, our change, our wildness. But I do not fear it. I carry it in my blood."

I paused. There was a long silence at this indictment. I could smell carrion, the rotting flesh of corpses after a few days in the sun, the stench that hyenas carry around their grinning, gaping, gasping, black mouths and on their poisoned breath. My leopards could smell it also and were becoming angry.

"Who killed my people?" I raised my voice again. "Who wanted them dead? Before I left France, my Wóhólò Tagí said, I didn't need to search; my enemy, my people's murderer would find me. The hunter should be careful, before he becomes the prey!"

Ferrier was on his mobile talking to the client, Secretary of State for International Development, Sir James Mercantor.

"You can't help but admire him," Ferrier commented, "He's just admitted to killing several of your local private soldiers, if that's what you can call them, including their captain, leaving them in complete disarray.

He's fearless! And, he's just made a direct challenge . . . to you!"

"What happened in that forest was nothing to do with me, and don't you dare repeat it! My role as Minister is to help that country into the modern world through international investment." Mercantor was almost shouting. "This black tribal, whoever he is, has admitted to the murder of Ethiopian state police. Regardless of any disruption, arrest him!"

There was a cynical look of resignation on Ferrier's face: absolute power at distance producing decisions of rationalised insanity.

From one side of the hall there was a strange hissing, whining sound near to a panting baby's cry, even a laugh. People looked around to see what it was, where it came from, some even stood up.

"Are you OK, Chár?" asked Dieter, approaching me to offer both of us some reassurance.

Manson repeated the same question, "Chár, are you OK?"

I was quickly glancing around the room, expectant, apprehensive, at the walls, the pink columns, the windows, the blues and browns. This sterile place was not the jungle, nowhere to hide, no trees to climb into.

The audience were becoming increasingly agitated, like the waves of a troubled sea. Suddenly, a loud voice was heard to cry out.

"This is ridiculous! Why are we listening to this nonsense? Can't you see? This is just political staging to blacken the name of legitimate governments." It was Ferrier. He had stood up and was walking down wide steps towards the stage, pushing through chairs and guests.

On the other side of the hall, Jack DeLange was also lunging towards the stage, his dirty brown coat, smudged with grime and covered in torn threads, hanging off the material like the balding fur of a mangy dog, billowed out behind him, leaving an invisible odour of his sweat-covered, sickly flesh.

"By his own admittance, this . . ." Ray was shouting, "this . . . illegal immigrant . . . is a murderer! And killing members of the Ethiopian police, who were legitimately clearing government land of illegal squatters, makes him a terrorist!"

By now other members of the audience were on their feet attempting to restrain these two aggressors, who seemed intent on disrupting proceedings.

"Get your hands off me!" Ray shouted at the jostling crowd around him. He removed a gun from inside his jacket and immediately the crowd fell back like skittles. "Stay calm everyone! We are from the Police Antiterrorism Unit," he lied, "and have been investigating for some time these individuals!" he was panting and rushing his words in desperation to get them out before the room descended into further chaos. "As it is, the French police are questioning the people who smuggled him into France. He's under arrest!" His voice had reached an almost high-pitched scream. "Don't move anyone. I'm talking to you, you idiot!" he shouted at an old man on the floor.

The same whining cry which had so disturbed everyone in the hall earlier could now be heard in several corners of the hall. There was suddenly a loud bang and all the lights went out. Ray's agitation had reached such a point, knowing he had nothing to do with anti-terrorism and was just a cheap secret service agent, freelancing, that his gun started firing spontaneously in his hand. The bluff might have worked, but not now in total darkness with shouts and screams and panicking bodies scrambling to escape.

Dieter, who was right next to Chár, took his arm and with voice raised against the hubbub told him to run.

"I am sorry! I am sorry!" he cried.

Ferrier found himself on hands and knees, sliding in the blood of the old man he had just shot, when he felt the weight of two feet or hands, he guessed, land on his back. In the general panic of the blackened sightless chaos, he felt a sharp pain as the feet seemed to tear into his flesh. At the same time, teeth sank into his neck as his face was pushed into the old man's blood. With a violent twist there was a nasty thudding crack at the base of his skull. His body fell apart.

As for DeLange someone stabbed him in the heart with an elbow. A sharp pain shot across his chest, down his right arm and out through the ends of his fingers. He didn't even have time to scream before he collapsed, and his poisoned heart surrendered to the dark.

I followed my leopards as they ran, glowing with the same flames as Wóhólò Tagí. Outside, police cars were racing to crowd out the street with howling sirens and flashing red and blue lights. We ran up some stairs and from the roof, could see the brightly lit New Inn Yard. Still no trees, except a couple protruding from the barren pavement and both behind bars. It was easy to perceive a multitude of pathways through a jungle, some used by many different animals, some restricted to the few, but here there were none. I needed to escape to the dark. It seemed impossible to remain invisible were I to try to flee through that arid manufactured landscape. I could see a bridge at a short distance and the road underneath it was in shadow. Maybe the other side of that, along the embankment, I would find a hole to creep into, until everything calmed down and I could . . . what? There were people starting to flood out of the main entrance. Perhaps I should join them and use numbers to hide. No. I had already seen what had happened to my people when they were forced into a herd, surrounded. Kettling, the English call it. In any case, how could I get to that bridge through the mass of police, security services and ambulances?

I walked around the flat roof, checking each side to see if there was an easy escape. There were several strange metal boxes centred at different points on the roof, which were humming the cry of the unknown. Where the police cars had accumulated, there was a sheer drop to ground level before the cycle racks and the road, but on another side there were lower roofs above what I realised was the entrance, and from which, were I to climb down to them, reaching the street would not be so difficult. I lowered myself over the edge towards the higher of the two roofs, onto a narrow ledge, then peering over, saw a window ledge. I managed to just reach down to put my feet on it. From there I knew I would have to jump; the roof was not so far. The Amnesty building butted up against another much older building of dirtied yellow brick. In the corner between the two buildings, I found a black drainpipe I could climb down.

What would I do once at ground level? I knew I would have to steel myself against the cold night air. Moreover, I was in the territory of my enemy and his private security. My instinct told me to remain motionless and silent until the cacophony ended. Opposite, the other side of New Inn Street, was a tall building with a red door, which called itself, Seven New Inn. To the left of it were various graffiti. For a few minutes, my gaze was captured. There were several works, some overlapping each other. I was innocent of street art, having never seen it before London, but one figurative piece held my attention.

*   *   *

Many times I had sat on Juliette's bed, in her warm chambre intime[75], in the roof of the farm house, with its heavy beech beams, the walls and white plaster of the pitched interior ceiling, covered with prints of great paintings by the masters. I would spend time looking through books, either my own, whichever I was currently reading, or of works by painters of all time periods, while Juliette would sit opposite making sketches, paintings and studies. I had become her eternal model. Some were brief and quick, others taking much longer with considerable attention. I was mostly naked, which suited me, and which Juliette needed to develop her skills of life drawing and painting. She needed to learn how to represent bodies, she explained, and it was true the way she looked at me then was quite different, studious even, to how she looked at me when she wanted to seduce or be seduced.

One major intended work was to turn me into a black 'Cupid Victorious', 'Amor Vincit Omnia', love conquers all.[76] Of course, I loved that idea, love conquers all, and was charmed and delighted that I should be the manifestation of 'Love'. Looking at the Caravaggio painting, it was clear Cupid was only a boy; my genitals were of course bigger and I couldn't help grinning as Juliette posed me on the edge of her bed and splayed my legs wide open, as in the original painting. Love was definitely about sex, my naked sexuality. She smiled back at me, sharing my excited, amused pleasure at the overt, eroticism of both the original and her arranging of my seated position, legs wide open, head tilted provocatively.

"How do you want to arrange my búrrà and dormì[77]?" I asked, laughing.

Sometimes it wouldn't take long before she weakened, surrendered and pretending to adjust the position of my head, or turn my torso slightly, her fingertips would end up sliding down my chest, my belly, her face

<hr>

[75]   intimate bedroom

[76]https://commons.wikimedia.org/w/index.php?sort=relevance&search=amor+vincit+omnia&title= Special:Search&profile=advanced&fulltext=1&advancedSearch- current=%7B%7D&ns0=1&ns6=1&ns12=1&ns14=1&ns100=1&ns106=1#/media/File:Amor_ Vincit_Omnia-Caravaggio_(c.1602).jpg

[77] Balls and penis

ever closer to mine until we could taste each other's breath. My dormì, slowly swelling, would lift and rest upon my thigh, while, naked, I would delicately unbutton her blouse, moving slowly closer until my hot breath caressed her nipples, and I buried my face in her pretty breasts, both of us surrendering to our passion. Other times, it could be much longer and she was able to make considerable progress with her work and I would end up studying the pictures on the walls and then the books of prints she presented me with to distract me while she was working. Many times, also, I brought my own books, recommended by my teacher and sometimes those offered by Rémi. These were much more difficult, stuff that Rémi was reading even at university.

"Look! Stop moaning about how difficult they are and just get on with it! I do not accept that you should know less than me! Just force your brain to work and don't be lazy! You have to understand everything, eh?"

Even if I didn't understand, I just kept reading and then reading again, until familiarity presented me with new worlds, new thinking. Sometimes Rémi's impatience annoyed me and we would end up arguing, shouting at each other until Nathalie had to intervene, sending us in opposite directions to the ends of the garden, not that we were separated for long, but immediately sought each other out to laugh, play silly games and chase each other between the fruit bushes or end up wrestling on the lawn. Nathalie would just leave us to it. I hadn't lost the child in me and Tagí didn't want to either. He was definitely Suri, who were much more fun than these sensible aranjinya.

"Okay, you want me to keep up with you, read these books, learn this stuff, then I want you to learn Suri!"

"I can! I will!"

If anything such disputes brought us closer, such that sometimes, overhearing us chatter, Nathalie realised how much of a bond was growing between us when half of what we were saying was with smatterings of Suri, incomprehensible to her.

If the black wings of Eros/Cupid were able to emanate their own light, it was going to be possible for my black body to emanate light also. Juliette opted for the black background of the original to become shades of dark red, often a preferred colour of Caravaggio's for drapes and clothing in many of his paintings.

Initially, I wondered how it was possible to give detail to a figure, like my own, which was black. It seemed to me there was no shadow or variation in the black to show shape or form and this contributed to the quality I possessed of being able to become invisible, but when I looked at Juliette's paintings, I was amazed at the extent to which they were me, undoubtedly images of me. The number of different colours she had used was so surprising, different blues, reds, browns, yellows, whites. I looked at her with disbelief:-

"Are there so many colours on my skin?"

"Er, yes!"

"Here," I pointed at the picture, "my leg has some dark blue, but I don't see that on my real leg. Where is it?"

Juliette had understood that in order to paint chiaroscuro, it was necessary to focus on the dark shadows and lines of a figure, a white figure, hence, logically, with my black figure, she would have to concentrate on the light contours, lines and highlights.

"The colours move and change. Your skin doesn't have a colour, it reflects light, so the colour changes. At night everyone is black. Different skin reflects colour differently. White people think they are white, but no. They are pink, grey, yellow, green, blue, many different colours. People don't look. You have to look carefully. I am looking carefully at you! That you are hot, for example, your skin moist, sweating, I have to show that for you to become real in the painting."

At which point the memory faded and I found myself sitting on that roof edge once more, above Amnesty International, in Shoreditch, looking at the graffiti opposite, no longer in Great Britain, but nasty England. I felt a tightness in my throat, such that I couldn't breathe. My eyes were burning.

Looking again at the graffiti, the one image which caught my attention and had carried me back to Juliette, was of five abstract figures, all naked, and although they reminded me of paintings by Bacon and Auerbach, Bacon's tended to be about isolation and individual suffering and Auerbach's were simple portraits, often wise, beautiful, here, lit by a street lamp, were older men and women, misshapen by an unknown history, crowded together and supporting each other, one figure appearing to be slumped over, the blues and reds on their naked flesh like bruises or wounds. Were they being herded somewhere? Somewhere like Dibdib? Suddenly, it seemed right that this image was there opposite the Amnesty building commenting on the violence it opposes, violence which had been brought into my own home, my village. By whom? By what? And why? And there was someone, or something pursuing me, even now! What was it that was so bad about me, Chár? Why were they, whoever they were, angry with me? Were they angry? Were they going to kill me? The vicious spirit of Dibdib still seemed to be roaming the Earth in ravenous pursuit.

*   *   *

Many claims have been made recently about Caravaggio turning his studio, no less, into a gigantic camera obscura. Sunlight through a hole in one wall, possibly assisted by mirrors, focused onto his models and then that image of the illuminated subject projected through a lens onto the canvas. There have even been claims of traces of light sensitive chemicals found in the canvas primer on which a faint image could have been retained for several hours. Certainly, scratch marks have been found on canvasses delineating an outline to figures. Over the centuries, artists have used all sorts of techniques to produce realistic representations. Regardless of this primitive outlining of figures, the art is in the application of paint to produce the masterpiece. It, therefore, seemed perfectly reasonable to Juliette to use her camera and then project and delineate outlines for figures. Critically important now was the staging. If she wanted her art to contain the power of the Historia Sacre and mythological paintings, then it would have to illustrate a particular historical moment and tell the story of that moment, just as the Caravaggio paintings were used to illustrate religious history in contemporaneous terms. She discussed this with me and Rémi; we would be her models. But this painting would come from my history. Already in her mind was the religious symbolism of the slaughtered sheep, sacrificed by Abraham and Christ himself being perceived as the Lamb of God and then, my sacrificing of a sheep to bathe in its blood and wash away any remains of death that might be clinging to me. The coincidence was simply too great! And then Rémi, painted with the same black wings as Cupid, but as my Bodhisattva, surrounded by flames emanating from his skin, the fire of purification, anointing me with the blood of the sheep . . . . Positioning them for this tableau was now critical if she really wanted to create her painting, her representation of a new mythic incarnation of Dionysus. But when?

Printed in Dunstable, United Kingdom